Portals:

Book Two

Demons & Daggers

Travis I. Sivart

4

Portals: Book 2, Demons & Daggers

Copyright © 2020 Travis I. Sivart

All rights reserved.

Cover Design by Travis I. Sivart

ISBN: 9798682950089

Talk of the Tavern Publishing Group

6

Dedication

I dedicate this adventure to the minds that explore worlds beyond their own. Minds like yours, my dear reader.

8

Table of Contents

Acknowledgements

This book comes from the encouragement of many people, but two stand out in my mind. The first is Andrea, my constant companion, who laughs from the other room as I edit the story out loud. The second is Tara, my editor, who's more excited than myself about the characters and who encourages me every time we talk.

Beyond those two, there are countless folks who watch me write my stories while I stream on twitch.tv.

15

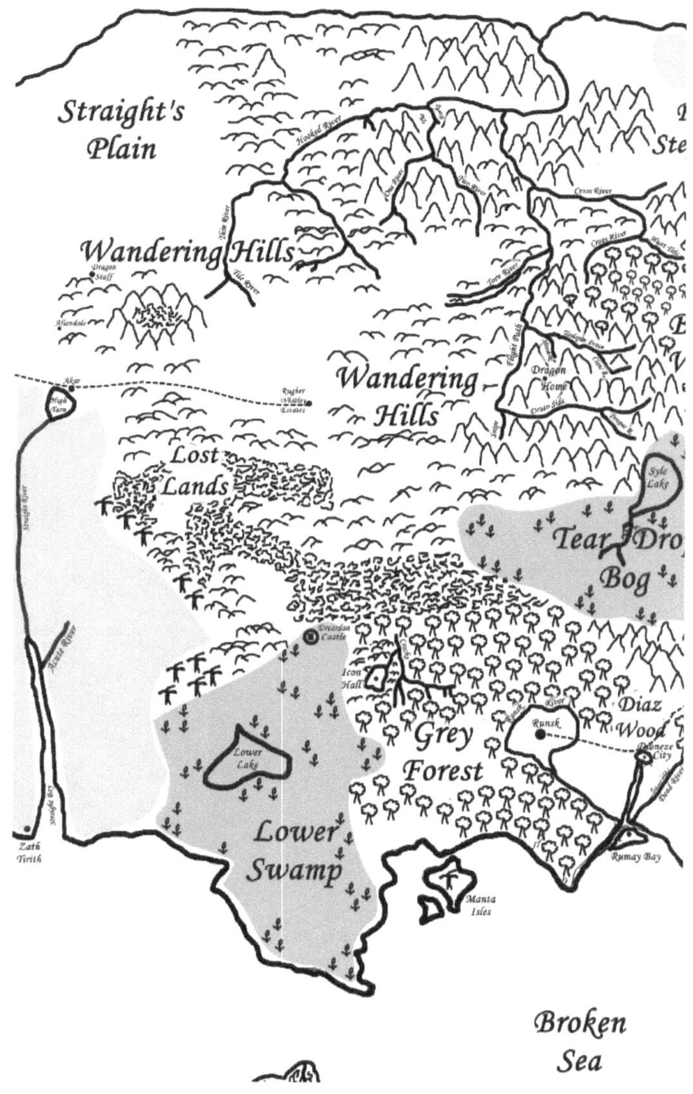
Straight's Plain
Wandering Hills
Dragon Staff
Aftendale
Wandering Hills
Akar
High Tarn
Rugher Whitley Estates
Lost Lands
Syle Lake
Tear Drop Bog
Straights River
Acute River
Dreardon Castle
Icon Hall
Runsk
Diaz Wood
Daoneze City
Grey Forest
Lower Lake
Lower Swamp
Zath Tirith
Straights Bay
Manta Isles
Rumay Bay
Broken Sea

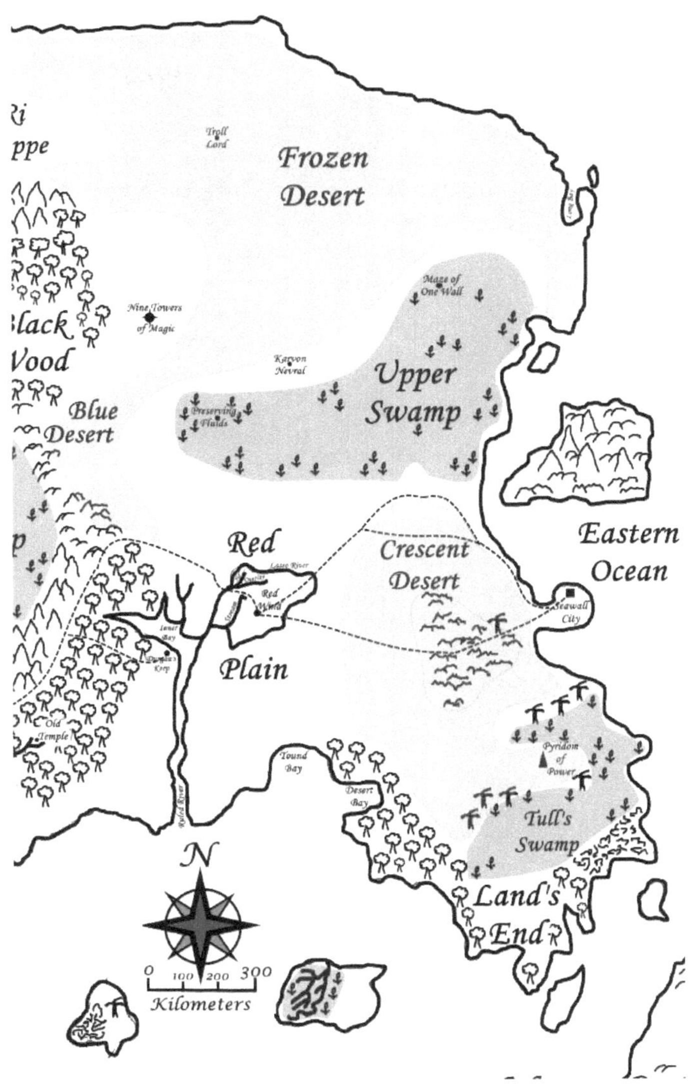

Ri
ppe
Black
Wood
Blue
Desert
Frozen
Desert
Troll
Lord
Nine Towers
of Magic
Karvon
Nevral
Maze of
One Wall
Upper
Swamp
Preserving
Fluids
Eastern
Ocean
Red
Crescent
Desert
Lazzo River
Red
Wind
Plain
Inlet
Bay
Dungeon
Krep
Old
Temple
Seawall
City
Tound
Bay
Desert
Bay
Pyrdom
of
Power
Tull's
Swamp
Rolvd River
Land's
End
N
0   100   200   300
Kilometers

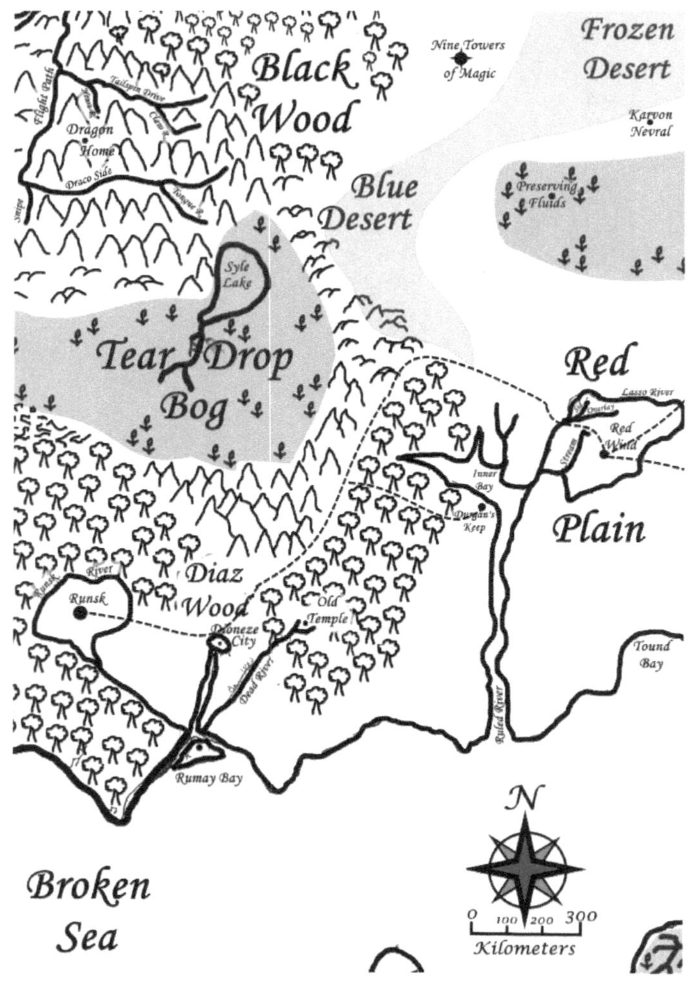
Frozen Desert
Black Wood
Blue Desert
Nine Towers of Magic
Karvon Nevral
Preserving Fluids
Flight Path
Tailspin Drive
Dragon Home
Draco Side
Tongue R.
Syle Lake
Tear Drop Bog
Red
Lasso River
Overlay
Red Wind
Stream
Plain
Inner Bay
Dungan's Keep
Diaz Wood
Runsk River
Runsk
Dioneze City
Old Temple
Dead River
Ruled River
Tound Bay
Rumay Bay
Broken Sea
N
0   100   200   300
Kilometers

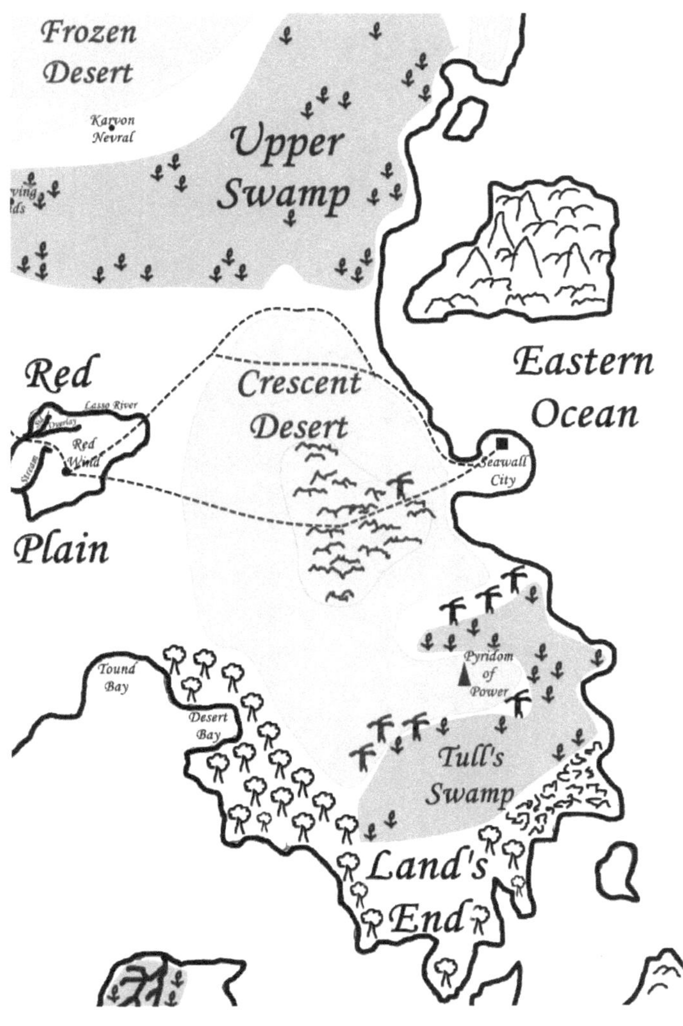
Frozen
Desert
Karvon
Nevral
Upper
Swamp
Red
Lasso River
Overlay
Red
Wind
Stream
Plain
Crescent
Desert
Eastern
Ocean
Seawall
City
Tound
Bay
Desert
Bay
Pyridom
of
Power
Tull's
Swamp
Land's
End

22

Chapter 1

Nathan tumbled heels over head, falling down the rocky slope, his backpack clanging and clattering, feet going out from underneath him again and again. His double-headed battle axe, torn from his grip, flew to one side as cooking pots scattered to the other. His face hit a rock, his nose popping with the impact. It sent him sideways in a tangle of limbs and straps as the world spun around him, like he was inside the world's largest coin-operated washing machine.

A moment before, he'd been staring down the muzzle of a double-barrel shotgun. Nathan's ears still rung with the echoed retort as the man holding the weapon pulled the trigger and emptied two rounds into his midsection.

It'd been a rough day so far.

Less than three hours ago, Nathan had woken up and got out of bed to the blaring digital scream of his outdated alarm clock. His coffee maker had stopped working after brewing a tepid half cup of Joe. But that was okay, since he could stop at the local Starbucks. Nathan got dressed in his white shirt, striped tie, grey suit jacket, and headed out the door.

Once he'd arrived, he had to work his way through picketers demonstrating for non-dairy milk to be offered. The protestors wouldn't let him into the building, though others pushed their way through. Nathan smiled and told them he understood, and he admired them for standing up for what they believed in.

He made a side trip to a 7-11 to get his coffee instead. The heavy woman behind the counter glared at him when the machine didn't read the swipe strip on his debit card, and sourly informed him she couldn't manually type in a card anymore. It was the slide or nothing.

Nathan offered to pay cash, but only had loose change on him, and had to get a smaller coffee so he could afford it. He apologized and thanked the scowling woman, wishing her a nice day, before heading to the door.

A mother and her three kids were coming in as Nathan left, and he held the door for them automatically. The mother marched by, her nose in her phone, ignoring his jovial good morning. The kids were jumping and screaming, and the middle one hit Nathan's arm, causing his coffee to slam against his chest. The lid popped off, and the coffee scalded his stomach and soaked into his suit jacket.

As the pain subsided, Nathan realized the woman was now screaming at him about touching her child, and how he could've given her poor baby third-degree burns with the coffee. She was threatening to sue him and ignoring his apologies. The sour woman behind the counter was yelling at him to shut the damn door.

He left, still holding his crushed coffee cup.

That was the first hour of his day.

The second hour wasn't much different.

Nathan arrived at a little neighborhood jewelry store—which he owned and had opened thirteen years ago—let in his one employee, Austin, greeting the twenty-something-year-old with a smile. The younger man shuffled sullenly behind the counter and checked his phone while Nathan went to the back to get ready to open. He set up the coffeepot to brew and opened the safe while waiting. Counting down the till, he found the drawer was $17.38 short from the night before.

When Austin came back to fill his coffee cup, Nathan asked him about the shortage. The younger man held the now full mug in one hand and the glass coffeepot in the other.

The twenty-something swung his greasy bangs out of his eyes with a jerk of his head and glared at his boss, looking the older man up and down through slitted eyes.

Austin took three steps forward, raised the coffeepot up to eye-level, and threw it onto the floor. The pot shattered and Austin began yelling at Nathan about accusing him of stealing, and how that shit wasn't cool.

Nathan tried calming the younger man, apologizing and trying to explain he was just asking what happened, but never got to finish as Austin yanked off his clip-on tie, screamed he was quitting, and stormed out of the back room with his still full coffee cup.

The bell out front jingled, and the door slammed shut. It was at that moment Nathan realized the coffee cup in Austin's hand was his, and not the employee's. Now he had no mug, and the coffee pot lay in broken shards in a puddle of coffee. When Austin had thrown it down, it had splashed across Nathan's slacks, staining them to match his shirt and jacket.

Nathan finished opening the shop, cleaned the mess in the back room, changed out of his ruined jacket and shirt, and put on the only other thing he had around; the ugly holiday sweater he'd bought to wear to a friend's party three months ago. He'd won an honorable mention with the sweater, just like everyone else. His friend didn't want to hurt anyone's feelings, so, at Nathan's suggestion, agreed that a participation prize was a good idea.

But the third hour of Nathan's day was, by far, the worst.

Nathan had been open forty-five minutes when three men burst in. Two wore pantyhose over their heads and faces, and both had a handgun in one hand, and a pillowcase in the other. The third man had a ski mask and a double-barreled shotgun. He seemed to be the leader and shouted at Nathan to give them all the money in the register and safe.

Nathan apologized and explained that he'd deposited the money the night before, and only had the hundred dollars in the register, minus the $17.38 it was short.

The man in the ski mask shouted that he hadn't stolen the damned money. That made Nathan pause, look at the robber, then ask, 'Austin?', before turning away at the sound of shattering glass.

The pantyhose guys were breaking glass cases with their guns and snatching rings, watches, necklaces, and other jewelry from the broken displays. The back of the cases was open, but the men still broke the glass instead of just reaching around the case.

Nathan tried to tell them they could just reach in the open door behind the counter, but ski mask jabbed the gun into Nathan's gut to get his attention. That's when both barrels went off.

Nathan had looked down and seen the gaping hole in his sweater—wondering what else he could change into—as the world spun and went dark.

In the blink of an eye, he was outside in the sun, and falling down a rocky slope.

He slid to a stop, laying on his back and staring up into a crisp, clear sky tinged with green. Blinking, Nathan thought his eyes were playing tricks on him. It was like his vision was blurry, but it made the color weird instead of the picture fuzzy. It reminded him of his grandparent's TV when he was a kid, with the corners of the screen losing their color tint and turning a bleary grey.

He worked his jaw, sand grinding between his teeth, and slowly moved each limb to see what condition it was in. To top it all off, he'd caught his beard in his chain mail shirt, forcing his chin to his chest.

That was when Nathan realized he didn't have a beard, or chain mail, or a battle axe a couple of minutes ago. But he had all those things now.

He jerked his hands in front of his face, his shoulders locking in complaint and tangling on the straps of his backpack. The orange dirt of this region of the Crescent Desert his thick, callused fingers, and hairy knuckles.

His mind grabbed at the name of the surrounding area, wondering how he could know that, and discarding the fact these weren't the same hands he had a few minutes ago.

A roaring noise blended with a dozen screeches, the former coming from up the hill, and the latter from all around him.

Sitting up, Nathan looked towards the roar.

A creature—a thing was a better way to describe it—stood nearly three-meters tall and lurched towards him. It had the head of a vulture, but jointed and segmented legs like an insect. The monstrosity's chest was a thick leathery barrel, creased with chitinous, overlapping scales, each the size of a dinner plate.

The screeching came from smaller creatures, something that looked like petite lap giraffes—from Sokoblovsky Farms in the Direct TV commercials—blended with the undead cat from Stephen King's Pet Sematary.

These things swarmed towards Nathan. He'd never seen them before, but he knew what they were. The big one was a crigth, and the small ones were jedth, and they were all bullies. Nathan didn't like bullies.

Nathan rolled to his feet and stood his full meter-and-a-half height. Something in his head niggled that this was wrong as well. He should be another half meter taller, and why was he thinking in metric instead of feet and inches?

His new body was already moving as his mind freaked out and questioned everything going on. He had pulled out two hand-axes—these also had double-heads, like his battle-axe—wading into the cat-giraffe things and laying about himself with the weapons.

Each time a swing connected, he kicked the creature away with a thick-booted foot, avoiding the acidic splash of blood that followed.

The enormous monster lumbered down the hill, coming closer.

Nathan looked around for his battle-axe. The weapon, lost in the fall, was far out of reach. The creature was between Nathan and his favorite axe, which he had named Marcid, which in Rokairn meant a female blacksmith.

He wondered, on top of all the other swirls of thought, what's a rokairn?

The knowledge was instantly there, and he knew what it was. It was him, a species of highly organized, skilled, and talented people who favored mountain and cave dwellings, as well as metal and jewel crafting. And they almost always had exceptional beards, even the women.

Nathan tucked his shoulders in and his head down, running towards where Marcid lay without thinking about what he was doing. The monster came towards him on long, lanky legs, listing far to one side and then the other with each step.

Nathan ran between its legs, and stood up when under the beast, throwing his shoulders back and his arms wide, causing the segmented limbs to fly akimbo and the thing lost its footing.

By the time the demon spawn had risen to its feet again, Nathan had Marcid in both hands and was chopping into it.

The creature fell under the attack, Nathan's steel nerves and stone-like muscles making quick work of it.

This monster didn't have the acid-blood thing, but Nathan still avoided the visceral spray, because it smelled really, really terrible, and reminded him of crushed stink bugs.

Some of it got on him anyway, reminding him of the coffee that stained his shirt a couple hours ago, or the spray of blood when the shotgun went off against his belly.

As his body slowed, the deed done, Nathan came back to his mind. He looked across the sandy field of carnage with a double handful of dead demonic things scattered about.

Movement in the east caught his attention, and distant howls reached his ears. The pack was on the move, and the hyena-headed man-beasts that worked with the demonic invaders would be upon him soon, along with the giant hyenas that always followed.

Nathan's stomach lurched, making him bend over and vomit.

Chapter 2

The Kid threw himself off the building and plummeted towards the cobblestone street below. He released a metal grapple attached to a wire and flung it towards the rooftop he'd just left.

Reaching out with his mind-magics, he grabbed the metal hook and thrust it towards a chimney pipe. It wrapped around the protrusion just in time to catch his falling body, reversing his headlong plunge into a graceful upward arc. He landed on the rooftop across the road.

Crossbow bolts peppered the wood and stucco wall below his feet, missing him by a hair. The Metal Hand Assassin Clan was hot on his trail.

The Kid laughed.

His pursuers took exception to him foiling their job earlier this afternoon. They'd set up the double execution of the new mayor of Durgan's Keep and the high priestess of Promethene, goddess of sound and light. The two public figures had sat lunching together; discussing how to create a new economy by making apprenticeships available to those leaving the religious order's orphanages.

What should've been an easy in-and-out job turned into five assassins dying by their own poisoned darts turned back on them, and the city watch taking four lookouts into custody.

The Kid made it public knowledge he caused the failed missions, exposing and embarrassing the clan at the same time.

The street thief, turned hero of the people, mentally tugged on his grapple and reeled it in, catching the self-coiling metal wire in his hand. His body shimmered and disappeared at a mental command.

The Kid pulled out a dozen newly made throwing stars. They were like shuriken from his world, and it surprised him no one here had made them before. But since no one had, they'd become his calling card.

He dropped them over the side of the building, leaned over the gutter, and took control of their fall with his mind, directing the projectiles towards the people following him and speeding them up as they flew.

The razor-sharp squares sunk into the flesh of throats, chests, and bellies. Men and women from the Metal Hand Assassin Clan fell under the onslaught.

This was what the Kid had been doing since saving the fortified city of Durgan's Keep from an undead invasion last autumn. He'd been harassing and ruining the professional life of the criminal underground—and taking very public credit for it.

Because of his public image, there were multiple contracts out on him, dead or alive. Thankfully, the common people loved him; he was their Robin Hood.

This was such a different life than what the Kid had lived back in his old world—where he was a woman in her late seventies dying of cancer—and he much preferred this new life over the previous one.

The Kid thought back to the people he'd met from his world and who'd helped him save this city. A self-styled time-traveler, Jack Tucker, claimed to have pulled each of them from their dying bodies into bodies in this world, which were also dying at the moment of transfer. From what Jack had said, the energy it took for them to come here also healed whatever body they took possession of. They kept all the skills, memories, and experiences their new bodies had before their arrival. It made for awkward moments in the street when the Kid would meet someone who claimed he owed them money.

Esperanza—priestess of Latress, goddess of weather, wind, and wisdom—had returned to her life in the world they'd come from. She'd been struggling against her faith from Earth, conflicting with her abilities granted by a goddess of this world. After saving the city from undead hordes, they'd escorted Torrents to where he was going, and met Jack Tucker, who opened a portal so Esperanza could return to her original life.

The Kid often wondered what happened to the body the priestess had inhabited here. He also wondered if the transfer back to the other world healed her original body, the way the transfer here had healed their new ones.

Torrents—the barbarian who'd also traveled with them—had gone to Dargaon's Hole, a community of people doing some crazy ass bidj. It was a place in the Wandering Hills where dragons—like real and actual huge reptilian, magic-wielding, intelligent beings— lived and thrived. These powerful creatures once allied with humans who raised livestock to keep them fed in exchange for protection.

Torrents, a massive barbarian, was now playing house with a transposed community of peasants for the past six months, rebuilding an ancient agreement and nurturing a new culture to rise in place of the old.

It was late spring now, and Esperanza had returned to the world that the Kid, Torrents, and the priestess had come from before inhabiting bodies in this world. That was almost six months ago.

What are you doing now? Edsumar's voice echoed in the Kid's head.

"I'm playing Batman," the Kid pulled the throwing stars back to his hands, using a secondary thought to wipe the blood from the sharpened blades before they reached him, "and taking out the bad guys so the city will be safe."

I thought Batman didn't kill people. The voice questioned. *And it sure looks like you're killing people. So, maybe you're playing Punisher instead?*

The Kid let out a heavy sigh and drew away from the edge of the roof.

"You're harshing my mellow, dude." The Kid rolled his eyes at the magical weapon that couldn't see his face, but knew what he was doing, anyway. "Don't you have some mystical contemplation that involves your thousand-year-old missing belly button, or something else you could be doing besides bothering me?"

Bothering you is my favorite pastime. The magical weapon's tone was upbeat. *I don't regret calling to you to recover me from that dank, dark hole I'd been lost in, not for a single moment. You may not have the skills and intelligence I'd hoped for, not to mention the moral compass, but you are by far the most interesting specimen I could've hoped for.*

"You're always so encouraging," the Kid muttered, moving to the other side of the building and crouching to find his egress.

Edsumar was the soul of an ancient dragon, magically imprisoned in a dagger, along with the essences of the five draconian priests who had performed the ritual. When bored, the being sage offered advice and juvenile snark to the Kid.

The weapon had shown some uses beyond stabbing people—allowing the Kid to see in the dark, returning to his hand when thrown, and a couple other things—but mostly exuded attitude at inopportune moments.

The Kid stepped off the rooftop and dropped towards the ground, three-stories below. Without thinking, he threw his cable and grapple over his shoulder and hooked it to the eave above him with his mind-magics.

His mental abilities also tied a loop in the metal cording, and it slithered around his foot. His downward momentum slowed as he touched down on the cobblestone street, the cord winding itself back into a loop with a second thought.

"Can I call you Alfred?" The Kid asked Edsumar out loud, causing people to turn and look, surprised at his sudden appearance.

Perhaps Microchip would be more appropriate, Edsumar answered, *as I'm the voice in your ear, not your butler.*

"I don't like the Punisher thing," people drew away at the words as the Kid passed, talking to himself, "I prefer to think I'm making this city safe, instead of just punishing the wicked."

Isn't it the same thing? By punishing, you make it safe, though you also give back to the community with kindness and coin. Edsumar's voice wavered. *There is something that requires your immediate attention.*

"What?" He drew the single word out to three syllables contained in a sigh, and the Kid rolled his eyes and turned to look where Edsumar mentally urged.

A stone fist caught the Kid in the midsection, knocking the wind from him, and throwing him backwards into a brick wall.

His vision swam. He pushed to his feet, stumbled to his left, and held up his arms to block any other attacks.

Drop! Edsumar said.

The Kid did as the mystical artifact commanded, and debris followed the sound of stone hitting stone, raining down on the prone thief.

"Dafuk!" Anger filled the Kid's shout. "What the hell?"

Yeah, Edsumar said, *yelling to attract your foes' attention when you're blinded is always a good idea.*

The Kid pushed to his knees, clenched his fists, and mentally pulled the detritus from around him. Rocks, stones, and pebbles combined into a cluster that, molded by the Kid's mind, took on the forms of weird, mutated crustaceans.

The largest was slightly bigger than a house cat, with eight legs covered in bristling spikes, and a carapace with razor sharp ridges. Two massive claws clacked, the dozens of creatures scuttling forward to defend the blinded rogue. Mirror images of the largest, the smaller ones each acted independently of the others.

The Kid heard screams of terror from around him, as his vision cleared to reveal a golem of stone and stucco standing over him. The illusionary creatures the Kid created swarmed the magical construct. Bricks made up each knuckle of the thing's huge hands, and the Kid followed Edsumar's advice and ducked as the limb swished past his head and shattered the wall behind him.

From his prone position on the ground, the Kid thrust his awareness into the thing in front of him, seeking the kernel of power at its center. The street thief's mind found the tiny pearl of energy at the core of the animated form, and wrapped his power around it, smothering it from the influence of its creator.

The magical energy surged against the Kid's mind-magics, the identity of the being in front of him pushing from the inside, and the control of the person directing it battering at the protective ball from the outside.

The Kid mentally scrambled for a way to win, knowing physical violence wouldn't work. He needed to make the monster stop struggling against him, but stop whatever was commanding this thing from regaining control.

He needed to hide the construct from whatever made it, and at the same time make the golem recognize the Kid as its master.

The illusionary lobster-like things crawling along the golem became starbursts of magical power in the Kid's awareness, which he locked onto. They burrowed into the golem, pushing into its stony hide and underneath the blocks and plaster that of pebbled monster's flesh.

People in the street backed away from the fight, shouting; the towering behemoth growled, a noise like stone grating on rock. The brick-and-mortar monster staggered, tearing at the stony hide covering its wood and iron skeleton, ripping chunks away.

The Kid pushed his magical creatures deeper into the thing attacking him, forcing his pets into the construct's center, seeking the core of power. Once they'd reached it, the Kid didn't have them attack it, instead he had them devour it in reverse, and make themselves become absorbed into the engine that sucked in magic to keep the golem running.

In the Kid's mind's-eye, he saw the ruby-red glow of the pulsing energy take on a blue-ish tint, changing as more of his illusions were sucked into its heart.

The rock monster tore into its chest, grabbing at the wrought iron bars of its rib cage and pulling it open to expose the rune-covered arcane ball at its center. It reached inside and wrapped a massive hand around its heart and squeezed.

The Kid created a shield in front of himself, using his abilities, and covered his face with his arms.

The construct exploded, shards whizzing into the crowd, cutting into flesh with conflicting red and blue pulses.

Stripped of their magic as they passed through his shield, the shards of rock pelted his arms covering his head.

When the dust settled, the Kid rose from his crouch to look around. Covered from head to toe with powder from the explosion, he batted at his hair and shoulders, knocking detritus to the ground and blinking to clear his eyes, trying to see what remained of his attacker.

He focused on the spot where the being had been and stared in disbelief mixed with a growing nervousness.

Where the monster had been was a stony creature, about the height of a medium-sized dog, with a chitinous shell made of layers of shale and brick, eight legs of intricately jointed wrought iron, and two massive stone claws that clicked a complex rhythm that countered the noise of its ticking feet.

Well, this is something new. Edsumar's tone dripped sarcasm and amusement. *What the hell did you do?*

"I made a-" the Kid gulped, trying to wet his dust coated throat, then barked out a grating laugh, "I made a rock lobster!"

The creature danced back and forth in front of the Kid like an excited puppy.

Chapter 3

Torrents growled and swung the huge maul at his target. It missed as the thin, beige, lizard-like creature darted to one side on its two hind feet, its thin forearms flapping at its sides, before falling to all fours and dashing behind the barbarian.

Five more twinglinds—that's what Trinity, the dragon, had called them—moved to flank him, even though he was over three times their size.

Two of the twinglinds darted between Torrents's thick legs, biting at the tender flesh.

The big man yelped and jigged sideways, trying not to crush any of the things under his feet.

The dragons considered the quasi-bipedal creatures good luck, and thus the local human population had adopted the annoying beasts as a sort of mascot for Dargaon's Hole.

If Torrents had his druthers—a word his grandmother had used a lot—he'd crush their little heads and fry them all up in a skillet. The bodies, not the heads. Because the heads would be crushed, and probably wouldn't be good eating, anyway. Not that the barbarian would ever get a chance to test that theory either way, since the creatures were bordering on sacred animals by everyone, and everything, he interacted with.

The barbarian had been here, with the refugees from Hope's Hollow, for months now. He'd had to get away from the Kid, who was just too reckless and carefree for his tastes. He needed to be doing work that meant something, and not harassing local thieves and assassins.

This commune—made up of the humans and the single dragon of Dargaon's Hole—had sounded like a good idea when he'd gotten the letter from the one person who had looked out for him when he had first appeared on this world: Axle.

Axle took the role of patriarch and co-mayor of the small community who had to flee its home after being overrun by undead. He worked closely with the hedge-witch, Rose, the matriarch, and the other half of the mayorship.

The people had survived a tough winter, living off supplies hidden deep in the cavern in the mountains known as the Wandering Hills. There wasn't much, and there was more beer and brandy than beans and rice. Most of the vermin disappeared when the human population was wiped out decades ago, and Trinity had done what she could to keep vermin from the supplies, but a dragon wasn't the best rat hunter.

Trinity also supplemented the community's rations with fresh meat…when she could find it.

Rebuilding had been more difficult than anyone thought it would be. The blend of restoring what was already there—but had fallen into disrepair—versus just building something brand new was always a delicate balance.

Torrents leapt atop a boulder, gaining the advantage of elevation to survey his surroundings, adding to his more than two-meter height. His olive-skin and rippling muscles were covered with a sheen of sweat. He wore a linen tunic, fur boots, and leather pants. His straight shoulder-length hair was plastered to his head in the unseasonably warm spring air.

His body in the other world hadn't been as tall and was much thinner, having lost his high-school jock physique after the accident that had put him in a wheelchair. As a black athlete, he'd dealt with admirers and haters in his sports career, but had a whole new set of problems once his father died in the car accident, changing his life.

Though he had chosen to stay in this world when given the chance to return home, he still questioned that decision. Esperanza, who he missed, had decided to return. The priestess who traveled with him and the Kid had done what neither he nor the thief could do, returned to face a world and life that had been killing them, but in very different ways.

Torrents still felt lost, but in a way that was unlike what he'd experienced in his previous life. Here, he was needed and was making a difference, but he didn't think he was really living life for himself. Which was the key to life, wasn't it? If you only lived for other people and their purposes, were you even living?

The hiss of a twinglind drew his attention. The creatures scampered away, throwing looks over their shoulders. But they weren't running from him.

Torrents smiled. He'd found what he'd come into the foothills to hunt. Wererats.

They were lycanthropes—from what Rose had told him—similar to werewolves, but with a rat as the root form. The barbarian had laughed at the idea, imagining an angry, humanoid sewer rat that stood about a meter tall, squeaky and shaking a little paw at him. Like Splinter from the Teenage Mutant Ninja

Turtles, without the ninjitsu. Axle assured him that wasn't what he should expect.

The wererats had been harassing the settlement, attacking groups of woodsmen during the day, or sneaking in and stealing supplies at night. It was more of a nuisance until they stole a supply of weapons from Dargaon's Hole.

Steel weapons were rare in this day and age, and someone who could craft them was almost impossible to find. The invaders had stolen a dozen short blades, a few swords, and some bows and the arrows to go with them. Without these supplies, Dargaon's Hole couldn't to defend itself, or hunt effectively.

Torrents had volunteered to go find the thieves, recover the items, and convince the wererats to leave the area. They'd either leave on their own, or he and his mallet would convince them.

Turning towards the direction from where that the twinglinds had fled, he saw a grey furry head looking out from behind a rock outcropping. It had matted hair; extended, rounded ears that were laid back against its skull; and a protrusion that was more of a snout than a nose.

The creature's eyes locked onto the barbarian's before it ducked out of sight.

Torrents moved without thinking, his head ringing with the warning of it being a trap, but his body acted on its own. He didn't care if it was a trap. He wanted to feel the burn of his muscles singing as he crushed something that was hurting the people he cared for.

Springing from his perch, the barbarian sprinted towards where the creature had disappeared, his maul held in two hands, his shoulders hunched as he barreled forward.

Reaching the hiding place, Torrents turned, gravel sliding under his feet as they went out from under him.

A woven hemp net dropped over him, and seven small people leapt atop him, jabbing at him with blades. A blow to his head made him stagger and reel.

Well, this was a bad idea, Torrents thought, dropping his weapon and covering his head with his meaty arms. Swords and daggers cut into him, but he forced his feet back underneath him and thrust upward.

He launched himself into the air with a roar, grabbing the net in both hands, and pulled it from over him. The wererats piled on top, tangled in the thick weave, and were thrown backwards.

Torrents, net in his fists, turned in a circle, spinning around a handful of times.

One wererat, whose feet tangled in the net, pulled itself free and flew over the side of the hill with a scream. The crunch of bones snapping followed.

Another entangled creature went silent. Its skull crashed against the stone outcropping, crushing its head and scattering flesh, bone, and blood over its companions.

Torrents released the net, and it flew another three paces before falling to the ground.

A blade slid into Torrent's midsection from his left, causing him to double over, grabbing at the weapon.

Three of the beasts leapt on him, stabbing him repeatedly in the back and legs.

Pulling the sword free with his left hand, Torrents reached down and picked up his maul with his right.

The creature holding the sword's handle lost its grip on the weapon as it was yanked off its feet and fell to the ground in front of him.

The barbarian smashed the creature's skull in with the pommel of the sword, still gripping the blade in his bloody hand.

Swinging wildly with the iron and wooden hammer in his right hand, Torrents felt the ribs of a wererat shatter under the blind blow. The creature spun away, flying backwards with the force of the hit, crashing into a second beast. The two crumpled to the ground and lay still.

Torrents swung a few more times, shaking his head to clear it, trying to get his bearings while the three remaining creatures scurried away from him, looking back and forth between one another.

"I'll cripple him," a sharp voice whined. "You two come at him from the side and back."

The barbarian's vision cleared, and he saw the voice had come from a slim ratman, who was drawing the waxed string of a long bow, sighting down the arrow.

The other two wererats moved in opposite directions, circling him, making it impossible for him to keep more than one in sight at a time.

"I'll be damned," Torrents growled, "if I'm going to let my career end because of an arrow to the knee!"

The big man dropped the bloody sword and took the maul in both hands. He crouched to make himself a smaller target and waited.

All four people burst into action when the bowstring twanged.

The barbarian moved the mallet low and leapt into the air towards the ratman, who was dropping the bow and drawing daggers.

The arrow thunked into the handle of the huge wooden weapon, cutting into one of Torrents's fingers, as he crashed into the beast.

Two behind Torrents skidded to a halt—he was no longer where he'd been—and adjusted their courses to attack him.

The ratman in front went down under his bulk, the handle of the hammer thrust sideways into the creature's mouth like a bit for a horse. Its head snapped backwards, its jaws forced open, and cheeks tore where the weapon pushed further in.

Twisting the weapon, Torrents snapped the wererat's mandible, and the fight went out of the creature as it gurgled a scream. The beast writhed under the barbarian, dropping his weapons and clutching at his face.

Pushing down with the handle of the maul, further crushing the leader's jaw, Torrents kicked backwards with a thick leg, and the ribs of the wererat poised to leap upon him collapsed under the big man's booted foot.

The last creature skidded to a halt again, sliding in the gravel and landing on its butt. Scrambling, the wererat backpedaled, turning to flee.

The beast gained its feet, moments before Torrents, and leapt on top of the original outcropping of rock that it had ducked behind to lure the barbarian into the trap.

Rising to one knee, Torrents turned and launched his maul through the air. It spun end over end, the head of the weapon smashing into the back of the ratman, attempting to leap to safety.

Spine and ribs cracked, bone tearing through flesh to glint in the afternoon sunlight. The beast crashed to the ground, twitching.

Panting, Torrents clutched the gaping wound on his side with his bleeding hand.

He smiled.

"Another one bites the dust, mother chuzzers."

Pushing to his feet, he winced at the dozens of minor cuts and wounds made themselves known.

He limped towards his weapon, reluctant to be without it in case any of the creatures survived. He'd have to find their bolt hole; these types always had some hiding place to shelter in.

Bending over to retrieve the maul, the ground shook, making him fall to his knees.

Torrents looked around, confused. He didn't think he was so injured that he should have a problem standing.

Then the ground quaked again.

Looking behind him, to the southeast, a green light expanded across the distant horizon.

"Oh bidj, what happened now?" the barbarian mumbled, turning and falling on his butt. "That's the Demon Front."

Chapter 4

Nathan was lost. He'd been running west, his short legs covering less ground than a human, but his rokairn stamina and endurance seemed to be endless. Between the two, he may not have moved as fast, but he needed to stop less often than most other people would have. It was the whole tortoise versus the hare thing. And he was traveling alone, which had its benefits.

He ran in something close to a trance, his breath coming in puffs—short, short, long, short, short, long—as he paced himself, letting his mind rest and focusing his awareness to obstacles on the trail in front of him. This must be what people back home called a runner's high.

The body he was in had a mission. It involved something called the Pyridom of Power and blocking the magics that demons used to invade this world.

Thirty years ago, there had been a comet—affectionately known as the Talisman—that had changed the face of the planet with magical radiation, causing summoning and necromantic abilities to increase tenfold. Armies of demons and undead had ravaged the land as a result.

Once the comet had moved on, the creatures and casters that had destroyed society waned and diminished. But three decades later, the world was a different place. That was the world that existed now, the world Nathan appeared in.

Nathan yanked his awareness back, fearing he'd interfered with the workings of the body he now inhabited.

"Sorry about that," the rokairn apologized to himself, "I'll try not to distract you anymore."

His speed slowed, his consciousness taking control instead of his body acting on muscle memory.

Nathan knew whoever he was inside of had just come from Seawall City, a place with a militaristic organization of priests and mages working together in a singular purpose of bringing their goals to fruition.

He was unsure what those goals were, but the body seemed to appreciate the methods employed by the society, similar to a rokairn mindset.

His rokairn brain mulled over the idea of a well-oiled government machine. A magocracy, a theocracy, and a stratocracy, all seamlessly blended to make a balanced council that functions as one.

The enchantments the priests and mages of Seawall City had imbued upon Nathan would only last a week, and his body had intended to go to the Pyridom of Power with these protections and enhancements to shut it down.

Nathan decided running away was a better idea and had been doing just that for the past three days. He'd slept in fits and starts, finding a hiding place—a gap between rocks, a shroud of scrub bushes, or anywhere else he could stop for a few hours—and then moved on.

The Pyridom was to the south, but the road led almost directly west from Seawall City to the city of Red Wind.

When Nathan and this body joined, it had been on the southernmost point of the rocky crags in the center of the Crescent Desert. They'd been heading towards the magical focal point of the cone-like pyramid the demons were swarming over. The creatures were searching for secrets that would allow them to create a foothold, bring in more reinforcements to further their plans, and to overwhelm the societies of this world.

He'd diverted his path away from his southernly direction and instead moved to the northwest and back toward Red Wind. One man, or rokairn, against an army of demons seemed like suicide rather than a good plan of action.

Nathan avoided confrontation whenever he could. Confrontation led to things like a double shotgun blast to the belly, and not to a long, peaceful life.

The hyena men chased him, hounding him in the most literal sense, until he had changed course and headed west again instead of south towards the Pyridom.

These creatures brought to mind the Egyptian jackal-headed god of the dead, Anubis, and Nathan invented the connection of these scavengers to demons as minions and middlemen. He also associated the Pyridom with Egyptian culture, though it was a cone rather than a pyramid. It was like a warped version of the world mythos he knew, and the association allowed him to conclude that running away was the best plan.

His mind wandered over the coincidences and connections of his world mythology and what appeared to be reality here. Could this entire world just be in his mind? Was he actually dying on the floor of his jewelry shop, twin holes torn into his belly? Did his mind make up all this confrontation, hatred, and violence for some reason /to balance out what his life had been?

With a thunderclap, a woman appeared directly in front of him. She had skin that was a green so dark it appeared black, except in the brightness of the cloudless desert day.

She wore a ragged and rusted chain mail tunic that fell to her knees, divided at her waistline by a wide, worn leather belt holding a two-handed blade that dragged in the sands behind her.

Her hair was short and slicked back across her skull, shaded in a midnight blue that wouldn't be apparent in anything but sunlight. Her legs were bare, but hinted at lines of scales, and her onyx-colored boots rose to her knees. But the one feature that held Nathan's attention was her sea-green eyes that sparked, and orange flecks of energy rained down to the ground around her.

The rokairn slid sideways to a stop in the sand, reaching over his shoulder to grab his double-bladed axe. It came free with a tug. His mind screamed a silent, startled cry, but his body didn't allow it to escape.

"What the heck am I doing?" Nathan panted, not from exertion, but from his quickening heart rate. "I don't want to hurt you!"

He shouted the last words across the space between himself and the new arrival.

"I'm sorry," he said, trying to smile, his hands spinning the axe in a display meant to intimidate, "I meant I don't want to fight, and I'm just trying to get past. If you wouldn't mind, may I go around and leave you to your business?"

"Chuz you, little man," the woman's voice was acid on flesh, and his skin crawled with her words, "you will die because you need to, and I shall devour your remains in celebration of your defeat."

"That's extreme." Nathan's smile warped into a grimace and his left eye twitched. "I just want to get to Red Wind. There's no need for any violence."

The woman moved like quicksilver, not responding to his words, and the weapon at her waist appeared in her right hand, its blade the deep flaky maroon of rusted metal and dried blood.

Her left hand twisted, creating a rounded flame the size of a basketball. It burst forth and flew at him.

Nathan's axe came up when the woman gestured, and the fireball burst into a harmless flash around him.

The magics bestowed upon him disseminated it.

"I don't want to hurt you," Nathan growled, but recovered, surprised by his own words. "I'm sorry, I'm not threatening you. But I think we can settle this by talking. I don't even know who you are."

"You defy the master, and for that, you must die," the woman was now in front of him and swung her enormous sword down at him.

His own axe moved without conscious thought, catching her blade in the underside curve of his and knocking it aside. The sword bit into the ground, a black seething crevasse appearing around the cut in the earth.

She snarled.

"Who are you?" Nathan backpedaled, his weapon turning and slicing across her midsection. "And why are you doing this?"

Purplish tendrils slid from the wound, grabbing the edges of the opening and pulling it back together before disappearing back inside the thin line left on her scaled flesh.

She brought her sword up, twisting it in front of her in a defensive maneuver, readying for her next strike, but keeping the shorter opponent at bay.

"Klendrisia," she muttered, confusion creased her face as she fought against speaking the words, "daughter of the Demon Lord Ghlevid and human woman Delia, and I'm missioned with destroying the one person who could bring the end to our plans. I don't know why you turned away from the Pyridom, but I will not let some trick distract us from the threat you present."

"Demon Lord?" Nathan's axe drooped from its protective stance. "Is that really a thing?"

The woman's sword shot forward, turning away at the last moment as it hit an invisible barrier shielding him.

"The damned mages and priests can't protect you forever," Klendrisia snarled. "I will wear down those defenses until they collapse and then kill you."

"Why, though?" Nathan whined as he backed up, stumbling over his own feet, his axe rising once again. Narrowing his eyes, his voice took on an angered tone. "What did I do to you? I'm sure this is just a misunderstanding, and we can work this out without me destroying you."

The conflicting sides of Nathan showed through, his hands weaving the weapon in front of him with skill and enthusiasm, but his face and body looking afraid and muddled.

"My father commanded it," the woman drew in a deep breath, struggling, trying to hold back the information, and purplish energies coalesced around her, "and I must do as he commands or be destroyed for failure. My future within the legions depends on my success."

Klendrisia's voice was wooden and monotone, her face showing frustration at her confession and sharing deeply personal information.

The energies slid down her body and slithered along the sandy terrain like an oil spill of otherworldly power, creating a ring around the rokairn. Tentacles of the same color erupted from the ground around the short, stout warrior, writhing and stretching towards him.

Sickly yellowish sparks burst forth, centimeters from his flesh, but his magical barrier deflected the attack.

Nathan's mind warred inside of him as his body did on the outside. His nature urged an end to the fight and aggression, and a deep fiery instinct within him warned him of the danger he faced, demanding he respond with deadly force.

It overwhelmed him, and his vision swam.

Raising the axe, he swept it across the eldritch appendages, severing them in a shower of blue sparks that danced in the air before fading from sight.

Nathan roared, a battle cry coming from deep inside. It was an ancient phrase handed down from generations of holy warriors who had kept the peace through battle and diplomacy, and it carried the power of gods and rokairn with it.

"Kaleb triot, den'al venitier!" Nathan shouted and swung his axe in an arc.

His weapon impacted the woman's sword, and her blade shattered in a magical explosion.

Klendrisia stumbled backwards, the confusion on her face replaced with a mix of anger, surprise, and grim determination.

"Please," Nathan's imprinted his take on the words over his body's natural phrasing, "what the heck are you?"

"Cambion," the woman screamed, the words torn from her as she leapt backwards onto a dune, and slid sideways, "I'm an abomination to demons and humans, birthed from the unholy union of passion between a dweller of the lower dimensions and this fragile, rich plane you call home!"

The ground rumbled and shook, and the sky lit up with a wash of green energy.

Nathan looked up, turning, seeking the source. To the south, a pulsing column shot into the sky where he assumed the Pyridom of Power sat.

The rokairn's mind screamed at the telltale sign he'd dreaded. The demons had overtaken the monument, breaking into it to release its secret and gifts of magic.

Klendrisia stood and laughed.

"You've failed," she giggled, madness creeping into her voice as she spat the next words with venom, "and now I'm forced back to report to my father. Damn you for failing. I've tasted hope, and it is bitter."

The woman spun to leave and disappeared before she completed her turn.

Chapter 5

The Kid didn't know what to do, so he went underground, literally.

Hiding in the same basement apartments that once housed Jakdin—the crime-lord who'd betrayed Durgan's Keep to the necromancer who had attempted to conquer it—the Kid stared at the clattering, but cute, creature who followed him.

The rock-lobster—who the Kid had taken to calling Fred in honor of the lead singer of the B-52s and thinking of as a 'he'—had followed him through the city. The thing scaled the walls, clacked along the cobblestones, and even threatened a surprised puppy who had barked at the Kid.

Bringing the construct to life left the Kid mentally exhausted, his magics drained and weakened. He also had a splitting headache.

This means something, Edsumar said into the Kid's head, *and I really think you need to do something about it.*

"What does?" The Kid had talked out loud to the dagger, even though no one else could hear it, not caring if a passerby thought he was crazy. "You mean Fred? Or the dip in my powers? I'm sure it's temporary. I just need a good night's rest."

No, the dragon's voice contained a sigh in the Kid's brain. *I mean the magical creature that attacked you. That isn't Mezk's style, or in his repertoire. That's straight up holy magics, and someone with the backing of a church created a thing to kill you. And then you not only stopped it from accomplishing its mission, but you also destroyed it, and took its magical essence and made your own immortal minion from it.*

"I could name him Cuddles," the Kid mumbled, "after my Pomeranian, back home."

If it was a church, which no church has any reason for targeting you, then it was done because someone paid them a lot of coin, Edsumar said, *like if multiple guilds and clans decided they wanted to get rid of you and your meddling. Make sense? Maybe it's time to leave Durgan's Keep.*

The Kid grunted a noncommittal agreement and stared at the rock lobster.

Are you even paying attention? Edsumar's shout in the Kid's head made the street rat clutch his pounding head. *There's something larger going on than one city, and some petty vendettas. Now suck it up, quit hiding in this hole, and this city, and go do something more than messing with some local, small-time, mobsters.*

"You think I'm hiding?" The Kid looked up at the corner of the musty basement he was sitting in, picking at the barrel beside him with a dirty fingernail. "I've been doing things, not just hiding."

So, at least you admit that you're hiding. The dagger snickered in the Kid's thoughts, *and all you've been doing is staying out of the way of the world at large. Do you think you were brought here for the limited purpose of saving one city? Don't you even consider that there may be more? A man doesn't drag people from other realities to clean up one town. You do that for epic reasons, like fixing a broken world. And maybe even fixing a broken person in the process.*

"Broken person?" The Kid snorted. "And are you talking about me, or yourself? Are you hoping that Jack is secretly planning on restoring you to your formal draconic glory? Bestow on you some spare dragon body he has hidden in some closet somewhere?"

Deflect much? Was the dagger's only reply.

"Me? ME???" The sound of the Kid's voice echoed off the walls, and Fred backed away, nervous, clacking his stone claws. "You think I'm avoiding things?"

The Kid stopped. He moved his gaze from the corner to Fred, then down to the ivory-tooth dagger at his side.

He let out a long breath that spoke of decades of being tired and ready for something to change.

"Fine," the Kid said quietly, "maybe I am avoiding something. I just thought that when I came here, conquered an invading army of thugs and undead monstrosities, and rebuilt the government of a five-hundred-year-old city, I'd get to just relax and have some fun, you know?"

For a wise old woman trapped in a seventeen-year-old boy's body, Edsumar's tone was teasing. *You sure can be naïve. I mean, when has life ever gotten easier? If you want to grow, succeed, and accomplish things, then it's a constant uphill battle. Do you think I cherish waking up as a magical artifact? If indeed I even ever slept so I could wake up. I mean, I zone out, and my mind kinda shuts down, but I never really sleep. I don't have the needs of the flesh anymore, but sometimes I swear I still feel the urge to pee. Do you have any idea how frustrating it is to need to pee, when you don't even have a body, and you haven't had anything to drink in millennia? I mean, really, you like to think that having a bit of meat, or a popcorn shell, stuck in your teeth is frustrating? Try wanting to urinate when you don't even have a winky.*

"Did you just call your tallywacker," the Kid stopped picking at the barrel and turned to look at the dagger again, "a winky?"

Did you just call a Johnson, Edsumar's tone matched the Kid's, *a tallywhacker?*

"Did you just call a schmeckel," the Kid giggled, and the two continued their penis-name challenge, "a Johnson?"

You're a pemtie, Edsumar laughed, a deep-mentally throaty sound that made the Kid rock back on his heels, *but you're okay with me.*

"Ugh," the Kid moaned, "this is like bad 90s TV dialogue. Can we change the subject?"

Sure, Edsumar's tone was smug, like the dragon had won some secret battle. *How about changing it to you growing up, putting on your big-girl panties, and doing what needs done?*

"And what exactly," the Kid asked, and Fred scurried forward at the question, moving closer to his master, "needs to be done?"

The rogue paused, waiting for the artifact with the soul of a dragon to answer.

No reply came.

"You want me to answer this question?" The Kid stood and began pacing. "You want me to come to my own conclusions about this life, and what's going on?

"In one world," the Kid gestured with his hands, working through his thoughts, "I'm on hospice care, waiting to die in a sterile hospital room. I didn't even have my own house, or any family left to go to, where I could die in a home surrounded by loved ones. I have a Pomeranian, named Cuddles, who I see every few days. I still think Janice—who always reminds me of that Fleetwood Mac knock-off Muppet in Dr. Teeth's band—has taken my baby home to take care of her, but brings her in to see me. And yes, Cuddles is a her, though I'm also pretty sure I've heard Nurse Janet calling Cuddles Rowlf, and a he.

"Hm," the Kid stopped pacing for a moment, "this definitely has shades of Veterinarian's Hospital to it."

The Kid shook his head to clear it, then continued pacing and talking.

"Here," the Kid smiled, "I'm a free-styling champion of the city. An urban Robin Hood. Hero to the poor and downtrodden. Okay, well, maybe that's a bit of an exaggeration. But I thought, I felt, like I was doing something here. Something good. It didn't feel like I was just hiding and avoiding things, but maybe I was.

"I lived life through TV shows before," the Kid was speaking directly to Fred now, who clacked his stone claws in response to the words, "experiencing it through Alice and Dingbat in Mel's Diner. Happy Days, CHiPs, Hart to Hart, Columbo, Kojak, MASH, Bob Newhart, and others, all showed me it was okay to laugh. How I related to Vera, who always had her head in the clouds, never gave up hope, even when Mel yelled at her. It was like my life at home, except Mel never hit Vera. And if he had, then Jolene would have knifed the bastard behind the restaurant.

"But I didn't have a Jolene," the Kid sighed, and wiggled onto a barrel to sit. "I didn't have anyone, really; I wasn't allowed to have people. Not until he left. And right after he left, my son needed me, right up until he went to college.

"I supported my son through that time, too," the Kid was staring into the distance now, "eight long years, I worked three jobs so my boy could get an education and live a life better than mine.

"You know," she said, "I've never told you his name. He's Dennis. Dennis Michael. I don't like to use his name, because we named him after his father, who was never around since my son was nine years old. And I guess it's easier to think of him as my son, then give him his own identity.

"But here," he said, "I get to be more than I was there. I'm like a superhero and can do things that no one in my other life could ever do. I leap tall buildings, well, sorta. I made a difference to people here.

"I guess I made a difference there, too, but I never felt it. Does that make sense? Do you know what I mean?"

The Kid paused in his introspection, but there was no answer to his questions.

"It makes me question staying here," the Kid jumped down from the barrel and began pacing again, "is it for selfish reasons? I know if I go back to my world, it won't be for long. I'm on the Reaper's short list.

"But you know what?" The Kid cocked his head and put one hand on his hip, very reminiscent of his behavior when he was Jen in the other world. "I *did* make a difference there. I helped others, supported them, and not just my son. I touched a lot of lives, and gave hope to some, and made others laugh. Or maybe I just made them feel better about themselves by them looking down on me and my life. Doesn't matter, I made a difference.

"I should acknowledge that and give myself credit where credit is due."

The Kid smiled, but it was half-hearted.

"But what should I do now?" he asked. "Live selfishly for myself, or help others, or is it something more than either one of those?

"I think it's both," he said, pulling Edsumar from the sheath at his hip and looking at the ivory blade, "and neither. This is a new life, and a new chance, but it would be pemtie to ignore what I've already learned. So, I should take all these things into consideration, enjoy each moment of this second chance at life that I've been given, but still do what I enjoy most, which is helping others.

"Is that what you meant?" the Kid pointedly asked the artifact.

No, the Kid could swear that Edsumar's voice had a smirk in it. *I just meant that you should go investigate that magical disturbance.*

"What magical disturbance?" the Kid scoffed. "I didn't sense anything."

The building rumbled and shook, dust and dirt raining down from overhead.

The Kid ran out of the door, bolting down the long hallway, and towards the exit. The newly made minion skittered in his wake.

The thought of being crushed under a falling building made him move faster, but the excitement of seeing what was going on was his real motivation.

He'd found his place and loved the idea of adventure. The Kid knew he'd gotten comfortable with Durgan's Keep, and it was easy to continue doing what he'd been doing here in this city.

But there was more out there, and he took the stairs up to the ground level two at a time. Bursting into the courtyard outside the door, he could see the green tint to the sky outside and to the southeast.

That…disturbance, Edsumar sounded smug again.

The Kid harrumphed, his run slackening to a halt, Fred slowing beside him.

And as a side note, Edsumar added, *I really hate that creature you made, and can't wait for it to be destroyed.*

"I'm going to need to find Torrents," the Kid sighed, "aren't I?"

It's likely, Edsumar answered. *It seems that the two of you, and others like you, are inexorably linked.*

"Others?" The Kid blinked. "Wait, there are more of us?"

Chapter 6

Torrents limped. He'd applied compresses to his various wounds, binding the ones that wouldn't stop bleeding. He headed west by southwest towards the valley in the Wandering Hills where the people he cared for waited at Dargaon's Hole.

The green light to the southeast still danced on the horizon like a sickly version of the northern lights, with purplish cracks appearing and disappearing throughout it.

Normally, he'd have made the run back to the cavern complex in less than a day, but his injuries slowed him down. The barbarian had been walking for a day and half since he had faced down ratmen and scared off the luck-bringing twinglinds.

"Some luck," Torrents muttered, using a branch he'd cut as a crutch. "Those damn lizard things don't bring anything except salmonella and infection. They remind me of those worm guys from Men in Black, always underfoot and yipping about nothing."

The big man sighed, working his way up a dew-covered hill.

"Great, now I'm talking to myself." He put his wrist against his forehead and nodded after holding it there for a few moments. "Yup, just as I thought, I have a fever. I also really want some coffee after thinking about those worm aliens."

The world jerked sideways, and Torrents wrinkled his brow in confusion. Then something hit him hard in the side, knocking the wind from him.

He lay still, catching his breath, trying to figure out what hit him, and why his side was wet and cold all of a sudden.

"Hmph," he mumbled, turning his head sideways, "I fell over. At least, I think I did. Either that, or the world suddenly flipped vertical."

He pushed himself to an upright sitting position, doing it slow so the world wouldn't spin faster. He picked bits of grass off the side of his face.

"Why is there dew in the middle of the afternoon?" His voice sounded weird in his ears—like it was full of overcooked egg noodles—distracting him. "Did that rhyme? Dew, afternew…oon. Hm, maybe not."

He twisted where he sat, looking around and trying to get his bearings.

"Okay," he pulled the makeshift crutch closer, and set it to help pull himself up, "I think I fell down. Not just down, like to the ground, but down to the bottom of the hill. I'm gonna to have to stand, and I need to walk. If I don't, then no one will find me."

He pushed to his feet, using the crutch as, well, a crutch. Standing, he swayed, closed his eyes, and held onto the thick branch for balance.

"Oh chuz," he shifted his weight for better balance, felt hot pain shoot up his leg and into his gut, then yelped, "oh chuz! That hurt. But I gotta move on, or no one will find me."

He moved forward with a lurch, his backpack sliding and throwing his balance to one side.

"It's like I'm playing the worst game of hide and seek, ever," panting for breath, he shoved the bag with his elbow, and it shifted to the other side, jerking him backwards, "because no one is actually looking for me, and I'm not…really hiding."

Torrents lumbered forward, pushing his breath out with each purposeful step. He made his way up the hill, sloping to one side, making the journey of this hilltop, into more of an orbit of it. He went up at an angle, never quite reaching the top, as his satchel's weight pulled him to one side and came down at a similar angle.

He didn't realize that he'd only gone about a quarter of the way around the hill before reaching the bottom again and set off in a direction that led away from his desired destination.

The barbarian couldn't talk anymore, saving his breath for breathing, and moving forward, one step at a time.

His lips moved, his thoughts wandering through and around the concept of stopping, making a fire, and boiling water. It would have to be a defensible spot, because he wouldn't be able to move far for a few days, at least.

That was his intended thought process, but his fevered brain kept roaming in different directions, pulled by the weight of the infection, much in the same way his body was being pulled by the weight of the equipment on his back.

He looked up and saw stars coming out in a dusky sky.

"When'd…that…happen?" each word was a separate gasp for air.

He sighed and shook his head, which almost caused him to topple.

Coughing, slow and light at first, but then catching in his throat, it became harsh and grating.

When he finally stopped, he was panting to catch his breath, and realized he'd fallen to his knees.

"Damn it," his words were little more than a moan, his lips not even coming together in his exhaustion.

Torrents rolled the pack off his back and onto the wet grass.

He crawled around, scraping loose leaves, twigs, and some small brush from the ground, piling it up.

Leaning back and taking his crutch in both hands, one at each end, he put his booted foot in the center. Pulling with his hands, he pushed with his foot. It took three tries before he got the stick to break in half.

He fell back onto the wet grass when it broke, one piece in each hand and his legs stretched out. The effort exhausted him, but he knew he couldn't pass out yet.

Sitting up took all the effort he could muster.

He tossed the two pieces towards the pile of brush and tinder, then pushed them into place with his feet.

Torrents pulled his pack to him, fumbled with the leather ties, and after almost a minute, got it open.

He rummaged through the bag, tossing anything flammable onto his makeshift campfire. Pulling out a metal flask that held oil, he pushed the satchel off his lap and to one side.

The barbarian broke the wax seal around the cork, threw the cork and wax into the unlit fire, and poured the oil on the moist kindling and wood.

Dropping the flask to one side, he fumbled for a bit of flint from a pouch and drew a dagger. Striking the one against the other, causing sparks to fly, he prayed to Torr the fire would light.

With a pop and whoosh, the small pile of flammables went up in a mini inferno, throwing him back in surprise.

"I think I may need to find new eyebrows," Torrents muttered, panting, "but first, I have to get up and get more wood."

Ten minutes later, he lay and watched the flames jump two meters into the air, praying to Torr the fire would last long enough.

He passed out, shivering in the heat, moments later.

Torrents's eyes fluttered open when something cold, wet, and rough touched his armpit. His vision swam as he tried to focus on the figure bending over him.

He jerked away, attempting to sit up.

A firm hand pressed to his chest, holding him in place with almost no effort.

He was as weak as a tissue paper golem in a downpour and crumpled back onto the furs he was lying on.

"Easy, big guy," a man's voice said. "You're okay, you're safe, and you're with friends."

The voice was as familiar as someone shouting through a crowd of cotton dolls during a rave.

Noises pounded against Torrents's skull, and colors swirled into darkness.

His stomach lurched with his attempted movement, but was empty and had nothing to lose.

Torrents closed his eyes and grabbed the wrist attached to the hand that was stroking his chest soothingly.

"Can you stop that, Axle?" he mumbled, wheezing. "This feels awkward."

The hand patted his chest and moved away, replaced with a damp linen washcloth. The cloth scraped against his skin like wet sandpaper.

"Stop cleaning me, too," the barbarian said, his eyes still closed.

"But you stink," Axle's voice was clearer and closer now, "and if someone doesn't clean you, I fear the council will choose to throw you into the wild and let the hyenas have their way with you."

"You should just put him out of his misery," another familiar voice said. "Badass men make the worst patients, even worse than doctors."

Torrents sighed.

"What the hell is he doing here?" the barbarian opened his eyes, searching for the unwanted face that he was pretty sure was looming over him.

The Kid's smile came into focus, holding up one hand and waving his fingers at the warrior in the sickbed.

"Miss me?" the Kid asked.

"Like the plague," Torrents spat, then broke into a fit of coughing, pushing himself to a sitting position with the help of Axle.

"Drink this," Axle said once the coughing fit subsided. "You need fluids."

"Yes," Torrents rasped, "Doctor Mom."

The barbarian accepted the wooden cup held to his lips, and slurped loudly, trying to gulp the offered water.

Axle held the cup at an angle do the big man could only get sips instead of mouthfuls.

"Too much and you'll get sick," Axle said sagely, "and no one wants to clean that up. Speaking of cleaning things up, what the hell did you get in to?"

"Ratmen," Torrents said, holding himself up to look around.

He was in a familiar cavern with a high ceiling and walls that had been worked long in the past. A fire was glowing and crackling in the hearth across the room. He lay on a cot of furs and blankets, a table and chair beside him. The table held jars, pitchers, a large bowl, and a wooden cup. The chair held Axle. On the other side of the bed were his pack and weapons.

People passed through the public space, glancing over at the barbarian and his companions.

The Kid stood at the foot of the cot, arms crossed, and his smug little smile right where it always was.

"Poison?" Axle asked, washing the big man's back now that he was sitting up.

"Maybe," Torrents growled, "or just infection from dirty weapons being stabbed all the way through my abdomen. And stop washing me!"

The barbarian batted uselessly at his friend's efforts to clean the crusted sweat off him.

"Oh, let him do it," the Kid's tone was mocking, "you big baby. This isn't a movie where you can just get up and walk away from the kind of injuries you had."

Axle gave the Kid an odd look, but the two of them had gotten used to such looks when they mentioned things from their home world.

"What are you even doing here?" Torrents gave up on trying to stop Axle from his task and instead glared at the Kid. "How'd you even get here? I thought you were playing cops and robbers at Durgan's Keep."

"Trinity," Axle said, "after she saw your signal fire and brought you back here, she said she heard some sort of dragon god calling to her, and that she had to go. She came back with the Kid."

"How long was I out?" Torrents winced as Axle scrubbed at the healing cuts and bruises on his back.

"Three days," Axle said cheerfully, "since we lugged you in here and tossed you on the cot. You took a hell of a beating, and rightfully should be damned dead right now."

"Well," Torrents pushed Axle away, threw his legs over the side of the cot, and stood up shakily, "I've got to go, something's happened at the Demon Front, and I don't think it can wait."

Torrents, one hand on the side of the bed for support, gathered his pack and slung it over his shoulder. As he bent to pick up his weapons, Axle snickered, and the Kid out right laughed.

"Don't you think," the Kid pointed at Torrents's groin when the big man looked at him, "you should get some pants first?"

Chapter 7

The bustling city of Red Wind overwhelmed Nathan. A little by the mass of people and the activity, but mostly by the smell. He'd been a proud business owner in Denver, Colorado for over a dozen years, and had visited places like Las Vegas once or twice, so he'd seen crowds of people doing what they do in a city.

But he'd never smelled anything like the people of this city. He wished he were upwind of the whole place.

It was the dirt roads, the animals, the lack of sanitation services, but mostly the unwashed masses.

The whole town was a sprawling mess. It didn't have a building taller than three stories except for the fifteen watchtowers marking the original border, and seven of them were nothing more than dilapidated ruins at this point. Four of the remaining eight were strongholds of powerful cartels within the city, and the government and its meager watch still controlled the other four.

The town comprised mostly brick buildings with some stucco and wood structures, and half of it had been razed and burned to the ground about a dozen years ago. Nathan noted that the smell of wet smolder and mildew still moved through the air when the wind was right.

In the two days he'd been here, he'd learned some of the history of Red Wind and the Red Plains. It was semi-protected by the Lasso River, which snaked around, having been a trading post a hundred years back. When guilds came to the town, it blossomed into a tent city, and later—as it grew, and proper buildings replaced most of the tents—to a merchant run government via a council of money-hungry vultures in human form.

It rose to power as a financial behemoth when the organized crime families took over and opened a booming drug trade. They manufactured the drugs produced from the red flowers that gave the Red Plains their name.

When the war came, following the Talisman, the town fell into chaos, as did most of the continent.

The march of undead armies and demonic hordes scouring the countryside affected criminals and law-abiding citizens alike. Slaughtering them.

The town was now run by several criminal factions who had branched out into protecting its people while trying to build a financial infrastructure from the ruins of their civilization.

Nathan moved through the dusty, crowded street, dodging and weaving around people, wagons, and anything else that pressed past him, ignoring anyone who was in their way.

It was difficult to see where he was going with the reduced height in this new body. It hadn't been an issue when jogging through the plains by himself, but in the swell of stinky residents, it became a challenge.

Dust clotted his nose, blocking some of the smell, but made him cough every time he took a deep breath. He held a kerchief to his mouth and nose, which turned his apologies to barely audible mumbles as he moved out of people's way.

He'd taken up residence in an inn—named Bluster's Boil, a ramshackle establishment that barely passed for a building—and he'd left it that morning on an outing to find a map of the local area. He really, really didn't want to make this his permanent home.

He made a beeline for a jeweler's shop that caught his eye.

Nathan opened the stout door, entered the shadowy shop, and slowed to a stop. He wasn't sure if he'd come in because he was a jeweler himself, or if his rokairn desire for shiny things and craftsmanship combined had called to him.

The small antechamber, which didn't hold any products, had a single curtained doorway catty corner from where Nathan stood looking around.

A man with a bent nose and dark, greasy hair—combed over to cover his balding pate—looked at the rokairn with a squint.

"Whadda you want?" the man leaned on the counter, glaring at him over a dented goblet, and a plate with a hunk of meat as greasy as the man's hair, a lump of cheese, and a chunk of bread.

"Um, sorry to disturb your lunch," Nathan shuffled from foot to foot. "It looks really hunky-dorie."

Nathan smiled.

The man glowered.

"I just came in to look around," the man turned even more sour, and Nathan backpedaled, "no, no, you see I'm a jeweler, too, and just wanted to admire your craftsmanship. I miss it, you know?"

The man's look didn't improve. In fact, he hunched his shoulders further and outright scowled, then jerked a thumb towards the curtain.

Nathan hurried through the cloth and bead partition, keeping his eyes on his feet until he was in the next room. Once inside, he lifted his gaze and looked around.

The room was dark woods and red velvet. Ornate couches with silk cushions were set into alcoves, and alabaster columns accented the areas between the private niches and the main room.

Shorter columns held matched sets of necklaces, rings, bracelets, and other jewelry. They lined every display with black velvet in the center and delicately wrought silver and gold ornamentation along the corners.

A bored looking, broad-shouldered man with his arms crossed stood in one corner, continuously scanning the room.

Two women, draped in diaphanous white silk, lounged on a divan in the center of the room. They rose as Nathan entered, one picking up a silver tray of grapes and cut melons, the other lifting a matching silver carafe and goblet from a marble table. Both slinked towards him with soft smiles and hooded eyes.

An older, effeminate man who was exceedingly thin stood on the other side of the room, his smile a wide slit that ran from ear to ear. The man—also dressed in hanging silks, but his were purple, and reminded Nathan of a Roman toga—clasped his hands together, like he just won a beauty contest.

The man nodded his head in Nathan's direction, and fluttered a hand towards the serving women, indicating the rokairn should enjoy the amenities.

Nathan was stunned, backing away with his hands raised, his jaw trying to push out words his throat wasn't delivering. This place was such a dichotomous change compared to the ramshackle and dusty world outside.

He'd seen upscale establishments in his world, even been to jewelry conventions where the more successful companies would do up their areas like lounges. But he'd never seen anything like this.

The two women didn't speak a word, but offered the platter of fruits, a finely worked chalice of wine, and—by the silent suggestion of twirling fingers through and across the silks that barely covered them—much, much more.

"Talk about high-pressure sales techniques." Nathan waved the women away, flapping both hands like he was trying to shoo a flock of aggressive seagulls away from him on the beach. "No, thank you. I'm just looking. I don't want anything but to look at the craftmanship. I'm sorry, but thank you, I'm sorry, I don't want any of what you're offering. Though, it's lovely, and looks delicious. Not you two, I mean the food and wine. Not that you two aren't lovely, but I'm here for the jewelry, not an escort service."

He moved around the room—keeping his back to the wall and the women always in sight—towards the burly man standing in the corner.

"You here to protect the merchandise?" Nathan asked the big guy without looking up.

The rokairn saw the large man nod out of the corner of his eye.

The older man was sashaying in his direction, leaning down the closer he got to Nathan.

"Oh, you dear, sweet dwarf," the man simpered. "I'm Elequontius, your delighted host. No need to bother that brute. He's simple and can barely put a sentence together, and I shall cater to your every whim and need. If the women bother you, I shall take care of everything myself."

Something inside Nathan snapped. It was more of a click of a deep-seated instinct within the body that he inhabited. Nathan didn't like bullies, and though people might pick on him, he wouldn't stand by and let someone pick on someone else who couldn't defend themselves. He knew being nice wouldn't work with this sort of man, and the proprietor would keep pushing, taking any hesitation as encouragement.

"No," Nathan stood to his full height, his Rokairn accent coming out as he jabbed the thin man in the chest with a thick finger, "first, I'm Rokairn, not a dwarf. Don't talk down to me, and don't be a racist. Second, I don't want a suck up bothering me. I don't want some women throwing themselves at me in hopes that it'll lead to me spending more money. Third, I'll deal with the brute, and the brute only. Am I understood?"

"But, my good dw-rokairn," the man cleared his throat and went on, "this man knows nothing of the goods we sell…"

"Does he stand here each day, watching and observing?" Nathan growled.

"Well, yes," the man took a breath to go on, but Nathan interrupted again.

"I think that's good enough." The rokairn turned towards the guard, ignoring further protests from Elequontius, "you've been paying attention when you're standing here all day?"

The guard nodded.

"You know enough to show me things and answer simple questions, considering I'm a master jeweler?"

The guard nodded again.

"What's your name?" Nathan asked.

"Nob," he answered, but it sounded like he had a wad of cotton in both cheeks, "and I don't think anyone has ever talked to me in here. But I ain't no pemtie. I can help ya."

"But," Elequontius interrupted, wringing his hands and giving Nathan a sickly smile, "I don't think…"

"And you don't need to. Nob will do the thinking while I'm here. You go polish your…" Nathan pushed past the shopkeeper, Nob trailing after him, "goods. I'll only deal with this man while here."

Nathan drew out a pouch and undid the ties, walking towards a display, pouring an assortment of coins and gems into his palm, displaying them for the older man to see.

"Think this is enough to buy something here, Nob?" Nathan looked up at the big man.

"Yup," Nob smiled as he looked at the currency, "and I know they give you discounts when you pay up front. You lookin' for custom work, or just something to take away today?"

"I'm just looking," Nathan handed the man red gemstone and a few coins, "but you keep that for yourself since you're going to do such a fine job helping me, and making sure those other people don't bother me, okay?"

"Yup," Nob nodded.

Nathan spent the next twenty minutes inspecting pieces in relative silence, only breaking it to ask simple questions.

He held a platinum and sapphire cuff up to the light, inspecting the settings and cut of the stone, when the far wall shook from some sort of impact.

A scream filtered through the noise-dampening wall coverings, and the sound of steel on steel followed.

Nathan looked towards the noise, his brow furrowing. He thrust the band towards Nob, turned and strode towards the door, unstrapping his double-headed axe from his back.

He pushed through the curtain into the entry chamber, ignored the greasy-haired man behind the counter who stared at him with frightened eyes, and pushed through the door into the street.

Horns cut through the murmur of conversation on the street outside that hung in the air as thick as the dust.

The baying and laughing of the hyenas and their keepers drifted through the streets.

Nathan grunted, turned in the ruckus's direction, set his feet, pulled his shoulders back, hefted his blade, and moved towards it.

Chapter 8

Standing in the noonday sun, Klendrisia surveyed the city from a small hill on the outskirts, her dark skin glistening a deep green that betrayed her mood.

She hated how her skin betrayed her emotions to anyone bothering to observe her. She fought an inner war, battling herself and her heritage, to overcome her passionate nature and exert control over her mind and reactions.

The demon-spawn watched her gnohls, led by Ghe'hak the Ravager. He was an experienced pack leader, having had the position for almost four and a half months. A full season without being killed.

She remembered when he'd first changed and became a gnohl, and how he'd fought amongst the pack for his place. He was cunning, and chose his rivals with keen ability, taking them out and making his climb to pack leader.

But that wasn't why Klendrisia was fond of him. She liked him because he didn't kill without discretion. The gnohl killed easily and with pleasure that was more than bone deep, but he always did it with a reason rather than delight.

It was the beast's weakness. Someone would exploit it. The keen intelligence that haunted Ghe'hak would be his downfall, and that might come during this battle.

The other gnohls swarmed towards the city walls, now broken and shattered, remnants of a once powerful landmark in this part of the land. The hyena-headed creatures ran forward—some on two legs, others dropping to all fours and bounding over eroded battlements and earthworks.

Packs of snarling hyenas, some as large as a human at their shoulder, wove through their bipedal counterparts. These animals killed without a thought, devouring any human, rokairn, or aeifain they could find. Their reward for massacring the enemy was the chance they'd evolve into a humanoid and become a gnohl who could better serve their demon masters.

Klendrisia shouted commands that were lost in the dull thunder of hundreds of her minions charging forward, a cloud of dust marking their passage. The orders didn't matter, anyway; these troops weren't assembled for surgical strikes against an enemy. She brought them together as a horde, meant to sweep across the landscape and leave a swath of devastation to bring fear to anyone who saw, or heard of, their passing.

Klendrisia shouted the orders because she enjoyed it. It was part of her nature, to organize what she had to make it more efficient, to help her overcome anything in her way. It was against her demonic side and instead came from her mother's side.

Her mother had been a holy warrior of Jonath—the god of honor, earth, agriculture, and protection—taken prisoner by Klendrisia's father. The woman had been a prized trophy and eventually impregnated. Klendrisia didn't know the details, only that her mother died giving birth to her.

She took after her mother in some ways—or so she understood.

Her sire hated this about her, which was why he'd sent her out with just a single pack of gnohls and hyenas to hunt the rokairn warrior, Nathan.

When she had succeeded in diverting him from his task, two things happened; they tapped into the Pyridom of Power, allowing a new doorway between realities to open and bring in new demons and troops from the Abyss; and Klendrisia had been—reluctantly, by her father—given this new mission.

Hunt down the key to open the gates of the next portal, so her father's armies could spill into this dimension and take it for their own.

Just over a hundred years ago, the first portal had been reopened. It was in the south, on the peninsula named Land's End. Thousands of demons had poured through, but the majority of them were minor beings with no leadership. Heroes rose and fought them back and they made little progress in the way of an invasion. The portal had been shattered, but some remnants remained and allowed more powerful beings to creep through.

The problem with that, though, is the ones with armies backing them wouldn't risk coming through to this world without their armies, and the ones who did come through were rogue elements.

Klendrisia smiled as her forces reached the edge of the city. The meager guard at the border went down in a flurry of carnage, and her troops spread into the city.

She moved forward, drawing her two-handed blade with one hand and raising it above her head. Using her magics to amplify her voice, a simple task, she screamed her fury, so it echoed throughout the town.

Entering the city, the smell of animals and human waste reached her nose. Smells in Gehenna and the Abyss were bad, putrid, and foul, but the human worlds had their special portfolio of reeks, stenches, and fetid aromas that weren't matched in any of the other known dimensions.

The sounds of screams, blending terror and death, reached her ears. She noted screams about death rarely came from the receiver of the gift, rather it came from observers who were too pemtie to run, and instead stood and watched. It was an open invitation to be the next candidate in line to receive the blessings of eternal rest.

Klendrisia didn't have to put effort into the killing. People merely presented themselves for a task she thought of as mundane. She ran her tarnished blade across their bellies, chests, thighs, or whatever was presented as they bolted from her horde. Their enemies fell, leaving a trail of bodies and viscera behind.

She didn't bother to kill them all, just to take them out of the fight. Leaving some alive allowed them to suffer and spread the tale of her and her army crossing the land. It was marketing at its best, in her mind. Eliminating them from the fight, but still being around to spread the word of her conquests.

Ghe'hak had a small group of elite gnohls with him, and striding into the town, she saw him picking out any person who dared make a stand against her and her army.

Heroes fell, dashing themselves against the onslaught of wholesale butchery. Brave men wielding blades of their ancestors died in a split second, ending their legacy and family lines.

Klendrisia smiled. They were pemties, throwing their lives away against an unstoppable force.

The pack leader howled in the fervor of killing, inciting his followers into a blood rage.

The demon half-breed moved through the streets, cutting people down without prejudice. Her actions were almost an afterthought. When she killed a group of five adventurers, her only thought was that they shouldn't have drunk so much that they stumbled when leaving the pub, where they'd been spending their money made in the blood of other creatures.

Loot, my ass, she thought.

She strolled through the gore-ridden streets of Red Wind, spotting a familiar figure. A short, stout man stood at a crossroads, wielding his double-headed battle axe, and occasionally pulling out a hand axe and throwing it into a gnohl.

Nathan, the rokairn she'd encountered in the Crescent Desert, stood beside an equally broad-shouldered human with a hand-and-a-half sword.

The two cut down every one of Klendrisia's minions that came within their blades' arcs, and a handful that didn't.

She watched in fascination as the short, bearded man worked his weapon in arcs, figure eights, and wild swings. It was like watching an artiste performing a brutal, ritualistic dance to the gods themselves. The man focused and zeroed in on a target, launched an attack, and then moved to another before the first crumpled to the dusty street in front of him.

But the street wasn't so dusty anymore. It was a gooey pool of blood and grime, a thick, viscous soup of death and determination.

In Klendrisia's eyes, it was a thing of beauty. Every movement was passion incarnate, as this rokairn defended strangers from death.

Of course, it was useless. There was no overcoming the challenge she presented. But if anyone had a chance, it would be this warrior.

She watched his focus break when a gnohl tore a chunk from the big human beside the rokairn. A surprising burst of concern broke Nathan's concentration as the human fell under three of Klendrisia's attacking legion.

The little man was vulnerable. He cared about the creatures dying around him.

The realization surprised the demoness, if she cared to consider herself in that light, and she wondered about it.

How would she feel if Ghe'hak fell? Would she care? Wasn't he just another pawn in this game, a thing to be used and discarded when his usefulness passed?

Why would anyone ever allow themselves to care if someone else died? That was akin to becoming emotionally attached to your sword. It, and they, had their use, but once that expired, why invest any more thought into something no longer useful?

It just felt so…self-destructive and pemtie.

She raised her sword from the dusty street, thinking to step in and end the ignorant rokairn's suffering.

Why should she care if he was in pain? Why did she want to show him mercy and kill him, so he no longer had to face the inevitable distress of watching those he knew die?

This was one of the things she often considered, blaming her human heritage for her weak thoughts.

Why would anyone ever care if someone else died or suffered? It was a ridiculous concept, and self-defeating.

Something drew her attention, and she looked away from the dance in the distance. Something called to her, niggling at the edge of her awareness.

A tingle crept along her dark flesh, like a dozen spiders running up her arm. A sharp, but distant, ringing came to her ears.

The key. It was active, and it sung to her.

She reached out with her mind, searching for the artifact that would open the next portal. Her mission goal, once accomplished, would be instrumental in bringing the full might of her father's forces to this realm.

It called to her again.

Like a hound on a scent, she stepped forward without conscious thought, knowing this one thing must come before anything else.

She tore her awareness from the distant, sweet siren call of the magic that would achieve what no one else could and looked one more time at the rokairn.

Nathan was staring at her, the big human, leaning heavily on him as the man's breath clenched in his chest, and he struggled to live another few moments.

Recognition dawned in Nathan's eyes, and Klendrisia could see the man's jaw working, trying to make sounds to ask questions.

They always questioned, these despicable, pathetic mortals, whenever they were cut down like stalks of diseased grain.

You didn't let the weak survive. It made sense to hew the lesser, so the strong may thrive. Why didn't the beings of this place understand that simple rule of nature?

The demoness saluted her foe, smiling with a smug expression.

She would let him live, today at least. Perhaps he'd be challenging and give her some small distraction during the overly simple task of recovering the artifact she sought by killing anyone in the way.

Four humans swarmed around the distracted rokairn warrior, one taking his wounded companion, and another placing a hand his shoulder. The newcomer touching Nathan spoke words Klendrisia couldn't hear. The rokairn turned to look at the hand on his glowing spaulder.

Priest of Jonath, Klendrisia thought, *isn't that a quaint coincidence? The very organization that my own dame belonged to, coming to help my nemesis. Oh, I have a nemesis now? Interesting.*

Nathan had turned back to look at her through slitted eyes, but the call of the key was stronger than the unspoken challenge.

Klendrisia buffered her voice with her magics once again.

"Come to me," her screech shook windows in buildings, and the nerves of strong warriors across the town, "kill all in your path, but join me as we seek our goal."

Swinging her sword to her side, she secured it into place with her other hand.

She threw a look over her shoulder at the rokairn, who was running towards her, the four humans behind him shouting in dismay.

She smiled at him, turned away, and moved with inhuman speed towards the northwest, and the song that hung in the air, beckoning to her.

She knew he'd follow. She'd have her chance to kill him soon enough. And hope would die on her blade.

Chapter 9

"Chuz!" Torrents yelped, collapsing to the ground beside Trinity's foreleg.

The dragon looked down at the tawny-skinned man.

"My apologies?" The dragon said sarcastically. "Perhaps it's my fault you chose to leave the conclave before being well enough to travel?"

The Kid snickered, a bit louder than what would have been considered accidental.

"It's the stitches in my belly," Torrents pushed the words out through clenched teeth, "they might have ripped when I slid off you. And it's not nearly as smooth a ride as I expected on the back of a dragon. I mean, damn it, you jerked up and down with every wing stroke, and any breeze caused you to lurch to one side or the other."

"I can kick you in the knee," the Kid offered, "and that'd help you forget about the pain in your gut."

"Go chuz yourself." Torrents didn't bother looking up from checking his bandages, swearing at the other rider, who was still atop the dragon's back. "Maybe that will distract me enough that I forget the pain in my ass. And by that, I mean you're a pain in my ass."

"Thanks for explaining that one," the Kid slid down the side of the silver-white, winged reptile, landing with a flourish beside Trinity, "otherwise I might've thought you meant your own head being up your ass was causing discomfort."

Fred slid down the dragon's back, following his master.

"Children," Trinity stretched her neck between the two, "I think you'd better consider where you'll be spending the night rather than bickering."

"Children?" The Kid raised an eyebrow. "You realize I'm almost four-score years old in the other world, and in my other body?"

"Yes," Trinity bobbed her head in respect, "forgive my brash, impulsive youthfulness. I am a mere four centuries old. I apologize."

"Whatever," the Kid muttered, walking in a circle around the grassy knoll they'd landed on, "it's quality, not quantity, that counts."

"Oh?" Torrents stood upright, wincing. "So, hiding from life because your kid died and your husband left you is now considered quality?"

"Like you're one to talk," the Kid spat back, his voice turning high-pitched and mocking, "constantly whining how life broke you and took away all your natural gifts, when you killed your own father and put yourself in a wheelchair?"

Torrents's turned towards the Kid, his hand reaching over his shoulder for the double-handed pommel of his massive sword.

"Now that Esperanza is gone," Trinity sighed, "you two will kill each other long before any demonic forces can. I brought you as far as I could without attracting unwanted attention. I'll leave the two of you here, at the southern border of the Black Wood, and wish you luck in surviving your own bickering."

The dragon crouched, then launched herself into the air. The down stroke of the wings kicked up a cloud of dust, causing the two below to cough and cover their eyes. Fred clacked his claws, attempting to snag one of the many leaves that swirled through the air at the dragon's departure.

"I've missed you," the Kid grinned at Torrents, "at least with you I could say anything and get away with it. But I have a splitting headache right now. It's been lingering since I created Fred."

"You're a jerk, and cranky." Torrents sighed, "you know my temper. Why'd you push me? If I was into beating up old ladies, or young punks, I'd have a field day with your face."

"That's what he said?" The Kid raised an eyebrow. "Is that a thing? It started after I was too old to care, but can we do 'he' in that phrase instead of 'she'?"

"Just stick to quoting movies," Torrents bent to pick up his pack and supplies he'd dropped from— what they affectionately called—the luggage rack on the back of Trinity, and winced with the movement, "it'll be easier on all of us."

"Fo-shizzle," the Kid watched the barbarian move around the hilltop, "you should have stayed in bed more than three days, dude. You weren't ready for this, and two more days on and off a dragon didn't help you."

"I'll be fine," Torrents stiffened, trying to hide his discomfort, "and once we get to PepperGarten, I'm sure he'll have something to help me."

"Yeah, I guess," the Kid picked up his small pack, and Fred scurried over to him, allowing him to strap the bag to the construct's back, "but really, who hunts dragons? Can they really be that much of a threat?"

"I'd think…" Torrents began.

"That'd be refreshing change," the Kid interrupted.

"I'd think," Torrents said with a growl, "that you'd be a bit more cautious of anything a dragon fears. And she explained how her kind has been hunted in the east since the Wizard Wars."

"But that was like a thousand years ago," the Kid scoffed, turning to survey to the south, "you'd think they'd lose interest by now."

The hill they'd landed on was bare except for dew-ridden grass, though it was afternoon. The long-lasting after-effects of the comet Talisman had made weird climate changes that had long-lasting repercussions.

A few trees dotted the hillside below, and a stream trickled to the east, the runoff from the mountains to the north feeding the foothills to the south.

Birds took to wing in the south, an enormous flock of egrets who'd taken to sticking together for the herd-mentality protection.

The Kid pondered for a moment before turning to Torrents.

"Why would a bunch of birds suddenly take off when we're nowhere near them?" the Kid asked.

"Predator?" Torrents stepped around Fred, adjusting the sword on his back and looking in the direction that the Kid was staring.

A cloud of dust appeared in the distance. It was small and faint, but it was a definite indicator of something large. Or of many smaller things moving as a unit.

The laughing bark and howls wafted across the distance.

"What was that?" The Kid fingered his magical dagger without being aware he was doing so.

Gnohls, Edsumar's voice answered in the Kid's mind.

"Gnohls?" the Kid echoed.

"What the chuz are gnohls?" Torrents shaded his eyes from the mist-hazed sun above to get a better view of whatever it was in the distance. "Is that cloud headed towards us?"

Hyena and demon hybrids, Edsumar mentally informed the Kid, *formed from the broken corpses and spirits of humans they kill. And yes, I do believe they're coming this way.*

"Uh huh, they're bad things, hyena-men with demon heritage," the Kid mumbled. "I have a bad feeling about this."

"Star Wars?" Torrents sighed, reaching over his shoulder to free his weapon. "Really? You're doing that now?"

"Do we run? Hide?" The Kid looked around for cover. "Or do we wait here and hope they're not coming for us?"

"Why would they be coming for us?" Torrents scoffed. "We just got here. They might keep moving past this hill."

The two watched in silence for a few minutes, the cloud turning more in their direction.

"Or not," The Kid drew Edsumar from his sheath. "Looks like someone was waiting for us to arrive. Why do they always have to be looking for us?"

"Because we're awesome," Torrents shrugged, "and know we can kick their ass, and want to take us out for the street cred?"

"So," the Kid sighed, "we're fighting then?"

"Unless you have a better idea," Torrents shrugged again.

The Kid looked around, hoping to see a better idea laying in the calf-high grass. He didn't see anything to help. No cover, no defendable area, no way to take out a large group without getting his hands dirty.

"Maybe they're on our side," the Kid suggested, looking tired, "and are coming here to recruit us to help their worthy cause."

"It's always delightful," Torrents rolled his eyes at the Kid looking up at him, "and wonderfully naïve when you say such things. When have they ever not wanted to kill us? This world is bidj when it comes to good guys, and a chuzzing buffet when it comes to bidjwads wanting to do horrible things."

"Okay then," the Kid sat down on a stone jutting from the ground, "I guess we wait for them to get here, and hope that the high ground is enough advantage to get through this. Can you fight in your condition?"

"Do I have a choice?" Torrents's answer was bitter. "Can I just hang back while you take out something big enough to raise that much dust?"

The two looked into the distance past the approaching danger; they could see where the threat had most likely come from.

The green light to the southeast was getting bigger. It spanned almost a quarter of the horizon in that direction now, with a dark nimbus of greasy smoke ringing it.

Whatever had come through to this world, to the Demon Front, was now burning things and creating a wasteland as they moved further across the continent.

It took almost a half hour for the two to see the forerunners of the horde: a wedge of huge, primitive proto-hyenas burst through the tree line at the bottom of the hill, the shadowy chuckles of the beasts causing the two on the hill to take a deep inhalation of breath.

The phalanx of the creatures surged up the hill, loamy soil churning under their claws, leaving a swath of bare earth behind them. Each beast was almost the height of a man at its shoulder.

Torrents, his lips a grim smile, stepped forward. He chose the stance he'd face the oncoming enemy with a double handed grip in front of him, which would allow him to swing into the bodies of his foes while still blocking their attacks.

The Kid tossed his dagger, Edsumar, into the air, causing it to flip once, then catching the handle again. He did this repeatedly, waiting for the enemy to close the distance.

As the beasts approached the crest of the hill, the Kid stepped behind the barbarian, drew his arm back, and threw Edsumar past the big man.

The dagger cut through the air, its path true, and pierced the eye of the lead hyena. The monster fell to its side, and slid to a stop along the turf, the rest of the creatures darting around it or leaping over their fallen pack member.

Torrents drew his blade up slightly, adjusting for his first strike, and winced at the pulling sensation of the injuries in his abdomen.

The first wave hit the duo, the line of monsters crashing into them.

At waist level, the barbarian swung his weapon in a wide arc. The blade cut across the chest and forelegs of the two lead beasts, severing muscle and sinew from bone. The two went down, but not before one of them locked its teeth onto the warrior's forearm.

Torrents knew fighting a four-legged predator was very different from fighting a man with a weapon. You had to watch out for teeth and claws, rather than blocking or dodging a weapon. Some people fought like their blade was an extension of their body, but most used it as the tool it was, and often that was the way through their defenses.

Animals were different; they reacted in a smooth flow, every movement and reaction connected without separate thought.

The animals the barbarian had struck weren't dead, just injured, and they continued to fight.

Torrents shoved at the one on his right with his booted foot, rolling the beast backwards into its companions and causing them to stumble.

The one on his left locked its jaws around his arm, shook its head, jerking one hand from the barbarian's grip on his sword.

Edsumar appeared in the Kid's hand in the blink of an eye, its innate magic returning it to the rogue.

Fred—the rock-lobster construct the Kid created—waded into the fray. Stone claws tore into thick hide and matted fur, ripping chunks away from the attackers in sprays of blood.

The Kid reached out with his mind, using his magics, and concealed himself in a spray of illusionary mist, ducking under the snapping jaws of the hyena bounding at him.

He came up under the beast, slashing across its belly and spilling entrails onto the wet grass. The creature snaked its head under its front legs to bite at the thief, only to receive a dagger slid across its jowl and along the side of its head, turning the attack away.

Torrents pulled his arm free, blood gushing from the wound, and caved in the hyena's skull with the pommel of his sword.

The barbarian dropped to a knee, returning his second hand to the pommel of his weapon, and thrust it down into the open maw of another of the monsters. Twisting it, he pulled it to the side and jerked it out.

The beast gurgled and stumbled, tumbling down the hill.

The Kid grabbed a handful of gravel from underfoot, held it in his open palm, picked them up with his mind, and shot them forward. The grape-sized stones turned to deadly projectiles, ripping through another beast, made a sharp turn like a tiny, deadly flock of stone birds, and tore through two more.

Fred scurried from one fallen hyena to another, his claws cutting into the beasts' throat and tearing through their jugulars and larynxes, taking them out of the fight as they died in a gout of their own fluids.

As the stones flew from one monster to another, the Kid launched Edsumar at the furthest one, embedding the blade into the creature's ribs where the heart should be. The beast skidded to its side in the grass, fighting for breath and to rise before Fred moved to end its life.

Torrents jumped over the fallen beasts in front of him, bringing his double-handed blade down on the head of one of the three remaining, crushing its skull and spine. The beast fell, twitching.

Moments later, the last two died, one by dagger and stones, the other by a length of steel through its body.

The two companions looked at one another.

Torrents was panting, his arm a ragged, bloody mess, and held to his injured stomach.

The Kid was rubbing his temples, wincing in pain. He smiled, but it was a shaky smile that lacked his normal bravado.

They nodded to one another, then turned to look in the direction where these things had come from.

Dozens more were flooding from the tree line at the bottom of the hill, accompanied by almost as many gnohls. They all bounded up the hill towards the Kid and Torrents.

"Chuz me sideways," Torrents muttered.

Chapter 10

The ground rolled and tumbled past Nathan's feet as he glanced down. His dark brown boots blended in the blur of loamy earth below his feet, moving in a constant tattoo to the bellows of his breath.

He'd been following the demoness and her murderous crew for days, sleeping when they rested, ready to move on before they were.

He knew he couldn't take them out alone, but whatever they were up to had to be stopped.

These creatures committed wholesale slaughter on a city just because they were passing close to it. They'd murdered men, women, and children just for the joy of it. They hadn't looted, hadn't taken prisoners, or even destroyed everyone in Red Wind. They'd killed while passing through. Just for fun.

That made no sense.

Why kill at all, let alone without a purpose other than the joy of it? His human mind fought with that, struggling to make sense of a senseless act. He wanted to know the reason, so maybe he could understand the actions of these creatures, though he'd never be able to accept them. His brain tumbled it around, grasping at the slippery ideas like a dog trying to catch a fish flopping in a boat during a hurricane. He just couldn't get it.

Nathan shoved the thought aside, letting his rokairn brain took over. Why worry about something you can't even conceive? That's not how you get things done. If you want answers, but can't get them, then find the next step that will get you closer to them.

That's how you do anything in life, one step at a time. Follow these beasts. Study them, fight them if needed, and find a way to stop them. That was the rokairn way, one step at a time. Take the next hammer stroke, to create the tool you need to do the job that needs to be done. One step at a time. There was never any reason to run in circles, mentally or otherwise, when it wouldn't get you closer to your goal.

The rokairn body soothed his human mind, calming and lulling it in the rhythm of movement and the task at hand—running. All else faded, barring the small thoughts dashing around his head like lightning in a bottle; thoughts of his well-being, his breath, how his legs felt, how his gear bounced, and how to make sure none of those became an issue.

Nathan didn't run fast, but he never stopped. One step at a time. He was the tortoise, and like a force of nature, he would win this battle against an extra-dimensional hare set on destroying a world that he'd been forced into.

He stumbled, physically tripping over an errant stone or root, the thoughts of his human side pummeling the reality of the rokairn side. Memory of the age-old adage, 'A journey of a thousand miles begins with one step,' or the old joke, 'How do you eat an elephant? One bite at a time.'

It all meant the same thing, just keep moving. One step at a time. There was no other way to do anything. People liked to think they can multi-task, but a body can only do one thing at a time. And it's always easier and more efficient to complete one task before starting another. Doing two things at the same time splits your attention—and creates extra work as you adjust your mind, tools, body, or whatever—to switch between doing more than one thing at once.

It wasn't just Nathan's thoughts that had pulled him from his reverie; a scene was unfolding in the distance. The sounds of the laughing barks of the gnohls and their hyena pack was the first thing to catch his attention and was often how he followed the pack without being detected. The second most common way he tracked them was by the damage they left in their wake. Torn earth, broken trees, and dead bodies.

He'd learned to keep a respectful distance after discovering they almost always sent out forward scouts, but sometimes also sent out a rear scout to make sure nothing was following.

That lesson had been a rough day.

He'd been trundling along in his fugue of concentration, not paying attention. A gnohl had appeared in front of him, launching itself from a thicket, screaming as it came at him with a pitted blade. Without a conscious thought, he'd bent under the weapon—the creature aiming poorly because of Nathan's smaller stature—and came up with two hand axes. He'd sliced across the beast's belly, opening twin vents in the thing's guts.

That hadn't stopped it, though; the monster went on, manically laughing as it chopped and hacked clumsily at Nathan.

The rokairn had pivoted, kicking the feet out from under his foe, while cutting a hamstring, and the artery in the bastard's thigh, with two separate cuts. The monster died loudly, and not easily, as Nathan danced in and out, wielding his twin blades as precisely as a surgeon would use scalpels.

The creature died, though, but not before it attracted the attention of two more gnohls and a handful of their proto-hyenas.

Nathan knew he could hunt them. He could kill them. But that would've drawn the attention of the others, and he wasn't ready to face a score and half of these things alone in a place he didn't know well enough to create a reasonable defensive position.

He'd ran, he'd hid. He created false leads and trails, making them run in circles, or just in the wrong direction. This wasn't easy, because the giant hyenas could track by smell. He'd ended up hiding in a stream, in the tangled root system of a fallen tree, to cover his scent and tracks.

They eventually gave up and returned to their war band, but Nathan had learned: keep extra distance. Watch for scouts and stay to one side rather than following the main path they'd left behind.

Now, the band was about a kilometer in front of him, its focus on something on a grassy hilltop.

He broke away without hesitation, circling the hill as he approached. There was a value in coming in behind the group and cutting them down when their focus was elsewhere. But he couldn't risk the chance they'd set out someone to watch for exactly that.

He didn't move to the opposite side of the knoll. Instead—in his mind, the gnohls were at the six o'clock position—he moved to the nine o'clock position of the hill and came in at an angle.

Atop the mound he saw a huge barbarian with a sword taller than the rokairn himself, the man bleeding from his left forearm, his stomach, and other places. Beside the barbarian was a younger man, skinny and wiry, dancing about. The smaller man only had a dagger, but seemed to use some sort of magic.

Dead hyenas and gnohls surrounded them, as well as the rest of the war band, which outnumbered the dead, and the defenders, by a lot.

Nathan's human mind shuddered, drawing the body he now inhabited to a dead stop.

"This is insane," he muttered, trying to talk himself out of what he was about to do. "I should turn west and keep going until there's nothing that wants to kill me within shouting distance."

He'd reached over his shoulder, without conscious thought, and freed his double-headed battle axe. He was spinning it in his hands, a grim smile on his face in anticipation of what came next, even as his voice argued against it.

"Do you want to risk dying to save someone else?" He asked out loud, unsure which part of his mind the question came from. "Or do you want to risk living while making a difference in the world?"

His feet were already carrying him forward, crouched as he moved, making himself less obvious. He didn't have a chance to answer himself; he'd already taken one step and wouldn't stop now.

He could have circled back around to the rear of the war party, but then he'd have to face them all at once. Well, any that weren't directly involved in the battle already.

Instead, a flanking maneuver seemed best, and he moved into a position where he'd be able to see the two men and support them, as well as get support from them.

"Kaleb triot, den'al venitier!" he roared, propelling himself into the side of the attacking force.

It had a chanting quality to it, the rhythm matching the beat of his feet.

Twenty sets of eyes—two from the defenders, the rest from the attackers—turned to look at him in surprise.

His axe was a blur as he spun around the gnohls and their minions. Three fell in as many steps, and another toppled backwards with a shattered knee from the rokairn's boot.

The two men rallied, the big one with the huge sword screaming to the god Torr for blows that strike true, and the smaller one shouting to someone called Fred to take care of the fallen and crippled enemies.

The three pushed the gnohls back, surprising them with their fervor, but the hyenas pushed forward.

The man-height beasts came in low, three snapping at the rokairn's arms. One caught the shaft of the axe in its jaws and tore the weapon away. Another bit into Nathan's wrist, clamping down on the bracer and chain mail covering it. Something popped, and the rokairn wasn't sure if the sound had come from him or the hyena.

Raising the arm with the hyena attached, he punched it in the throat, crushing its larynx. He twisted his wrist, freeing it from the gasping creature's mouth, and grabbed its head in both hands, and spun.

The hyena lifted off the ground as Nathan spun— reminding the rokairn of doing the same thing with his niece years ago, but by her hands, not her head—and when he released his grip, the creature smashed into another hyena, both flying backwards.

The third beast took advantage of this distraction, locking its teeth onto the back of the rokairn's neck, lifting him from the ground, and shaking him like a rag doll.

Small projectiles tore through the hyena, and Nathan saw the smaller man directing the path of the missiles with his hand.

A huge stone lobster clambered across the body of the beast that had released Nathan's neck, and tore out its throat with thick, rocky claws. The smaller creature dropped off the body of the hyena and to the ground with a thunk, skittering to the next fallen enemy to repeat the maneuver.

Nathan bent and retrieved his weapon, noting the damaged shaft that would need replaced. He hefted the axe and took one step, then the next step, towards a foe.

Nathan watched as the smaller man flung a dagger with the hand not guiding the stones, and the weapon flew at a gnohl's head with unerring precision.

A form coalesced in the path of the magical weapon, snatching it out of the air, and wrapping it in thick burgundy material. A shimmer radiated outward from the dagger and the cloth that covered it. A dull boom, barely audible over the combat, echoed across the hilltop.

The person holding the weapon and cloth was the same he'd met in the Crescent Desert and seen in the battle at Red Wind. She smiled at him, winked, raised her head and screamed a cry, then faded from sight.

The sound of the hideous, broken laughter of hyenas filled the air, and the gnohls raised their heads to join the pack in what felt like celebration.

As one, all the enemies turned and bolted to the north, dodging away from the defenders and making their escape from the hilltop.

The demoness appeared a quarter of a kilometer away, at the tree line at the bottom of the hill. Her wave caught Nathan's eye, and then she turned and disappeared into the forest.

The gnohls and hyenas loped down the hillside, following their master, leaving their dead behind.

"Who the chuz are you?" The deep baritone drew Nathan's attention back to the two men.

Chapter 11

Nathan turned to answer and saw the barbarian with his weapon held high in combat stance.

"Really," the smaller man's voice sounded strained and panicked, "what're you, like fifteen? Like it matters who he is? This guy shows up from nowhere to save us, someone steals Edsumar, and you're worried about him?"

"He's an unknown," the big man growled. "He could be a plant."

"Yeah, genius," the small man said, "he might be a philodendron or a radish. No! He came in on our side, and I've swept his mind. He's one of us, not from here, just like Edsumar said. We're tied together. Chuz Jack Tucker and all his bullbidj."

The rokairn looked from one man to the other, his brow furrowed, lifting his axe defensively. The shaft cracked noise as it split, the head of the weapon toppling to the ground.

"Nathan," he muttered, looking at the ground where the important part of his weapon lay stuck, blade first, in the soil, between the bodies of dead and dying enemies.

Fred scampered between the gnohls and hyenas, continuing his task of cutting throats, removing the threat of a foe rising again.

The two were staring at the rokairn, waiting for him to say something else.

"I'm sorry, I'm a jeweler?" Nathan mumbled. "And followed that war band to stop them from…"

The rokairn verbally stumbled to a halt, looking back and forth between the two men.

"A jeweler?" The bigger man asked, lowering his sword. "Your shop must be gangsta as chuz."

"That's what you're worried about?" The Kid shrilled. "I just had a priceless magical artifact snatched, and you're asking about some damn guy's store that sells watches, necklaces, and engagement rings to deluded twenty-somethings?"

Nathan and Torrents looked at the Kid.

"You have a magical weapon?" Nathan asked.

The Kid threw up his hands, huffed, and turned in a circle.

"We need to go after them," the Kid shouted.

"No," Torrents said, "we don't."

The Kid spun to face the barbarian, his face pale and incredulous.

"We don't," Torrents continued, "because I'm tore the chuz up. This guy has a broken weapon. And you, you're a mess right now. And how're you even going to fight when the weapon you always use is gone? Right now, we get somewhere that we can regroup."

"And where exactly is that?" the Kid sneered.

"PepperGarten's," Torrents said, "where we were headed, anyway. He'll know things, too; he always seems to know things."

The kid huffed and threw up his hands again.

"Um, I'm sorry," Nathan interrupted meekly as he dug his axe head out of the ground, "do I go with you?"

"I don't care what you do," the Kid sniped. "Follow, go, whatever. But I say we go after these bastards and get Edsumar back."

"We will, but," Torrents's voice was rising now, "I think we need to go to PepperGarten's first."

"If it counts for anything," Nathan said, and the others turned to look at him, "going after them right now would end up getting everyone killed. One step at a time. And if you can't move in the direction you need to go, then move in the direction that will give you what you need, to do what needs done."

Torrents and the Kid stared at Nathan.

"See?" Torrents shrugged. "He agrees with me. I say we keep him. We can always kill him later if he turns out to be a douchebag or something."

"Thanks?" Nathan gulped.

The Kid harrumphed and turned away.

"Whatever, fine," the Kid sulked, "but I can't even hear Edsumar. Whoever that woman was, she's got him blocked somehow."

"Klendrisia," Nathan offered, and the two looked him, so he continued, "I'm sorry, she's a demon half-breed. Her father is someone named Lord Ghlevid, and her mother was a human named Delia. She's opening portals for demons to come here and take over."

An awkward moment of silence drew out as the two stared at the rokairn.

"How do you even know all that?" the Kid asked.

"She told me," Nathan shrugged, "back in some desert I was in while she was trying to kill me."

"Do people always get so chatty around you when they're trying to off you?" Torrents asked, wrapping his bloody forearm.

"Not sure," Nathan shrugged again, "people never used to try to kill me, not until recently. In the past week, it's happened way more than I'd ever even thought it could. It's like living in an action movie."

"Can we walk and talk?" The Kid moved south across the hilltop, stepping around the dead bodies scattered across the grass, Fred clattering to match his pace. "If we're going to get Edsumar back, we should get going."

"Okay," Torrents nodded, tugging the end of the cloth into the rest of the bandage around his arm, "but you, Nathan, keep talking. I want to know as much about you as we can before we trust you with a watch when we're sleeping."

The barbarian scooped up his pack he dropped during combat—the Kid already picked up everything he needed to carry—and the two began walking down the hill.

Nathan scrambled after them, undoing the leather harness around his chest designed to hold his axe on his back. As he walked, he attempted to lace the head to the holder, leaving the broken shaft on the ground behind, and get it into place on his back.

"Keep talking," Torrents said when he caught up. "The Kid said you're from our world, and came here just like us? Through some magic?"

"I guess," Nathan said. "When I got shot in the belly, suddenly I was here, in this body, falling down a hill."

"Shot in the belly?" the Kid winced.

"Yeah," the rokairn nodded, "double-barrel shotgun from an employee robbing my shop right after he'd stormed out. I guess he quit. He didn't have to. I just asked about the seventeen-dollar shortage from the night before."

"You think you'd fire him," the Kid snickered, then rubbed at his temples, wincing at the pain in his head, "especially after he fired on you."

"Well," Nathan was flustered and hesitated, "it wasn't like that. Not at first."

"Don't pay the Kid any mind," Torrents said, "just keep talking and ignore him. And, by the way, my name is Torrents, like a torrent of water, but with an 's' at the end."

"Um, okay," Nathan glanced up at the big man, then continued, "I came here, and had an urge to go to some pyramid, the Pyridom of Power, and stop someone or something from opening a portal to let demons into the world. It sounds even crazier when I say it out loud instead of just thinking about it. And it was pretty crazy sounding in my head."

The group worked its way up another hill, the land in front of them an endless series of rolling hills, mostly green and grassy, turning to brown and sandy dunes to the east, and to mountains to the west, leaving the forest behind them in the north.

The sky had an ominous green glow to the southeast, and it looked like the rain to the southwest was headed their way.

"Anyway," Nathan went on, "she came at me soon after I came here, and for some reason told me that stuff. I think I had some magical spells on me, because some of her magic spells didn't work on me. That sounds so weird, but they just bounced off me.

"She left when that green explosion happened. I knew I should go stop it, but…"

Nathan stopped, realizing he sounded like a coward.

"I left," he said, stronger. "This wasn't my fight. I don't like to fight. So, I ran away. I ran until I hit a town. I guess it was a city. Somewhere called Red Wind. I was there less than a week when she showed up with a whole lot of those things and killed most of the town."

"Is that why you followed her?" The Kid asked. "I thought you didn't like to fight?"

"Yeah," Nathan nodded, "it was, and I don't fight."

"You did okay back there," Torrents gestured behind them with his head and wobbled on his feet from the effort, feeling the repercussions of his injuries and slowing down.

Fred pushed through the underbrush to one side of the group, peeking out for a moment to check on them before disappearing again.

"Apparently," Nathan sighed, "I can fight, but I never could before. Never really tried. But when I saw hundreds of people being slaughtered for no reason, well, it wasn't about me anymore. I don't like bullies. I can handle being picked on, but I don't like it when others who can't defend themselves are attacked. It just…makes me mad."

Torrents and the Kid nodded in empathy and understanding.

The Kid had given the larger man a shoulder to lean on, helping support him through the difficult terrain.

"I tried to protect people," Nathan shook his head, "but there were so many of those dog-headed things, those gnohls, and they were killing everything around them. Those huge, prehistoric hyenas ran through the streets in packs, tearing through people, not even eating what they'd killed.

"I tried to stop them," the rokairn continued, "but I got stuck in an intersection with them coming at me from all sides. There was a guy with me, he worked in the jeweler's store I'd stopped at, his name was Nob. He stood back-to-back with me, or maybe we were side by side, but he was there, and they got him.

"I watched him," Nathan's voice broke. "He was trying to help, because of me, and I watched him get torn apart, an arm's length away from me. I watched these monsters rip into him, and how they laughed. That damned hyena laugh coming from the men things and the beast things…"

"Hey," the Kid's hand was on Nathan's shoulder, shaking him gently, "it's okay. You did good, man. You did what you could, and that's all any of us can do, okay?"

Nathan realized he'd stopped walking, and the other two had stopped as well. He was shaking, his face contorted as he tried to bring himself under control and failed.

The rokairn cracked, and clenched his jaw, and shut his eyes, a sob ripping from him and tears streaming down his face.

The other two comforted him, Torrents awkwardly patting him, and the Kid hugging Nathan close to his chest and smoothing the rokairn's hair.

"That was a good, ugly cry," the Kid said a few minutes later, when Nathan cried himself out.

"Sorry about that," Nathan mumbled, wiping at his face with the back of his hand, "I haven't done something like in a long time."

"Sometimes," the Kid held a square of linen cloth out, and the rokairn took it, "that's what we need. We're in a weird world, and it takes time to get used to it. Throw some of the things we see on top of it, and it can break you. But that's why we've got each other. I guess."

"Yeah," Torrents looked away, leaning on a tree and breathing heavily, "what the Kid said."

The Kid laughed and turned to look at the barbarian, a retort ready, but when he saw the big man swaying, he cut it off.

"You ready to go?" the Kid asked Nathan, who nodded. "Good, then help me with him and keep talking. It helps keep his dumb mind off the pain."

Nathan nodded.

The two moved to Torrents, positioning themselves on each side to help him walk.

"What happened after that," Torrents panted, the words coming out one by one, "how'd you get here?"

Nathan took a moment to collect his thoughts.

"As Nob was falling," Nathan gulped, "to the street, four people rushed out to help us. They had magic, too. They did something, and one of their hands glowed, and I felt better. Revived, refreshed."

"Sounds like holy magics," the Kid said, and Torrents nodded.

"That's when I saw Klendrisia again," Nathan steadied the barbarian, "she was watching me, smiling. Then she turned and left, letting out a scream like she did today. All the monsters followed her.

"These people, the holy people," Nathan hesitated, "priests, I guess, carried Nob away. I don't know if he made it, but I sure hope he did."

"They said they were part of the Church of Jonath," Nathan continued, "the holy people who helped us, I mean. They gave me a mission, well, they did after they let me clean up. They also offered to fix up the holes in my chain mail and bang the dents out of my bits of armor that needed it. They did more magic stuff to me, and even gave me a necklace with their little god icon on it."

"That's called a holy symbol. And what mission?" The Kid urged, trying to keep him talking.

"To hunt the demoness," Nathan sighed, "to stop her from hurting more people. Maybe even all the people. They said if I did good, they'd even make me a member of their church or something."

As they crested the next hill, the three saw a massive willow tree, and a tiny, thin man with a white, scruffy beard. The man stared at them, hands on his hips, with a sour look on his face.

Chapter 12

"So," the wiry man's voice was high-pitched and urgent, "you got rid of the cranky lady, eh?"

Fred pushed forward through the knee-high grass toward the new person, his claws clacking.

"We didn't bump her off," the Kid was supporting Torrents as they moved down the hill, shouting at the old man below them, "if that's what you mean."

"Naw," the man danced from one foot to the other, shaking his hands above his head, "she'da kicked allya asses anyway, so PepperGarten knows that means she got tired of you and bailed on ya."

"It didn't quite happen like that," the Kid rolled his eyes.

"PepperGarten sees you got a replacement, didn't have anything in your size?" the old man cackled, "And what the hell happened to the big dumb guy?"

"Hello PepperGarten," Torrents's words slurred, "I was hoping you'd be out or something so I could come here and die in peace."

"He got in a fight with some ratmen," the Kid sighed, "got poisoned, wouldn't stay in bed to get better, took a two-day flight on dragon-back, fought some gnohls, and then walked for a couple hours to see you."

"Yeah," Torrents breathed, "that last one is the worst part of all that. Can we go inside?"

PepperGarten cackled and jigged in a tight circle.

"No sense of decorum," PepperGarten said, "aren't you going to introduce PepperGarten to the new guy?"

"Yeah, sure," a wide smile crossed the Kid's face. "Nathan, this crazy old coot is PepperGarten. PepperGarten, this is Nathan. Say hello to my little friend!"

Torrents coughed out a laugh, and his knees buckled.

The Kid and Nathan squeezed in tighter to stop the big man from toppling.

"Don't make me laugh," Torrents wheezed.

"Let's get him inside," PepperGarten danced to one side and gestured towards the massive willow tree, "before we end up having to get the shovels. For his grave. To dig it. Because he died. Right here. Before we took him inside."

"Yes, yes," the Kid began helping Torrents forward, "we get it, you don't need to explain it. It's not funny if you have to explain it."

"Maybe to you," PepperGarten giggled, "but to PepperGarten, it's sometimes even funnier when PepperGarten explains it."

Nathan looked around as he helped the Kid walk Torrents in the direction the old man had indicated.

Fred ran around PepperGarten's feet, who let out a squeal.

"What the heckity, heck, hecking, is that thing?" the old man screeched.

"That's Fred," the Kid said over his shoulder. "He's my rock lobster. I made him."

"Interesting." PepperGarten leaned down to inspect the magical construct closer. "PepperGarten sees threads. Fred has threads. Fred threads. He might come in handy one day, but PepperGarten bets you have one hell of a headache. Good job, lad!"

The Kid glanced sideways at the old man and grunted as he guided Torrents forward.

They were on a lawn of sorts. It had the feel of the yard of the old lady Nathan remembered from his childhood. The woman never mowed her lawn or trimmed anything back, making her whole yard one continuous garden.

The rokairn saw vegetables, berry bushes, wildflowers, and a small clearing with stones—large enough to sit on—surrounding a fire pit. Chest high hedges wove their way around the perimeter of the area.

Squirrels and chipmunks darted through the trees and underbrush, and birds chirped and called from all around.

The tree itself was high up on the hillside, its wide, drooping roots and branches hiding the entrance to the earthworks under its boughs.

The four stepped under the tree's protection as rain started falling; a fox darted past them and into the man-sized hole in the mound's side, curtains pushed to one side of the opening.

Torrents collapsed to the hard-packed earth of the floor, and PepperGarten capered past the trio to wooden shelves jammed into the dirt walls.

The Kid flumped onto a grassy tuffet, pulling off his boots, and shaking the loose contents collected on the journey onto the floor.

"Hey!" PepperGarten screamed, and the fox looked up from cleaning her belly, "who do you think has to clean that up?"

"No one," the Kid said without looking up, "it's a dirt floor and you don't own a broom."

"Oh yeah," PepperGarten's face brightened, and he turned back to the shelves and began pulling down herbs, "smart of PepperGarten, wasn't that? Cut off his wrappings, would ya, Nathan?"

Nathan watched the old man plop berries and moss into a large wooden bowl on top of the herbs.

The rokairn squatted down next to Torrents and swung his satchel from his shoulder. He drew out a small knife, unsheathed it, and began cutting away the bandages.

"Do you have any water, please," Nathan asked, "so I can wash his injuries?"

"Yup!" PepperGarten answered with an upbeat tone, then began whistling and humming at the same time, creating an off-key melody that couldn't be followed.

"I'll get it for you," the Kid stood and patted Nathan's shoulder, "PepperGarten can be a bit…difficult to communicate with."

The Kid moved across the cramped space to a hole in the wall that served as a window and picked up an earthenware bowl.

The smell of rain wafted in, acrid and sharp, and birds crowded under the bow of the tree outside. Three groundhogs sat on their hind legs in the doorway, watching everything going on inside with dark, beady eyes.

PepperGarten was adding bits and pieces of the ingredients he'd gathered to a smaller bowl cradled in the crook of his arm. Picking up a mortar, he crushed them into a paste, all the while bouncing from one foot to the other.

The Kid set the bowl down next to Nathan and dropped another linen into it.

Nathan nodded, and began wiping the crusted and caked dirt, blood, and other matter from the wounds.

Fred crept into sight, just outside the door, his rock legs clicking on the steppingstones, then rushed past the groundhogs, causing them to bark and scatter. The fox looked up from her grooming to watch the new animal.

Two ferrets scampered across the floor, coming nose to carapace with Fred. The rock lobster was the size of a medium dog and outsized the two curious creatures many times over.

Fred clacked his pincers, and the two ferrets did a little bouncing, bounding dance that reminded Nathan of how PepperGarten moved.

The Kid moved away from where he'd been standing over Nathan and Torrents, rubbing his temples. He stopped, facing the corner, sighed, and ran his hands through his hair, plastering it to his head and pulling on it.

Releasing his scalp, the Kid turned around, put his back to the wall, slowly slid to the floor, and rested his arms on his knees, dropping his face to stare at the ground between his feet.

PepperGarten glanced at the Kid, slowing his little dance to take in the young man's posture, still mashing the mixture in the ceramic bowl.

"How'd you lose him?" PepperGarten looked back at his mixture, pretending indifference. "He leave you for a troll or something?"

The Kid looked up, startled. His mouth twisted with a retort, then went slack with a long outtake of breath.

"No," the Kid's voice was soft and far away, "I wish. That'd be easier. Some demon-lady took him, but not sure why."

"Klendrisia," Nathan offered, "that's who took him."

"Oh," PepperGarten drew the word out to three syllables, "she's a tough cookie, that's for sure. And since she's already got the Pyridom primed, but we aren't swarming with demons, PepperGarten would guess she's looking to open the network."

"The what?" The Kid tilted his head and squinted up at the bald man.

"Network," PepperGarten cackled, moving around the room and lighting candles in the dim light of the storm outside, "like a computer network, interlinked machines, or maybe networking at a party where you make connections you can call upon for purpose, or maybe like your neural network. You know, millions of interconnecting nodes of information and resources set to trigger specific events within your brain? It's like that, but spans more than just your brain, more than just this solar system, more than the Milky Way, and even more than our one remote universe. In the best terms, it spans the multi-verse."

"Multi-verse?" the Kid asked.

"Like in the X-men," Nathan offered, "or scifi. Parallel universes, or just other realties that can bump into ours and interact on some level."

"Eggs-actly!" PepperGarten beamed at the rokairn like he was a prize-winning heifer. "But the X-Men were just a group of masked kids when PepperGarten last read them in the 70's. Oh, as for the network here, the Pyridom of Power was a doorway to these things. Just like the Highest Spire and the Nine Towers of Magic, though they just tapped the energy of that network. Like a cosmic set of ley lines, and the mages would just syphon off the magic—or so they called it, but it's just energies that humans and others evolved the ability to sense and use—to do bigger and better experiments with. But it can be used to open doorways to other places. Like Hell, Limbo, Gladsheim, Nirvana, Gehenna, the Abyss, the Ethereal Plane, the Astral, and so on."

"What?" the Kid was still confused. "Why? Why would they want to do that?"

"Oh, any number of reasons," PepperGarten added a splash of vinegar to the mix, "to get our resources, take over our world for slave labor or food, or even just make a jumping point to another reality. The troöds have been working on it for almost 70,000 years!"

"Troöds?" the Kid asked.

"Yeah," PepperGarten nodded somberly, "alien, shape-shifting folk, sorta squid-like, but most people think they're reptilian. They waged full war against us about thirty years ago when the Talisman was around. You know, that magical comet that got stuck in orbit and made necromantic and conjuring magic go uber crazy?

"But enough about that," the old man moved to stand over Torrents and shooed Nathan away, "PepperGarten has some healing to do before things go sideways."

The old man knelt by Torrents's side and slathered the mixture into the barbarian's wounds.

Green sprouts pushed their way through the gooey mess, knitting around one another and pulling the injuries tight.

Torrents winced but smiled through gritted teeth.

"Thanks," the barbarian said to the old man with a nod.

"Why're you the one always getting hurt?" PepperGarten asked. "Don't you got enough sense to get out of the way of things trying to kill you?"

"Apparently not," the Kid quipped.

"How about this?" The hermit stood to his full height and stretched. "How about PepperGarten shows you how it's done?"

"And how are you gonna do that, old man?" Torrents asked, smiling despite himself.

"The next murderous bastard to come through the door," PepperGarten cackled, and turned to face the opening as if expecting it happen any moment, "PepperGarten will be their target, and you can see how PepperGarten doesn't get hurt because PepperGarten isn't dumb."

"Great," Torrents sighed, "PepperGarten doesn't mind if Torrents just lays here while we wait, does PepperGarten?"

"Why you talking like that?" PepperGarten shot an annoyed glance over his shoulder at the barbarian. "You sound like a pemtie."

"I'm talking like you do," Torrents grumped.

"No, you're not," the old man turned back to the door, "because when PepperGarten does it, PepperGarten doesn't sound like a pemtie."

The hermit put his hands on his hips, lifted his chin, thrust out his chest, and waited.

The Kid and Nathan exchanged glances, and the Kid smiled and shrugged at the rokairn.

A boom of thunder rattled the room.

The animals in the room went silent, turning towards the door. They stopped moving, licking, scampering, or playing. Even Fred went still.

In a flurry of movement, the creatures in the room bolted for cover, except for Fred, who moved to stand between the Kid and the door.

The doorway darkened with a figure, a glowing red blade in its hand.

Chapter 13

Lightning flashes and sheets of rain silhouetted the tall, thin form in the doorway, his carrot-orange hair glowing in the afterimage.

Water glistened on the black leather of the man's armor, and a short sword hung at his side.

The Kid gasped and leapt to his feet, his hand reaching for Edsumar, the magical weapon that was no longer there.

Torrents moaned and passed out as the medicine took its toll and worked its healing magic.

"Told you something bad was coming," PepperGarten snickered, raising his chin further, "this guy is bad news."

The man in the door moved forward with inhuman speed, crossing to the old man in a blink, slashing across PepperGarten's midsection with the glowing blade.

It sparked, the red of the dagger blending with green druidic magic in a purplish burst.

In a flurry of movement, the man struck the druid again and again.

Gashes appeared in PepperGarten's chest, belly, and face. Lines of violet eldritch energy appeared, connecting with one another, and becoming a dull green glow.

PepperGarten collapsed to his knees, hooting.

"That's," he gasped, clutching his midsection and cackling, "how you take a hit. Now, do the thing…"

The old man fell face first onto the dirt floor, rolling to one side.

"Avenge," he said, his voice soft, "PepperGarten."

The room grew quiet.

"Where's the Dragon's Dagger, boy?" The newcomer rasped.

"Edsumar?" the Kid said, pulling two daggers from sheaths. "You came here, for Edsumar? Why, Mezk?"

"To add it, and your corpse," Mezk growled, "to my collection."

The intruder moved again, his form blending with the shadows as candles guttered in the wind created from his movement.

The Kid raised his weapons, barely in time, to deflect the soul-sucking blade Mezk wielded.

Metal struck metal, and the Kid cried out, a burst of energy flaring with each strike on his weapons.

One blow struck true, and bit deep into the Kid's shoulder.

"No!" Nathan screamed, running forward, a hand-axe in each hand, slashing at the leather-clad enemy.

Fred charged at the intruder's ankles, his stone claws missing as the tall man danced around the attack, lifting his feet like he was tiptoeing through puddles and not wanting to get his dark boots wet.

The fox screamed its cry and ran at the intruder, snapping at his knees.

The remaining animals scurried for cover, hiding from the fight.

"Don't let PepperGarten die in vain," PepperGarten giggled, rolling into a ball, vines growing from his body and wrapping around him to create a cocoon. "Make it count for something."

The Kid pressed his attack, moving Mezk back across the small chamber in his furious series of strikes.

Mezk drew the short sword from across his body with his left hand, swinging wide and causing the Kid to bend backwards to avoid the slash.

Kneeling as he parried the Kid's blows, Mezk stabbed the magical dagger into PepperGarten's body again and again, draining the druid's soul. The Kid remembered the man doing this in Durgan's Keep, even to his own fallen comrades, taking their spirit to power his demonic weapon. The red of the blade dimmed each time, and rose in intensity when withdrawn, purple light flashing each time he struck the old man.

Mezk was gritting his teeth and glaring at the Kid.

The Kid focused his magics on the enemy, searching for a mental chink in the man's mind. The dagger stabbing into PepperGarten's body pulsed and brightened.

The Kid felt his attention drawn to the weapon as it called to him, and the mind-mage responded without wanting to. The Kid's concentration zeroed in on the blade, watching the heartbeat-like pulsing that matched his pounding head, and being drawn into it.

A sharp sensation of pain cut across the back of the Kid's head, but inside the skull, just as the dark blade in Mezk's hand burst into a flare.

The Kid felt his mind slip. His eyes rolled into his head, and his body crumpled as his knees went forward, and his shoulders fell backwards.

The Kid hit the floor with a dull thump, his head bouncing twice on the hard-packed dirt before he lay twitching and spasming, thick white froth creeping through his lips.

Nathan was upon the foe, setting his feet wide, and chopping at the carrot-topped attacker.

Mezk weaved to one side, then the other, dodging each blow without effort.

"We don't have that cursed weapon," Nathan shouted. "Did the demon-lady, Klendrisia, send you to get it? It's too late. She already got it."

"You don't have it?" Mezk hesitated, and Nathan's axe sliced into his shoulder.

Mezk grunted and returned to the defensive, standing and swatting Nathan's weapons away.

The man struck out with his dagger and slashed across Nathan's face.

The rokairn screamed and stumbled backwards, dropping his axes to clutch at his cheek.

Pulling his wet fingers from his face, Nathan looked at them, then looked around the room. Torrents was unconscious, the Kid was having some sort of fit, and PepperGarten was a broken and torn mess in the middle of it all.

Nathan hated bullies; he'd dealt with them all of his life. People who pushed others around and took whatever they wanted just because they could. This man, Mezk, with his glowing blade, had shown up here to take something that wasn't his. He'd killed PepperGarten just because the old man was in the way. The intruder wanted to do more than just hurt the Kid and would do so if no one stopped him. And Nathan was the only one left besides a few scared animals.

The fox was still nipping at Mezk, dancing away to stay out of the reach of his weapon.

Nathan felt pressure building up inside of him. His head had a dull thumping at the base of his skull. It matched the pounding of his heart and the intake and release of each breath. But it was peaceful at the same time, like when you accept something that's inevitable.

He pulled all that in with the next breath, held it—not tight inside of himself, but gently, like holding a baby bird in your cupped hands—then he released it, and a wave ushered out and away from him. It wasn't a burst, and there wasn't any physical indication that it happened, other than Mezk stumbling backwards and his dagger dimming for a moment.

Fred darted in, clamoring over the Kid's still spasming body, and latched onto Mezk's ankle and the bone crunched under the stone claw.

The thin man wrenched his leg from the construct's grip and limped backwards. The magical glow of the dagger in his hand intensified, bathing the room in an eerie light. The sound of bone and sinew knitting—a crackling sound like cartilage popping—filled the area, and Mezk sneered and moved towards the door.

"Then I will have to collect the souls from your corpses," the street thug said, "and revel in imprisoning them some other time."

His form bled into the shadows, and he was standing outside in the rain a moment later.

"PepperGarten dies, again," the fallen druid muttered. "Avenge me, so PepperGarten may live, again."

The rokairn looked from the dissipating form outside to the form on the floor, encased in writhing vines and branches.

When he looked back at Mezk, the man was gone.

"Ungh," PepperGarten's voice was faint in his cocoon, coming in broken phrases, "so poorly done…PepperGarten…would have beat him up…more better. The…better-est."

The man on the floor sighed and went silent.

The fox ran to PepperGarten, scratching at the wooden carapace and whining. The animals that had hid in corners were creeping out to survey the scene.

Ferrets ran from the corners of the room, leaping onto shelves and knocking wooden cups to the floor. The groundhogs made a beeline for the door, pausing to raise on their hindquarters, sniffing the air, then darted outside into the storm, abandoning the scene within.

Nathan looked around, taking in the scene again, exhaustion coming over him. His weapons lay at his feet, and he moved away slowly until his back hit the wall, sliding down to a sitting position. Dropping his head into his hands, he sighed, his breath catching in his throat.

Nathan never had to take care of anything in his life, and now he had the dead and dying surrounding him. It was overwhelming.

He'd been responsible for mowing the lawn when he was younger. It was a job, of sorts, at his grandmother's house when he was fifteen. She paid him ten dollars every week to show up and mow.

He started out, like any teenager, grudgingly. But with time, he came to like it. It took an hour to do— she had a large lawn, and he'd used her mower that had been his grandfather's—and he'd put on his headset attached to his music player and spend an hour in isolation with nothing troubling his mind. He'd walk back and forth, mowing and getting that time to himself with no other worries in the world. He came to love that solitary time, collecting his thoughts without any other pressures.

The memory was a light touch on his mind, making him smile, and oddly enough, reminding him of his turtle, Sheldon.

Sheldon was a box turtle, nothing special, just a run-of-the-mill turtle. He had (at least Nathan had assumed it was a boy, but it may have been a girl, he never had it checked) raised Sheldon since he was tiny. That turtle, who he'd gotten in sixth grade, was the first creature that had ever relied on Nathan.

He'd found him in a mall parking lot, gingerly moving across blazing hot asphalt, looking like he wouldn't make it to safety.

Nathan picked it up, and showed it to his parents, tears in his eyes, crying about how the poor thing wouldn't survive the cold northern winter. His parents let him take home but insisted he pay for the ten-gallon tank, and other necessities, from his allowance.

He'd agreed, without argument, wanting to see the little guy survive and be happy. Making trips to the local pet store and library, he searched for books on how to care for Sheldon. He'd bought all the leafy greens the turtle ever needed, shredded carrots, and even had given treats to the turtle.

Later, he learned his parents didn't always take the money from his allowance, but he paid for most of it.

He'd kept Sheldon for almost two decades before passing him on to a reptile preserve when he'd opened his business and couldn't care for him any longer.

It broke his heart to give up his little friend; he was the one being in the entire world who'd ever relied on him for his every need.

And now, two unconscious men, a dead guy, and a bunch of panicked creatures who needed him surrounded Nathan.

Nathan wasn't used to being needed. He was the quiet guy who no one ever expected anything of, but he always liked helping others.

He choked, literally. The pressure overwhelmed him, and a racking sob came out. He had to step up, or everyone he'd met in this world—except for the ones who'd tried to kill him—would end up dead. Most of them lay at his feet at that very moment.

The rokairn sat, sniffling on the outside, but a flood of emotion on the inside. He knew what had to be done. He'd done difficult things before, but it was always for himself. In fact, opening the jewelry shop was a way to push others away from him. It allowed him the perfect excuse for not going to a movie, or dinner with friends, or to see his family. The business always needed him.

Now, someone needed him, and he couldn't run or turn away.

Nathan stood, wiping at his blood-streaked face with the back of his arm. The cut from the magical blade had already closed, cauterized from whatever burst from him and made Mezk leave.

The Kid first; he needed the most help. Torrents passed out in a healing way, or something like that. PepperGarten was dead, so he could wait until last.

Nathan glanced around for a shovel, knowing he'd need that before the day was done. Then he scolded himself, mentally, for the caustic thought that at least PepperGarten came with his own coffin.

Chapter 14

Klendrisia held the small, burning sphere in her palm, the orange glow matching the setting sun through the broken archway to the west.

Ghe'hak the Ravager barked orders, literally, as the primitive hyenas circled the area on chaotic patrols, their cackles echoing through the hills. Meanwhile, the gnohls built campfires and squabbled amongst themselves.

The demon half-breed stared into the globe of energy above her hand, watching the human with the red soul blade moving through the rainstorm to the south, tracking her and her war band.

She debated killing him, toying with him, or using him. The smart option would be the first or third idea. Her father would say to toy with the mortal. He'd insisted their demonic lives were so long and extended that if you didn't play with your lessers, then you'd die bored when they finally killed you. He'd also point out that if you're involved with their lives, they can never truly sneak up on you. And if they do, then you weren't paying attention, and deserved steel between your shoulder blades.

When her father pushed her, she wondered if she was merely another lesser to be toyed with.

She sighed, knowing she didn't have to wonder; that's exactly what she was to him. She just wanted to be more in his eyes. Someone he'd appreciate, rely on, and even respect. He'd never given her any sort of encouragement, saying she'd done well, or that he was proud of her.

But she didn't care about that stuff, not really. She thought about it, but that didn't mean she cared. It twisted her gut when she thought too long about it, but that was because she couldn't stomach his arrogance at not recognizing her worth. Eventually, she'd make him admit to her value and abilities, even if it meant steel between his shoulder blades.

He'd never see it coming from her. It wasn't that he thought she didn't have it in her; he didn't think that far ahead and never even considered her true potential.

It was the lack of consideration that made her decide to turn her mission from him into her own agenda.

Maybe this other human, the one tracking her, could be a useful tool.

Klendrisia shifted, her dark-green skin tones paling into a deep olive hue, her clothes melting to something the man following would find more appealing. Her rusted chain mail melted away into a high-collared leather corset, crisscrossed lacing knitting down her sternum. Her wide leather belt melted from brown to black and stretched down her legs to form an open-fronted leather skirt attached to the corset with polished silver rings.

The demoness's hair lengthened and spun around itself, become a replica of large horns on her head, beaded tassels looping downward in a decorative fashion popular in the southern continents of this world. A ring appeared in her nose, matching those on her corset, and similar rings popped into existence, lining both ears, as a chain grew along her left cheek to connect the two.

Men were weak in that respect; appearances. They thought they could be the stronger sex by sheer force and muscle, never realizing the value of strengthening their minds as well as bodies. They trusted their eyes instead of their guts, especially when it came to women. Not because they were dumb, but because they never even gave a second thought to the idea that a woman could best them, deceive them, or break them through their own pemtie, limited arrogance.

Klendrisia had done exactly that many times. Sometimes with steel, sometimes with her will, but the result was always the same. She won.

She wasn't prone to losing; it didn't suit her. In fact, she'd claim she'd never lost. Not once. Any time she didn't come out on top, whatever man thought he'd won, lost all ability to think of her as a threat. They wouldn't kill her, didn't imprison her, merely thought they'd beat her down like some dumb bitch of a dog, and that she'd simply be cowed and follow along behind them without complaint.

Most of them had died with a surprised look on their face, but some never even had a chance to do that much. She wasn't pemtie, like men seeking vengeance. Her purpose when killing someone was to remove an obstacle, not feed some pathetic egotistical need to be recognized in that person's last breath. What did it matter if someone knew you were the one who killed them a few seconds before they died? It served no purpose and presented the chance for the enemy to react. Better they only see the floor rising to meet their face before dying. The most they could do then was to put out their hands to break their fall, before feeling the pool of their still hot blood gathering around them.

This man coming for her would be no different. She knew he'd failed to kill the rokairn. There was something different about that warrior; he smelled of foreign magics. No, that wasn't quite right, it wasn't magics he smelled of. It was reality. He wasn't from this place, and she was curious if he could lead her to somewhere else. Somewhere her father and others weren't already competing for. Somewhere the people would never expect a demonic invasion. If such a place existed.

What sort of backwards plane of existence could ever be ignorant of other realities waiting to attack at any moment?

Mezk slogged along the muddy swath left behind the army of creatures who had wounded the Kid and his group.

What happened got to him. He had to run. Not that he hadn't run away from a fight before, that wasn't the issue. It was the fact they were supposed to be weak, and the prize should have been laying there, easy pickings, just waiting for him to snatch it up.

The barbarian—who'd been sitting in a boat beside him, six months ago, as Mezk sized the man up—had been unconscious on the floor. The old man just stood there, waiting to be slaughtered. And the Kid, oh the Kid, he was supposed to be the only one there who mattered, and that was to be his true reward, killing the damn Kid.

Mezk had paid for the golem to be created, its only mission to kill the Kid and recover the Dragon's Dagger. But it had failed, and the Kid had transformed it into the creature that followed him now. The mini construct's magics were not unimpressive, way more powerful than the Kid realized, and were constantly being fueled by the Kid's abilities. It crippled his mind-magics, and Mezk had to wonder if his enemy realized what was happening to him.

That snot-nosed runt had been a thorn in his side for years, pulling the carpet from under his feet way too often. You expected rivalries and competition, but the Kid never even took it seriously. He never cared if he won or lost, just that he'd messed up somebody else's plans.

Six months ago, that'd been stepped up even more. When the Kid saved Durgan's Keep, but when he'd stuck with his new friends instead of gathering the scattered forces of the criminal underground, people had whispered. When the Kid left Durgan's Keep helping his friends, people had talked. Eventually, the Kid returned alone and began disrupting every criminal and illegal act he could find, and the people rejoiced.

After that, no one feared the gangs, the mob bosses, the enforcers, or any other arm of the underground. Well, they did if you were in their face, but once you were out of sight…the public was getting way too ballsy. The Kid was the reason for their newfound self-reliance and needed to be taken out.

The Kid had a bounty on his head, too, and it wasn't anything to sneeze at, either. But that wasn't the real reason Mezk wanted his nemesis dead.

The Kid had a magical dagger, though no one was sure where he'd gotten it from. It did cool tricks, which was enough for most folks, but not for Mezk.

His own dagger—the Demon Seed, a soul stealer—hungered for the other weapon. Mezk's dagger couldn't communicate, besides the urge of base emotions and wants, and it was pushing him to find this other item that housed an intelligence. If the blood dagger could absorb the Dragon's Dagger, it could grow into something much more powerful.

The wielder of such an artifact would be in an extremely unique situation.

Mezk knew what it was like to not be powerless. When he was a child, he saw the man—who may or may not have been his father—beat his mother and send Mezk to the streets to bring home coins by begging or stealing. He'd done this, as commanded, hoping the man would become his best friend and give him smiles instead of beatings.

Mezk lost two fingers in his seventh year. One to the constable, who caught him stealing a fish to eat. The other to that man who lived in his apartment and beat him until he could only gasp instead of breathing.

His finger was cut off when he failed to bring the requisite thirteen coppers or more home one night. The big man—breath reeking of rotting and the sour bitters he drank by the quart—held the boy's hand down to the table. The blade used wasn't very intimidating. It hadn't been especially large, and definitely wasn't very sharp. It took nearly three minutes for the large man to saw through the digit, rubbing against the still healing nub of the finger the constable had taken much more swiftly.

The pain was incredible, but it wasn't the worst part. That went to the dull, passionless stare of the broken man doing the deed.

Mezk didn't even remember the man's name, but he remembered the hollow look as the man sawed off his finger, like some sort of automaton. The man didn't even seem to know, or care, what he was doing. It was just something that had to be done, like breathing or bidjing.

Since that moment, Mezk had seen men revel in torture, and glorify the pain they gave to others. That, he could understand. He could respect the passion and high that came with the power and control over others.

But he'd be damned if he'd ever be like the nameless, slack-jawed bastard in his mother's house.

Mezk left that night. Stumbled out into the hallway, dizzy from the loss of blood from a finger that hadn't been cauterized or bound.

The fevers came in a day or two, and the boy had laid in an alley; shivering, vomiting, and bidjing on himself.

An old woman had found him and took him in. At the time he'd thought her old, but now that he'd passed her age, he knew she'd just lived a life that crumples a soul like a scribe with wasted parchment. He'd thought she was kind, and he was lucky.

Until a couple weeks later, when she took him to market, and sold him to a sallow-skinned man who beat the lessons of the street into the boy who thought he'd had it rough before.

In the beginning, he went hungry more often than he ate, having to fight for every scrap. He learned to find food in piles of scraps dumped into alleys, fighting cats and rats to get enough to stay alive, and how to avoid the things that would cause him to lose everything he ate, out of one end or the other.

He learned to wash enough that he could approach a mark, but not so much that his target thought he had a real home. He learned to hear the muted clink of coin in a pouch, and how to tell which leg would collapse easier if he fell in front of someone limping.

And then he learned to kill.

Killing changed everything. In a few months, with a burst of puberty, Mezk went from a starving street rat to teen runner working for a boss. All because of a few stiff bodies.

But there had still been a layer above him, standing on his back, keeping him down. He fought his way up that, too. Only to find there was another level above what he'd thought was the top.

That was when he met Zklypyllik, a demon claiming to wield great power, with the ability to free Mezk from his earthly restraints. They'd made a pact, and Mezk was freed from the bonds of the world he was born into and shackled with the bonds of his agreement and otherworldly restraints.

Now, he sought to break those bonds, to be chained to no one else ever again. Not to the man who'd cut off a child's fingers, not to some back-alley rat herder who used children to fill his beggar's pockets, not to a guild master of assassins, not to some demon, and not to the specter of the Kid who laughed at life.

It wasn't fair that the Kid got to live like that, and never pay the price. So Mezk would steal the Dragon's Dagger, feed it to the Demon Seed—a weapon given to him to use as part of the pact—and then he'd be free. No one would control Mezk ever again.

But until then, the weapon came at a price. It could heal him—as it had done with his missing fingers, and in the druid's burrow when that magical stone lobster had shattered his ankle—but there was a cost. It fed on him—if he didn't give it others to feed on. And right now, it was sick. Feeding on the cocooned druid had done something to the dagger, and waves of urges and illness randomly ebbed and flowed from the extra-planar weapon. It fed on Mezk's mind and soul, seeking something to sustain itself until it could heal.

Mezk slowed to a stop at the apex of a large hill. In the distance, three hillocks away, was a camp writhing with activity. Gnohls and hyenas swarmed around the base and crown of the encampment, barking and yelping. There was a meal worth offering to the Demon Seed.

And a single figure, an orange globe of crackling energy levitating above her hand, waited on the hilltop between him and the camp. He could see her smile in the setting sun as she watched him.

The dagger pulsed, and the urge to move towards the woman overwhelmed him.

Chapter 15

He'd searched the shed-like lean-to outside for a shovel and dug a grave for the vine-wrapped old man. By the time the other two woke, the next morning, Nathan had buried their host, and built a stone cairn over the grave. He'd pulled rocks from the hillside, the innate senses of his body knowing where to look for them, and how to hammer them to break them to a useable size.

Once he'd built the memorial, a single wooden shaft grew from the rocks within an hour. It rose as high as his shoulder, vines wrapping themselves around the bottom, middle, and top. No branches sprouted, and no leaves grew from it.

When Nathan reached out to touch it, it fell into his hand, and he later swore it was warm to the touch. It had startled him, and he jumped backwards, scared he'd desecrated the grave of the man who'd saved the lives of the two men inside.

As he stared at the short staff, runes glowed amongst the vine wrappings, their familiar script catching his eye. Moving closer to look at them, his mind twisted at the sight. They weren't in the rokairn script, or the common human trading language, they were in English.

"Life grown from stone," the familiar words read, "tended with care, brings together the elements of earth, water, and air. Use it as passion, in the art of war, use the fire, to meld with steel, and to protect evermore."

Nathan hadn't believed in magic, but he'd seen enough since…arriving—if that was the right word— in this world. The memories of his body related stone and earth to the god, Jonath, water to Jonath's daughter, Tarra, air to Jonath's wife, Latress, and passion, war, and fire to Jonath's son, Torr. The idea of protecting people made Nathan's blood sing.

It felt weird.

Nothing in Nathan's life made his blood sing. He hadn't thought of the concept. But when he read the words on the staff, his body—and perhaps even his soul—reacted.

His pulse quickened, not in the cardiac event sort of way, but in a way that made him stand taller, with determination and purpose rising inside him. It called to him, it…sang to him. And the way only music can, it inspired him.

He was chanting in rokairn, and it was solemn, full, and rich. It held generations of meaning and resolve. He lifted the short staff from the ground, and the thought of Marcid—his double-headed war axe that was missing a shaft—flooded his mind.

An hour later, he stood bare-chested in front of a pyre, wood piled taller than he was, and burning to twice his height, even in the constant drizzle. He wasn't sure how he'd gathered the wood, or how he'd gotten it lit. He just knew he was pulling Marcid from the flames, as they were both surrounded by the four elements of these gods, and his beloved weapon was whole again.

Her blade gleamed in the lightning, blessed by Latress. Tarra washed away the soot and cooled the passion of the flames that came from Torr. And the steel and root of the tree had been the gift of Jonath.

Then Nathan felt the need to nap. He was exhausted. His head was muddled and swimming, like he'd been disconnected and in some sort of trance.

Torrents shook Nathan's shoulder and called his name, as the Kid leaned against the wall, watching.

Nathan was curled up to Marcid and had been snoring gently. The rokairn jerked awake, blinking his eyes as he looked around.

"Come on, man, we need to go," Torrents said, turning away and gathering his things.

"Where's PepperGarten?" the Kid asked.

"Um, sorry," Nathan muttered, his eyes turned down and studying his hands. "He didn't make it. I buried him outside."

Ten minutes later, the Kid kneeled over PepperGarten's grave, sobbing openly. Torrents stood quietly, holding his face up to the rain as they both paid their respects.

To one side, Nathan shuffled his feet, looking anywhere except at the two men.

Torrents laid a hand on Nathan's shoulder, drawing his attention up to the man's face. The barbarian gripped the rokairn's shoulder for a few seconds, looking into his eyes, then nodded.

Torrents turned away, and the Kid was standing behind him, wiping at his face.

"That's his way of saying thank you," the Kid snuffled. "I do it a bit differently."

The Kid hugged Nathan, muttering 'thank you' a half dozen times, a sad smile on his boyish face that spoke of years of pain from losing people.

The three gathered food and supplies from the hole under the tree.

That's all it was now. The animals were gone, disappearing into the grey weather. The interior was just a damp, chill hole. The life inside had come from PepperGarten and was gone now.

They left in silence, only the glup-slosh of their footsteps in the mud marking their passage. Within minutes, the slumped willow tree and the paradise beneath were nothing more than a shadowed memory.

Nothing more of interest happened that day, as if the gods themselves were bowing their heads and giving the friends a moment's peace.

Nathan, Torrents, and the Kid walked dejectedly in a line, shoulders hunched against the hail. The rain and balls of ice pattered and pounded on the hoods of their cloaks and the surrounding grass.

The rain started six days ago and hadn't let up. It had been a steady, grey drizzle since that PepperGarten died.

Nathan had checked on the Kid's wounds, binding them as best he could. It hadn't been easy; they were deep and probably needed stitches. The rokairn did the best he could, scraping the last remnants of the concoction the druid made into the deep gullies of flesh carved by the glowing red dagger.

He'd even said a prayer—clutching the symbol of the god, Jonath, the priests in Red Wind gave him—asking that the two men who seemed to share his belief of helping others, not die, and maybe even recover.

They camped in gloom, finding what shelter they could, tossing tarps over the low branches of a cluster of trees in the Black Wood.

They made good time, each lost in their thoughts, no one in the mood to talk for the first couple of days.

The Kid remembered people she'd lost in her other life.

Her son, who'd killed himself with poisons you bought over the counter. She had never drunk another drop of alcohol since. She didn't see the need for that loss of control. Life had too much to offer and didn't need to be drowned to be enjoyed or escaped from.

Her husband, who had left when life became too hard, and he thought he couldn't be happy working to support a wife and child who adored him. It was too mundane, too normal, to suffer through. So, he left to find himself.

He found himself with the help of his young secretary, and the used-car empire his wife had financed when they were married.

The Kid, known as Jen in that world, had lived carefully and alone after that. She'd watched her friends die of old age, or self-abuse, but she'd lived on. Until cancer finally got her.

Once she'd come here, she lived differently. She reveled in every moment, delighting in every danger. She laughed whenever she could and said anything that came to mind that might bring a smile to her, or some else's, face. As a bonus, she could also pee standing up now.

It was hard watching people die. Even once she was here and was the Kid—a teenage boy who was a healthy, vibrant, mind-mage—she'd lost people. Esperanza sprung to mind. The young woman, in her twenties, was a powerful priestess of Latress in this world, who chose to return to her life in the other world. And there were others, like the people of Durgan's Keep, who the Kid had fought to protect, many who died in the invasion of undead.

Now he'd lost his magical abilities, too. And Edsumar was gone. He didn't know if the two were related, but he was pretty sure the damned dagger Mezk wielded had done something to him.

The wounds in his gut and shoulder throbbed and felt like they were leaking. But there was no blood, no puss, no discharge of any kind. His headaches were gone, but he could no longer feel of magic within his mind.

Torrents hunted, taking down a fowl or rabbit, as he silently stalked far to one side of his companions. The Kid wouldn't have scared off any quarry, but Nathan trundled along, his axe bumping and scraping his metal armor, making enough noise to warn away a regiment of German tanks.

The barbarian learned he needed to live for himself. Not to please anyone else, and not to merely survive. Since arriving in this world—transported at the moment of his second life-changing car crash—he'd been on the path of realizing the value of choosing your own way.

He'd found self-worth in helping others. First, his friend Axle, then the people of Hope's Hollow. He'd went with Esperanza and the Kid because he thought it was what he was supposed to do. But along the way, as he fought zombies and giants and rotting ghosts that could drain the life-energy from anything living, he'd realized he needed to live for himself.

Once he'd helped save Durgan's Keep, and Esperanza returned to their world, he'd went to Dargaon's Hole to help the refugees of Hope's Hollow survive the winter. Not because it was expected, but because it was for him. It made him feel good, feel useful, and feel whole.

Torrents tried to convince the Kid to come along, to give purpose to both of their lives. But the Kid just wanted to play. He loved messing with other people and making their lives miserable. Sure, it was the crime lords and gangs that the Kid targeted, but that felt petty and hollow to Torrents.

Helping a group of simple people, not just survive, but thrive, in somewhere that the elements alone would have killed them, gave him a sense of belonging and purpose.

He'd left Dargaon's Hole because of the green glow to the southwest, a portent of a danger that would sweep across the land and threaten the very thing Torrents had protected.

His home. His people. His responsibility.

He'd abandoned all the people he cared for, so he could protect the settlement before the danger reached them. That was why he left, and that was why he now moved through this dammed week-long rainstorm with a rokairn he barely knew, and a self-centered brat.

The three traveled northeast, following the swath of destruction left by an army led by a demon half-breed. They found ravaged caravans; the people murdered for sport. They found small villages torn to the ground, brick by brick, timber by timber, and bone by bone. Never any survivors.

One thing which united the three: the drive to stop the mindless horde crossing the land and killing for what appeared to them to be no reason at all.

They crested a hill on the morning of the sixth day, and the rain stopped, as if some great being turned off the tap. The sun crept from behind darting clouds, and the humidity began rising from the ground instead of falling to it.

In front of the three companions rose the broken structures of the Nine Towers of Magic. Greasy smoke wound its way into the air from dozens of campfires.

The sound of the gargled laughter of hyenas and gnohls rolled across the hills to meet them.

Chapter 16

Edsumar couldn't breathe. Not that the spirit of a dragon residing in an enchanted weapon with the souls of five reptilian priests needed to breathe, but that wasn't the point. It felt like he couldn't breathe.

He couldn't reach out with his mind to contact the Kid, or other dragons, or anyone or anything else. Ever since this cambion wrapped him in that cloth, it was like being smothered, something he hadn't ever experienced, even in life. He'd been one of the most powerful creatures on the planet, allied with many of his peers and equals in magical ability and political influence.

He'd worked closely with the mages that built the Nine Towers of Magic, one structure for each 'school'. There weren't nine schools of magic, but the human mages who built the towers categorized them that way, and it was fine, even if they were wrong.

There were five primary types of magic: mind, ley or elemental, alchemical, summoning or conjuring, and holy. Other types of magic came from combining one or more of the five primaries, for example, necromancy combined all five.

They built the Nine Towers as an elite magical school and testing ground, meant to bring the best together in a place where no one would bother them. They constructed them on a nexus of ley lines, feeding magical energies directly into the Towers that acted as conduits for that power. It was one of the five most powerful magical repositories on the planet.

Mistakes were made, hence why the Blue Desert now existed, the sand's color changed by magical runoff and pollution.

The Towers had another purpose, though, to lock away foreign magic and the invaders who sought a foothold in this world. It had done its job well, teaching generations of humans and protecting the realm.

Then the Wizard Wars erupted, and he'd had to go to 'Plan B', which turned out to be a botched attempt to put all his knowledge into an easily transportable item. It finally worked when the Kid came along and finished the ritual.

The mages, sorcerers, wizards, witches, and other magic wielding humans—who all had remarkably brief lives, thus were short-sighted—decided there was a better way. To drain life essences of powerful magical beings and harness (aka steal) their abilities for their own uses. The Wizard Wars.

After the wars, those running the towers fell to infighting, destroying everything they'd worked hundreds of years to build. One group left and went to the coast, founding Seawall City, while the remaining groups scattered, too small and broken to hold the Towers by themselves. The Towers fell into disrepair, though many magics still lingered on, and in, the grounds.

Edsumar could feel the Towers; like a vibration rattling his cloth cage. The muffled sensation gave him the closest thing he'd had to a headache in almost a millennium. He felt it less than a year ago when the Kid and his friends had come here to stop the necromancer that later attacked Durgan's Keep. They'd failed, as shown by the later attack on the walled city.

Edsumar's awareness expanded as someone removed the cloth around him. He could feel the Towers all around him, and the magical shell barrier—invisible to the naked eye, but obvious to anyone with magical senses—that extended to the perimeter surrounding the magical structures.

The Dragon's Dagger pushed his awareness out, trying to pass through the shield, but it came up short. He never could move past it; the well-constructed shell did its job.

Edsumar could feel the cambion as she gripped his leather-wrapped handle and called upon his powers. Her mind was closed to him, and he was unsure if it was due to her nature, a magical protection, or just her raw willpower. As he wrapped himself around her astral form encased in flesh, Edsumar felt his energy slowly sinking into her, like sinking in quicksand.

The dragon spirit calmed himself, knowing struggling would only make it worse. He reached out with his ethereal senses, seeking help, some sort of psychic branch to grab onto, before he disappeared completely.

Dozens of gnohls and their requisite proto-hyenas were moving around the area, their tainted magic emanating through the air like a stench hanging over a swamp or a trash dump. The creatures reeked—or the equivalent of the sense of smell for the magical dagger—of rot, filth, and decay. Their hunger washed over Edsumar, and he experienced the closest thing to nausea he'd felt since he'd had an actual body.

His mind warped and twisted in Klendrisia's grip, feeling himself being harnessed, enslaved, and forced to move his abilities into the closest Tower.

Edsumar knew he was the key. That's how the mages set it up. No single human, or group of humans, could fully access the Nine Towers of Magic without Edsumar opening the pathways for them. When the Wizards attacked, and he'd placed his attendants into stasis, the men failed to get the one thing they needed to access the full powers of the towers. Him.

But Klendrisia had him and was using her magics and the shielded area to force him into unlocking the full potential of the slumbering energies. The mystical dagger would be like a lightning rod, and properly activated, would draw magical energy from across the world to this spot. With that much power in one place, Klendrisia could do almost anything, including opening another gateway so that her father's demon armies could pour through to this world.

Edsumar's mind jerked again, the psychic equivalent of someone grabbing his head and making him look at something. His senses exploded in the awareness of the ley lines, invisible to the naked eye, intersecting above the magical wellspring. Eldritch threads of earth, air, fire, and water burst to overflowing, becoming torrents of energy that blended with the repository below them.

Something else tickled his awareness, something familiar and comforting. It was like catching the movement of someone's walk out of the corner of your eye: you knew a person even though you didn't see them. They had a rhythm to their gait you recognized anywhere.

The Kid's spirit—not her mind, but her energy, her soul—was a pinprick of light on the edge of Edsumar's awareness. The dragon spirit thought of the Kid as both female and male, because that's what they were, depending on the moment and what they were doing. On the outside, he'd seen the changes, too. The masculine exterior was blending with the feminine spirit, and the two were becoming one. The Dasism called it twin or dual spirits, the balance of male and female, completed in one form.

Edsumar reached out, breaking some small part away from what he was doing, and touched the Kid's mind. He felt, more than saw, the Kid look up, gesturing in the dagger's direction and rallying the two men with him to head this way.

Gnohls and hyenas threw themselves in the trio's path. The barbarian Torrents fought with willpower and drive that surpassed any normal mortal. The newcomer, Nathan the rokairn, set his feet and jaw, wading forward, knocking the demon's minions away with each forward step. The Kid was a desperate whirlwind, daggers twirling and spinning, slicing and cutting, surging away from his friends and pushing towards Edsumar.

The Kid's mind felt torn, like scar tissue that grew on a once healthy muscle. The mind mage's psychic powers were blocked after being injured badly.

Edsumar couldn't just watch this happen, a powerless puppet for Klendrisia's game.

The dragon spirit reached upward, drawing power from above, ignoring his instincts that warned which such an action would only quicken the results the cambion desired. Edsumar knew if he could help his friends, and if they could recover him, they'd be able to stop this event that would shake the world.

The magical energies the dragon spirit had deftly wielded when he had a body were now like grasping at steam. It slipped through his grip, burning him when he tried to snatch it and use it for his own needs. The cambion was blocking his ability on top of the limitations that came with being inside of a magical object.

Edsumar redoubled his efforts, and if he still had a head, he would've furrowed his brow in concentration, and his tongue might have even been sticking out from between his lips as he focused.

He linked to a ley line, fire, then tied to another, wind. Lightning flashed, forks coming down across the battlefield. Bodies of gnohls and hyenas exploded upwards, raining back down on the perimeter of the Towers.

He called down bolt after bolt, peppering the area. Something shifted, and drew the lightning to one tower, then another, and another. The Towers were pulling down the power of the ley lines, wresting it from his control. He could no more harness it than he could redirect a river with his bare hands…if he still had hands.

A new body entered Edsumar's awareness, a dark soul stained red with anger, hate, and fear. Those emotions pulsed across the shadow, like ruby red veins of power and destruction.

This shadow person slid through the battle, becoming like smoke, and reappearing to strike with the weapon that possessed him, rather than the other way around.

Edsumar didn't see the way a human, or any other mortal species, saw. He saw in energy, which included magic and emotion. This unknown figure was a ragged bundle of those things, and wasn't wholly in this world, or any other.

The Dragon's Dagger knew the Demon Seed knew he was there, and that it hungered for him.

This new enemy appeared in front of the Kid, and the energies of the two melded as they fought, bleeding into one another, becoming a blur to Edsumar's senses.

Nathan called upon his powers, but it was weak, disconnected. A burst of white energy, turning a muddy maroon as it washed outward, flew from the man and tossed aside the gnohls in its path. But not the hyenas. They surged forward to attack the rokairn.

Torrents stepped beside the rokairn—now that he was free of the gnohls he'd been fighting—his sword cutting into the beasts. The creatures didn't give ground, retreating wasn't in their nature. They killed, or they died. That was their sole purpose.

Edsumar's awareness dimmed as the demon's minions regrouped to attack the three people trying to rescue him.

"Mezk," the sudden sound of the cambion's voice startled Edsumar, "you've done your part, and you now get the agreed upon reward. Take it and follow me. We shall make our escape and live to fight again."

She wrapped Edsumar in the red cloth again, blocking his ability to see the energies and interact with the world around him.

He threw his mind into one last, desperate act. He drew down all the power he could grasp from the ley lines. Fire rained down, joined by lightning, hail, and frozen gusts that cut to the bone.

Gnohls screamed in guttural calls, and hyenas howled in pain. Forms winked out of existence in the downpour of power.

As the last of Edsumar's awareness disappeared, he felt the towers drawing in his power. Sucked deep within them, it erupted upwards.

He saw the Kid, clearly, not surrounded by enemies. The three friends were cutting down the last remaining monsters and moving towards him.

The world went, not dark, but dull. His awareness felt nothing besides the rumble of power from the Nine Towers. Then it felt a new sensation, the dark, pulsating red of the Demon Seed enveloping him.

Chapter 17

"Let's see what we've got," Torrents put his hand on the Kid's shoulder, surveying the dozens of dead bodies littering the ground around them, "looks a lot like it did when we were here before. Except for all the buildings that were blown up from all the lightning and fireballs. Man, what was that about? We were lucky none of them hit us."

"That was Edsumar, I think," the Kid slumped, his hands on his knees, watching the ground in front of him, panting, "I thought I could feel him reaching out for me, and wanting to protect us. I was trying to get to him, to help him."

Fred moved next to the Kid, resting a stone claw on the rogue's boot.

"We know, we had to run interference as you ignored everything trying to kill you," Torrents patted the Kid, "I think every hair on my body is curled up and singed from all that magic. I just got better, and now I'm bit and cut in a bunch of places from those things."

"They threw them under the bus," Nathan pointed at the place where the demon woman stood moments before. "They were right there. Klendrisia and Mezk just...disappeared. The demoness vanished in a blink. She'd been there one moment, watching me with a crooked smile, and was gone the next.

"I saw Mezk take something wrapped in a red cloth from her just moments before she vanished, then he turned and looked at you," the rokairn pointed at the Kid, "I could see him clearly even though he was a dozen meters away. I saw his lip curl into a sneer, like hate was twisting his features. It's so cliché to say something like that, but that's what it looked like. Then he'd slid sideways and melted into shadow. Like a video of a chocolate Easter bunny left in the sun, then put on fast forward, the man literally melted into shadow, and then was gone."

They stood in the middle of dozens of buildings surrounding five graceful towers, and the one chunky, crystalline black tower sat supported atop the rubble of four other towers. The broken structures looked like stubby legs under the massive black one.

"You guys have been here before?" Nathan turned to see the two nodding. "What was this place?"

"A magic school," the Kid stood, rubbing his face with both hands, "most of the buildings were administrative, barracks, or lecture halls for classes of elite magic wielders. They dedicated the towers to different kinds of magic."

"See the big, fat, black one?" Torrents pointed at the stubby tower that sat on the rubble of the four others, and Nathan nodded.

"That's what she said," the Kid mumbled half-heartedly, and received a glare from Torrents for the effort.

Fred clicked his claws in three rapid beats, a small space between the second and third.

"Cla-clack, clack."

"Did that thing just do a rimshot?" Torrents asked, looking down at the rock lobster in amazement.

"Just a trick I taught him," the Kid shrugged.

"Apparently," Torrents continued with a shrug, "that was some new, upstart god named Onyx, who came into power about a hundred years ago. He dropped one right on top of these to show off, I guess. Those black towers used to give out magic items to anyone who wanted one."

"Really?" Nathan looked at it in wonder. "Did you guys ever get one from it?"

Torrents and the Kid exchanged glances with one another, then looked back to Nathan and shook their heads.

"Why not?" Nathan was looking at the black tower, and the other two could see his mind working.

"I think there were always strings of some sort attached," the Kid shrugged.

"Like what?" Nathan took a step towards the tower. "Like you went crazy and murdered people, or that you suddenly had the urge to go door to door to talk to people about Onyx?"

"Not really sure," Torrents moved closer to Nathan, ready to stop him if needed, "we never found out since we didn't get any."

The ground shook, and the three moved their stance wider to balance themselves.

"Earthquake?" Torrents suggested once it subsided.

"Maybe," the Kid touched the big man's shoulder, turning his attention southwest, "or something worse."

The green light in the sky to the southeast had grown brighter, lines of red, blue, and maroon dancing inside the glow.

"Oh," Torrents said, "what's that?"

"I think that's what they were doing here," the Kid sighed, "and I thought we'd won. I thought we'd killed all the lackeys and chased off the bad guys. But now I think this was just one more step in their bigger plan.”

The other two nodded, still staring at the atmospheric show.

“Nathan?” the Kid nudged the rokairn, who looked at him. “Did you say you saw that woman give Mezk something wrapped in a red cloth?”

“Yeah, sorry,” Nathan gulped, “I did.”

“That would’ve been Edsumar,” the Kid’s voice cracked, “she gave him Edsumar.”

Torrents put a hand on the Kid’s shoulder again.

Fred moved protectively to stand beside the Kid.

“I’m sorry,” Nathan said again, looking down and shuffling his feet, “I wish we could’ve done something.”

“We’ll get him back for you, Kid,” Torrents rubbed the Kid’s shoulder, “even if we have to hunt those bastards to the end of the world, this world or another.”

“It might just be the end of the world,” the Kid sighed, deeper this time, “if we don’t find a way to stop them.”

“And speaking of that, how come there aren’t like dozens of groups like us,” Torrents spat on the ground, “even whole amies from different cities, out here hunting these people down before they destroy the whole planet?”

“Probably because they’re scared,” the Kid’s voice was quiet, “they’ve been through so much here from the stories we’ve heard. The world already ended once. They’re probably tired of fighting, and just want to survive. I’m guessing that just surviving the things they went through during the Downfall makes them a hero.”

The group fell quiet, each lost in their thoughts.

"Well," Nathan's voice broke them from their reverie, "sorry to ruin the moment, but do you still think it's a bad idea to get a magic item from Onyx's Tower?"

"Yeah," Torrents's answer was gruff, "I do. I don't trust it. Don't you think if it was a good idea, then others would be doing it? I mean, there were just two very slimy people here, and neither of them even gave it a second look."

"I don't mean to argue," the Kid looked up at the big man.

"Yes, you do," Torrents growled, "but go on anyway. You will, no matter what I say."

"True," the Kid gave a smile reminiscent of his old attitude, "but those two are already dealing with issues where they owe someone. Mezk made a deal with a demon from what the word on the street is, and Nathan said Klendrisia has daddy issues. He sounds pretty controlling, you know, being a demon lord and all."

"Does that mean you think we should go get something from the tower?" Torrents glared at the Kid through squinted eyes.

Nathan looked back and forth between the two as they discussed it.

"Could it hurt at this point?" the Kid shrugged. "We're going to need all the help we can get, and if we fail, we'll be dead, anyway. Even if there are strings attached, if it helps us survive, at least we'll be alive to face the music and deal with it."

Torrents stared down at the Kid, then his face relaxed as he sighed.

"Fine," the barbarian breathed, drawing the word out, and clipped the next word, "whatever. If we're gonna die, I guess we should go ahead and get every advantage we can."

The three gathered their gear, and made their way through the field of carnage, Fred scampering around their feet. Stepping around the burnt and mutilated corpses of the gnohls and hyenas, they picked out a route between the rubble of the shattered buildings along the weed-strewn cobblestone path.

"There are no magical constructs or energies wandering around the complex this time," the Kid noted. "Think whatever they did scared them off?"

"More likely," Torrents shoved a broken door from the pitted road, "whatever they did ate the things. It looked like a lot of magic was being harnessed and slung around."

"Uh huh," Nathan muttered, wanting to add something to the conversation. When the other two looked at him expectantly, he blushed. "Sorry, it's just that I think I could kinda see it. Just like I can see faint lines above us, and below us. It's like when you stare at a light bulb and then look away and you can still see it. Or when you watch a sparkler on the Fourth of July, and you see the trails it leaves."

"You can see the ley lines?" The Kid asked. "I couldn't even see those, and I'm what they call a mind mage. Guess that would make you an elementalist? Or is it because of your connection to the god, Jonath?"

"What?" Nathan looked surprised. "I don't know about any of that. I just know I'm in a dwarf's body, and can use an axe pretty well, and can see things that aren't there. I don't know how, or what any of it means. Is there a reason we're all here? A purpose?"

"Dude," Torrents said over his shoulder, winding his way through a tight cluster of rubble, "you chuzzing rock that axe! And don't call your people dwarves, it's insulting. Rokairn, or sometimes 'the rock people'."

"Stoners?" the Kid asked. "Can we call them stoners, or is that insensitive?"

"Cla-clack, clack," Fred clacked.

Torrents snorted a laugh, then glared at the Kid for good measure.

"And we're here," the Kid said haughtily, "because we were all dying, individually, and Jack Tucker used magic to bring us here to another dying body. And to what end, you may ask. We have no clue. To be heroes? To give us a second chance? Because he could? We don't know. I just know that I'm going to do something with it, even if it kills me. Again."

"That sounds reasonable," Nathan said, "and I'm sorry to ask this, but is it selfish to want to make a difference?"

"I don't think so," the Kid shrugged, "I've always loved helping others. Even when I worked in restaurants, just bringing someone some food they were looking forward to made me feel good."

"Damn straight it's okay," Torrents spat, "it feels good, and gets things done. Too many people go their whole lives only looking out for themselves, even stepping on others or using them to get what they want. Chuz those people, man. They're bidj. Helping others is the way to go, hands down."

"Sorry to ask," Nathan said, "I just don't want to be arrogant, like I'm better than anyone else just because I can do these things. And you think I have some sort of connection with Jonath?"

"I don't think you could be arrogant if you tried, Nathan," the Kid laughed.

"Really, man," Torrents sighed, "you're like humble all the way. And quit apologizing. Every other thing out of your damn mouth is 'sorry', and you ain't even done anything wrong. You'll know when you need to apologize, so chuzzing quit doing it all the time."

Nathan opened his mouth to say something, but the Kid interrupted.

"Don't say you're sorry," the Kid pointed at the rokairn, grinning, "you'll just piss him off, and barbarians are known for ripping the arms off droids, isn't that right, Torrents?"

Nathan snapped his mouth closed.

"Shut the hell up, Kid," Torrents was grinning, too.

"As for your connection to Jonath," the Kid went on, "I think it's obvious if you take a moment to look at it. First, you're on a first name basis with him and keep referring to him like he's an old friend. Second, those priests who gave you the holy symbol saw something in you, and they'd know, wouldn't they? And C, I'm bad at lists, but I'm sure there is something else, too."

Nathan opened his mouth to speak, but the Kid interrupted again.

"Oh yeah," the Kid held up a finger, "I remember now, you've been casting protection magic, and Jonath is a god who specializes in that sort of thing. Those invisible bubbles that were knocking the hyenas and gnohls away from us, and you said you did it back at PepperGarten's, too."

The three fell silent as they crossed into the shadow of the Tower of Onyx and slowed to a stop.

"Clack, clack, cl-cl-clack," Fred clacked ominously.

Chapter 18

They stood at the foot of the monolith, four crushed towers in ruin beneath, supporting it. Black, crystalline tendrils wrapped around the broken, stubby towers and sunk into the cobblestone courtyard, disappearing into the broken earth.

The ebon megalith rose forty meters into the air, on top of the six meters of the shattered towers that held it up. Though the five remaining towers—lingering in the distance—rose to more than double the height of the Tower of Onyx, all five could have fit into its circumference.

The three companions climbed the mound of rubble underneath to reach the center below the dark behemoth, Fred following. Pieces of the crushed towers shifted underfoot.

"What do we do now?" Nathan asked when reached the center. "Do we chant something?"

"Say a prayer to Onyx?" Torrents suggested.

"Make a wish," the Kid grinned, "and rub its belly."

The other two looked at the Kid to see if he was serious.

"How the hell would I know?" The Kid threw his hands up. "I'm over here wracking my brain, trying to remember what that crazy necromancer, Aku'ji, Mistress of Death and Wielder of Woe, did when she was getting the Scepter of Necropties from this thing."

"Really?" Torrents looked down at the Kid. "You used the full title and everything? How'd you even remember all that?"

"I'm good at crosswords," the Kid shrugged, "things like that stick in my brain."

"So, then," Torrents rolled his eyes, "what did she do?"

"I've no clue," the Kid shrugged again, "we showed up right after she got it. You rushed in, like you always do, and I had to save you, like I always do."

"Do not," Torrents muttered, "you just provide back up."

"Guys," Nathan interrupted, "sorry, but can we focus here?"

The two turned to look at the rokairn.

"You apologized again," the Kid smirked.

"Sorry, ugh," Nathan threw up his hands, "sorry, it's just that I, oh, no. Never mind. But we really should focus on getting whatever this thing can give us. Anyone know anything about this sort of thing from their previous body's?"

"Oh," Torrents gasped, the other two turning to look at him, "I think I do."

The barbarian reached up, holding his hands above his head, and they shimmered. The effect looked like heat rising off hot asphalt, but they were in the shade, and the ripples in the air were swirling around his hands instead of rising.

Torrents lowered his hands, and the three of them leaned in to look at what he'd received.

Something coalesced in his grip. It shimmered, then solidified.

A long, double-handed, black blade formed from thin air, laying across Torrents's open palms.

The three stared at it for a long moment.

"Wait a second," the Kid broke the silence, "isn't that your sword, but it's black now?"

"No," Torrents glanced over his shoulder, looking for the handle of his sword, but it wasn't there, "um, maybe?"

"It is!" The Kid squealed. "What a rip-off! This thing gave you your own sword, but with a new paint job. It doesn't even have cool racing flames or anything."

"It kills demons," Torrents's voice was low, "I can feel it, like an instruction manual in my head. The bond of a demon's soul is severed, sending it back to where it came from.

"Demons have souls?" the Kid asked.

"It makes sense," Nathan said, and the two looked at him. He swallowed an apology for interrupting, and went on, "the soul would be nothing more than the energy within us that makes up who we are. You know, your mind, emotions, and all the things that aren't your muscles, organs, and all that. That invisible stuff that makes you…well, you."

"Yeah," the Kid tilted his head and pursed his lips, "yeah, I guess that makes sense. Okay, move over, it's my turn!"

Torrents moved to one side, still staring at the ebon blade, while the Kid pushed forward.

The Kid raised his hands above his head, humming a little tune from an old cartoon that lingered in his mind.

Something appeared in the shimmering air around his hands, and a black cloth dropped over his forearms. He lowered his arms, and the three looked at the material.

"T-t-that's all, folks!" the Kid held up a circle of fabric.

"What's it do?" Torrents leaned in to look closer.

"It…" the Kid wrinkled his brow, "makes a hole, it seems. That's weird, it *is* like an instruction book in your head. Maybe that guy on that TV show, Greatest American Hero, should've got his instructions this way."

"Dude," Torrents moaned, "stop talking about old TV shows, and tell us what the hell it does!"

"It makes a hole," the Kid huffed, "just that. I guess I could throw it on a wall and crawl through to the other side. Or drop it on the ground and jump in and it would open another hole somewhere else, like another building nearby. It has to be close, though. I don't think it would let me go much more than ten meters or so."

"What if you dropped it on the floor," Nathan reached out to touch it, stroking the silk-like material, "and had a hole appear above it. Could you keep falling until you hit terminal velocity?"

"I don't know," the Kid's voice wavered high, then low as he did a verbal shrug, "maybe? I guess? But I don't think I'm gonna try it, though."

"Can anyone else go through it?" Nathan released the cloth, wiping his hand on his shirt without realizing it.

"Um," the Kid tilted his head in thought, "they're not supposed to, because it can have unexpected results. Okay, your turn Nathan! Let's see what you get!"

The Kid moved away from the center point of the tower, letting Nathan move forward.

Nathan reached up, stretching onto his tiptoes, and something hit his hand, then tumbled to the rubble below his feet, wedging into a crevasse.

"Oh my god," the Kid squealed again, "don't lose it before you even use it."

"What's with that noise you just made?" Torrents asked the Kid. "That's twice you did it. You never make noises like that."

"I used to," the Kid shrugged, "back home, in my other body. Maybe just more of me is coming out as I get comfortable in this world?"

Nathan pulled a matte black amulet from the rocks below him, holding it up for the others to see. It was in the shape of a small triangular shield, about ten centimeters by fifteen centimeters across. Light disappeared into it, and nothing seemed to reflect off it.

"It absorbs energy," Nathan's voice was subdued with wonder as he turned the artifact over in his hands, "like magic, sunlight, or other things."

"Do you just hold it up for it to work?" Torrents poked it with a finger.

"Well," Nathan pressed it to his chest, and it stuck there, "I think I just wear it."

"Wait," the Kid gawked, "you don't need a chain, or a clip to wear it?"

"No," Nathan shook his head, removing the amulet from his chest and sticking it to the bracer on his right forearm, "it just clings to wherever I put it."

"So, lemme see if I got this right," the Kid grumbled, putting his hands on his hips, the black cloth draping his side, "Torrents got a demon-slaying sword, and you got an amulet that blocks magic, fire, sunlight, and any energy coming at you, and I got a hole? Am I understanding this right?"

"It goes with the one in your head," Torrents grinned, "now you have a matching set."

"Your mom has a matching set," the Kid shot back.

"Cla-clack, clack," Fred clacked.

"Well, yeah," Torrents nodded, "she does. Well, she did, before she died. Thanks for bringing that up, jerk!"

"Oh, no, I'm so sorry for your loss," Nathan said, reaching out to comfort the big man, and saw the smile on his face. "Wait, is she really dead?"

"No idea," Torrents shrugged, "she left when I was a baby. I was raised by my dad. Single parent and all that."

"Oh, you," the Kid rolled his eyes, "the old dead mom comeback. It makes it awkward every time."

Torrents stopped, jerking his head up and looking into the distance.

"We got our presents from this jerk." His voice was low and quiet. "We should get away from the huge magical tower in the middle of everything. I think I just heard one of those dog-men cackle. They might not all be dead. We should get out of here, or at least somewhere more defensible, before they come for us."

The Kid and Nathan nodded. They picked their way down the pile of rubble and onto the street.

Fred scurried ahead of the group, scouting the way.

The afternoon sun was overhead, making the three squint when they left the shadow of the tower. Scavenger birds had circled overhead, and above them was a kettle of wyverns gliding on the higher air currents, both watching for the opportunity to feast. The smell of char and ozone pervaded the area, mixing with the stench of freshly dead bodies in the sun. Low drifts of oily smoke moved through the streets like they had a mind of their own, which was entirely possible in this place.

Rocks tumbled, the sharp clack of stone on stone drifting across the complex. Torrents looked in the noise's direction, raising his hand to shade his eyes, looking for the source of the sound.

A shout from Nathan was the only warning before the small man bowled the barbarian over, a wrist-thick spear cutting through the space where Torrents had been a moment before.

Seven figures boiled over the edge of a stone wall. The muscled, bare-chested men with hyena heads launched more spears at the group. Raising their thick, curved blades high, they charged with the gurgled cackle of their kind. Leaping over obstacles, they ran towards the trio. Four giant hyenas bounded after the gnohls, thick drool stringing from their jowls.

Torrents, catching himself before hitting the ground, saw his new and improved blade already in his hand. He didn't remember reaching over his back to pull the weapon free, but it was in his hand now. Did he even put it away? Had he been carrying it the whole time?

The blade moved through the air even before he finished his thought, ripping through the throat of the first gnohl, and burying itself into the ribs of the next.

The two man-beasts yelped, more like beasts than men, and an orange line appeared around each of their injuries. Their cries cut short as all life left their bodies the moment the blade freed itself. That same orange glow streaked after the blade as it pulled the creatures' souls free from their bodies.

The Kid reached out with his mind, seeking to guide the daggers leaving his hands. A sharp spike of pain thrust itself from the base of his skull, through his head, and ended at his right eye. The street thief screamed, doubling over, his daggers going wide. His abilities weren't just missing, using them now caused backlash. He'd reached for them without thinking, used to relying on them.

A hyena pounced at his curled-up form, and the Kid rolled away. The black cloth he'd been carrying opened underneath him, and he fell into the hole it created.

He dropped a meter, then hit the ground, landing in a crouch, the pain in his head dissipating. The two daggers he'd thrown were at his feet. The Kid snatched up the daggers and threw them in the same motion. Each weapon sunk into a different eye socket of the huge spotted animal as it turned to pounce again.

The creature fell.

The Kid started to pull the daggers back to him with his mind magics, but stopped. Reaching into the black hole on the ground beside him, his hands appeared in front of the Hyaenidae and he pulled the weapons from the creature's skull. Drawing his blades back through the hole, the Kid spun, threw them again, and dropped into the ebon aperture.

Fred ran back and forth, trying to keep up with the Kid as he disappeared and reappeared.

Hyper-aware, Nathan felt the attack before seeing it. The metal symbol of Jonath on his chest pulsed against him, pulling his attention in every direction that there was a threat.

The rokairn set his feet, squared his shoulders, and moved towards a clump of three gnohls. He ducked under the pock-marked blade of one, jammed the top of his double-headed axe into its guts, which tore twin gashes along each of the monster's sides. Intestines slithered free.

Nathan pulled his axe free and swung it to one side, chopping through the sword arm of another, severing it at the elbow.

Kicking out with his boot, the gnohl's knee bent backwards. As the creature fell, Nathan blocked the third creature's downward attack with Marcid.

Sidestepping, he caught the blade in the curve of his axe, and pulled the weapon to the ground, then punched upward with his left hand. The gnohl's face broke, its nose pushing in and up, shoving the shattered bone into its brain. The creature stumbled backwards, dropping its weapon and falling onto its butt.

Torrents stepped over the bodies of his fallen foes, thrusting his sword through the neck of another gnohl, its gurgled scream cutting off as he pulled the weapon free, the orange glow following the blade.

Nathan cut down the remaining gnohl, his axe taking out the creature's knees from behind. He flipped the weapon around and brought it down on the monster's skull, splitting it as the gnohl hit the ground.

The Kid popped up from his hole, now on the ground in a new spot, and sliced across the throat of a hyena, then spun and threw them into the ribs of another beast leaping at him.

The blades buried themselves into the creature's barrel chest as the Kid rolled to the side, avoiding the hyena's clawed feet when it came down where he'd been a moment before.

The proto-hyena spun, blood mixing with the saliva dripping from its jaws. It coughed, and its breath caught, unable to draw air in. It leapt at the unarmed rogue again but met Torrents's weapon mid-air. The ebon blade disemboweled the creature, who landed heavily on its side, gasping as its eyes went wide with pain and the struggle to breathe.

Torrents moved from one fallen gnohls to another, dispatching any still living with the magic of his improved weapon. The orange glow appeared with each cut, severing the creatures' life forces from this realm.

Nathan did the same with the hyenas, but with more effort and less flair, Fred assisted. It was the simple task of cutting throats.

"That went well," the Kid said, pulling his twin daggers from the now-still hyena, "better than I expected. No one even got hurt."

"Well," Torrents was staring at his blade, which didn't have a single drop of blood, or glob of gore on it, "we didn't get hurt. These bunch of gnohls sure did, though."

"What do you call a group of gnohls, anyway?" the Kid asked.

"Same thing you call a bunch of hyenas." Nathan cleaned his axe, wiping it on a corpse, then with a thick cloth, "a cackle, I guess."

"Really? A cackle?" Torrents looked at the rokairn. "You messing with us?"

"Sorry," Nathan met the man's eyes and smiled, "I'm not."

184

Chapter 19

The three, and Fred, traveled due south for the rest of the day and set camp shortly before sunset. Grey ash drifted from the sky, an atmospheric anomaly that wasn't as uncommon as it should be.

They found a small copse of trees on the edge of the Blue Desert, where they laid out their bedrolls and made a small campfire.

Once settled, they tended their injuries.

Torrents took most of the damage and changed the bandages on six different cuts from rusty blades. He had dozens of smaller scratches, but nothing worth a bandage.

Nathan only had minor injuries, his armor and magics taking the brunt of the attacks. But he still had the deep gash on his face from the Demon Seed, though the harmful magics dissipated when he used his holy magics.

The Kid's two wounds he received during the fight with Mezk back at PepperGarten's still showed but weren't serious. He spent his evening before bed playing with his gift of Onyx, the magic hole.

He popped in and out of it, practicing throwing his knives. Many weeds died, and he injured many trees during the exercise.

They slept in shifts, and woke early to start again, eating the leftovers from the previous night. Fred had kept watch with each of them, not needing sleep.

They spent the next two weeks in some form of repetition of that first day; traveling, camping, practicing, repeat. It took two days to cross the Blue Desert, then they skirted the western edge of the Upper Swamp while staying in the Red Plains. They hunted and caught what they could along the way. A sense of urgency built as the green lights in the southeastern sky expanded northward.

Whenever they came across a caravan or a small settlement, they bought or traded for what they needed most, and moved on. Villagers were always suspicious of strangers, and even more so since the activity at the Demon Front escalated.

Strange weather became common as they neared Land's End, where the otherworldly beings were. Rains of frogs, ash fall, dry lightning, or even normal rain that burned the skin were a few of the things they had to deal with.

It took two weeks to reach the road that led from Durgan's Keep to Red Wind. The Lasso River surrounding the latter.

As they got closer, they encountered more caravans, people fleeing the area with everything they could carry in fear of what was coming. These people would stare at them, watching their every move, but most refused to talk to them or trade anything, even information. The few that did only told them what they expected: demons appeared with more frequency and people were being taken in the night.

"I still think that we should have gotten some horses," Torrents grumbled. "It would've been faster."

"Not really," the Kid sighed, "we've been over this. They would've cost more than we have, they need more food and water, and they really don't go much faster than we do. We're all young and healthy. We've got this."

The Kid laughed, thoughts of her seventy-seven-year-old body in the Hospice care in the other world sparring with the image of her body now. Or would she be seventy-eight now? Were there cosmic time zones, or did time freeze, or move at a different rate in the two places? Unsure of how the time difference worked, the Kid laughed again and shook his head.

They could see Red Wind in the distance, just a few hours away. A dark cloud of smog hung over the city, which wasn't uncommon in this medieval world. Wood fires, foundries, and other things that used fossil fuels often created that sort of thing. But this cloud was different. It moved, swirling in one direction and then another. Tendrils reached out from it, touching the ground in small twisters, or sometimes going sideways.

Plants grew more withered and sicklier, the closer they got to Land's End; approaching Red Wind, that had become even more common.

Nathan had been quiet for most of the day. Torrents didn't know what to make of the man. The rokairn was a powerful warrior, capable of using holy magic, but was still meek and apologetic in everything he did.

That wasn't normal to the barbarian. Torrents had grown up doing sports, the closest thing he could associate with being a warrior, and had basked in the glory of being a local hero. Since he'd been here, he'd come to understand the value of being humble, but didn't understand saying you're sorry for speaking. It just didn't make sense to him.

The Kid watched the other two, hanging back to keep an eye on anyone or anything that might approach from behind.

The Kid kinda adored Nathan, appreciating his demure attitude, kindness, and concern with upsetting others. That sort of person was rare, but it did get on his nerves after a while.

Watching Torrents, the Kid could see the big man's frustration with the newest addition. Nathan never stood up for himself, always backing down from any confrontation. But when someone else was threatened, Nathan was the first to rise to their defense.

It almost caused an issue with a caravan they'd traded with. When the man they were talking to smacked a pre-teen boy who didn't move fast enough to get what he was sent to retrieve, Nathan had reached for his axe and stepped forward. A gentle hand and shake of the Kid's head kept the rokairn in check.

"That's how this world is," Torrents said later, when they discussed the incident.

Nathan glared at him.

"Look, Nathan," the Kid said, "that child will grow up and overcome these things."

"Kindness is a better way," Nathan argued, one of the rare times he did, "and there's never an excuse to hit someone to make them do what you wanted them to do."

"That's exactly what we're about to do with Klendrisia and Mezk when we catch them." Torrents pointed out.

Nathan shook his head and mumbled, "It shouldn't be that way. There should be another option."

"I want to agree," the Kid said, "but after a lifetime of abuse on both worlds, I don't think there is another way. I wish there was. There are no easy answers when the whole world responded with a fist."

Nathan eyed the horizon, watching Red Wind grow bigger.

"I like you guys," he said, "but neither of you seem to understand that I want to help others without resorting to violence. I've wracked my brain for another way, but I've already seen that the enemy we face won't listen to reason. Though maybe we could bring Klendrisia around. She had said almost as much, complaining that her people—and her father in particular—treated her that way, and she was tired of it. But she acted just like they did, not seeking an alternate solution, and instead doing the same thing they did."

The city crawled with movement, black specks darting around the outside of the crumbled defenses, and spots of fire visible from a distance.

Nathan picked up his pace to a jog, moving ahead of Torrents, his axe in one hand.

"You know," the Kid shouted, he, Fred, and Torrents matching the pace, "running will get us there a little faster, but a lot more tired. We may need to conserve our energy. Even stop for a meal before we get there. I don't think the taverns will be serving dinner, considering the circumstances."

Nathan ignored the comment, and moved at a steady, but faster, pace.

When they got within bowshot of Red Wind, a group of small creatures, about waist high to a human, broke away and came towards them.

"What're those?" Torrents asked, slowing his stride and reaching for his sword.

The weapon was already in his hand. He'd have to get used to that, or risk cutting his head off one day.

"Demons," Nathan's voice was a throaty growl, and he raised Marcid, "they have acid blood, so be careful when you cut them. Or bash and splatter them, whichever."

The creatures came fast, traveling on four legs, their spotted bodies thin and contorted. They resembled pygmy giraffes, if the spots on the animal were scabs and leathery flesh sluffing off every time they moved. Their rounded heads had pointed ears that swiveled all the way around, and large yellow eyes with slitted pupils. The things' mouths were full of needle-teeth in multiple rows.

The three of them had only a moment to see all this before the monsters swarmed. Then they were waist deep in screeching, biting beasts.

Fred launched forward, cutting at any enemy legs within reach.

Torrents's sword swung in wide arcs, tearing through the things easily, the orange glow of the weapon's magic trailing after. The little demons fell by the handful.

The Kid pressed his back to the barbarian, twin daggers in his hands, slashing to protect the big man.

Nathan laid about him with the flat of his axe, swatting two or three of the beasts away at a time. The long thin necks writhed around the shaft of the weapon, grabbing at it like a prehensile snake. Green light burst from the wooden handle of Marcid—PepperGarten's nature magic, destroying the foreign creatures.

Within a minute, the three moved away from dozens of the creatures that lay dead behind them. They brushed at bright red spots on their skin where the blood had splashed and burned them.

Reaching the broken city walls, hundreds of the minor demons ran through the streets, attacking anyone they could find.

Other forms were there, too.

Thin demons, almost as tall as a single-story building, with leathery, plated skin in shades of reddish-brown, moved around on segmented, stilt-like legs. The insectile creatures had four faceted eyes, and short, stubby antennae that resembled goat horns.

The group entered the city, cutting down any monsters that crossed their path. The companions fought their way between the buildings, following Nathan as he moved with purpose, heading deeper into the maze of chaos.

"There," Nathan pointed at a stone structure, short and squat, the symbol of Jonath carved into the triangle of the peak above the steps and doors.

Men and women formed into ranks in front of the broad, oak double doors, the ones in front defending the church with a shield wall, and the ones behind firing arrows into the demonic horde. Through the door, Nathan could see dozens of terrified families inside, every face looking towards the doors, or the hastily shuttered and blockaded windows along the side of the building.

"Kaleb triot, den'al venitier!" Nathan roared his battle cry and charged into the back of the attackers.

Fred crouched low, made a little leap, and scurried into the fight.

Torrents and the Kid exchanged quick glances, the Kid shrugging and Torrents giving a grim smile, before they followed the rokairn into the fray.

Chapter 20

Klendrisia appeared in the center of the encampment. Men and women dropped to their knees, prostrating themselves face down in the dirt and leaves. She moved through their groveling forms, smiling at their worship and dedication to her.

This was the slave lands. At least that was what she called it in her head. It was in the center of Land's End and the Demon Front, the peninsula in the south-easternmost corner of the continent of Teurone.

This land had once been a center of worship of her father, but the humans and dasism had come and wiped out the loyal followers who'd been working so hard to open portals for the abysmal armies. That was hundreds of years ago.

Just a couple hundred years ago, a foolhardy group of explorers—looters really—had come upon the abandoned keep in the thick of the woods hunting a vampire and whatever treasures it had hidden.

Klendrisia wrapped herself in the darkness again and reappeared outside of the broken structure where it had all started, this plan of hers.

One of the weak-minded fools had triggered the Ruby Door and opened one small portal that let hundreds of soldiers of her father's army through into this land. It also transported one human priestess of Promethene to her father. That woman became the mother of Klendrisia's half-brother, Nomed.

When someone rescued the woman, they stole Klendrisia's half-brother away before his birth. The woman died in childbirth, and an outcast of the church, a male, raised Nomed. The Church of Promethene only allowed female priestesses, and this man was an abomination to the church. But he raised a half-breed demon in the ways of the aeifain.

Nomed had grown to become quite a thorn in the side of Lord Ghlevid and even fought against the demon invasion to the west during the Downfall and the reign of the Talisman. Klendrisia's half-brother had manipulated entire countries to help block the contract between the troöds and the demons, who were working together to overthrow and enslave the people of this world.

Now, Klendrisia was in this ancestral shrine, and the humans here bowed to her and jumped to fill her every whim. Not her brother's, not her father's, but hers. She would succeed where all others had failed.

The people here would all die…or be transformed in the impending ritual. In a few weeks, the month would reach its end. On that new moon, Klendrisia would open a huge portal to this world for her father's armies.

She had manipulated the rokairn, Nathan, who was so hopeful about everything, to bring his friends to help with the sacrifice needed. Dozens of her minions had spilled tainted blood on the holy nexus of the Nine Towers, priming the magical pump so she could open the flood gates and redirect the ley line energies from across the continent to the Pyridom.

She stepped into the fold of the dark again, appearing at the foot of the Pyridom. The conical structure rose into the sky above her. The crigth wobbled past on their insectile legs, followed by clumps of the small, four-legged jedth.

Even now, the fledgling priest of Jonath would be fighting her demons, and then he'd raise an army to try to stop her. That army would bring the anger, hate, and fear she needed to taint the ley lines and turn the largest conductor of magical energy in the world into a beacon portal.

That was a very special sort of portal; it wasn't static, waiting for someone to use it. It called to them, drawing them in, even forcing them to pass through it. Yes, it would draw Lord Ghlevid's armies, but also the armies of the other demon lords, and the Inciter Demons—rogue demon warriors with no master— who sought their place of power as they roamed the realms.

The chaos would allow Klendrisia to gather control and allies to form her army. And the cost was small, just a single world.

The plan had many moving parts, but she'd orchestrated them well. The rokairn warrior-priest, the Dragon's Dagger to open the Nine Towers, the redirection of the ley lines, the demon scouts to draw in the enemy army, her army here waiting to battle, and the last piece she needed.

She called upon the cold void one more time, feeling it caress her, enfolding her in its nothingness, and stepped out into the center of the encampment again.

Mezk was there, sitting on a wooden throne he'd constructed in her absence, human women surrounding him. One fed him withered fruits—his face wrinkling with the bitterness—and two sat at his feet, rubbing on his legs like feral cats in heat.

The Demon Seed lay on the arm of the throne, and his fingers stroked it like a favored pet, or a lover. The red cloth that contained the Dragon's Dagger lay across his lap. The man never let either out of his reach.

Mezk smirked when he saw her watching him.

He inclined his head at her, and Klendrisia kept her expression neutral, knowing any show of emotion—anger, hate, or even a courteous reaction—would make the man feel like he was manipulating her, and that he controlled their relationship. She knew men like him all her life, but in this case, he was the one being manipulated.

Klendrisia raised one hand, motioning for Mezk to come to her. She turned away before he could respond, knowing that if she didn't, he'd gesture for her to come to him. She knew this game.

The cambion walked away slowly, letting the man catch up. When he did, his face was tight.

"When will I get what I've been promised?" Mezk said, falling in beside her and matching her casual pace.

"Soon, Mezk of the Demon Seed," she smirked, "the time will be upon us soon enough. Do you know your part?"

"Of course I do," Mezk growled, a sad attempt to intimidate her.

"Humor me," she purred, "and tell me one more time. I do so love to hear it from your mouth."

"Once the dwarf priest arrives with his army," Mezk's voice sounded forced, "I kill him with the Demon Seed on the steps of the Pyridom, making sure his blood washes the walls."

"Yes," Klendrisia smiled, "very good. Then, and only then, you may kill the two-spirit with the Dragon's Dagger. That should break the bond that keeps

Edsumar in this plane, and that will be the time for the Demon Seed to devour his enemy's energies. And that will release you from your pact. Isn't that correct?"

"Yes," Mezk growled, "and then I get to go, a free man, no ties, no pacts, no contracts. Right?"

"Oh, yes," Klendrisia stopped and turned to face Mezk, causing him to draw up short, "except one agreement."

"What?" Mezk's face turned red, ready to explode, "there is no other agreement, that ends it!"

"I just mean the agreement where I make sure you get out of here," Klendrisia smiled again, "safely and unharmed by me and any of my followers. That's all. You do still want that agreement to be fulfilled, right?"

"Yes," Mezk sneered, "of course. But that isn't so much an agreement, as an understanding."

"Oh?" The demoness looked up at the man. "Is that so? Well, I'm so pleased you clarified that. Words make a difference, especially when dealing with my ilk."

"Yeah," Mezk looked worried, wondering if he missed something, or if something had changed because of his words, "just make sure you keep to that understanding. Don't forget that I'll have two magical blades, and even without the consciousness in either of them, they'll still wield power. I'll wield that power."

"Of course," Klendrisia drew out the words, "consider me suitably threatened. And then, never do that again. If I feel I may come to any harm from you, all deals are off, and you may face new challenges that you never would have expected."

The demoness looked at the man, who glared back at her.

"Do we understand one another?" Klendrisia asked.

Mezk nodded.

"No, no, no," she moaned, shaking her head, "you have to say the words. You know that. Otherwise, it isn't clear. Do. We. Understand. One. Another?

"Yes," Mezk rasped, "we do understand one another. And I'll be free of all this, and I'll live a life with no one holding my leash ever again."

"You and me both, my sweet," Klendrisia's tone was solemn.

Mezk tilted his head, watching the demon-spawn turn and walk away.

The dagger on his hip, the Demon Seed, pushed the urge upon him to stab her now, while she wasn't looking. Kill her before she could set a trap for him.

The cloth wrapped Dragon's Dagger railed against its magical prison. The urges and thoughts from it were muted and blunted, but Mezk could still feel it trying to touch his mind and control him. It wanted out…and it wanted the Kid.

He'd give the dagger what it wanted soon enough, but on his schedule, and on his terms. Once the dwarf was dead, the barbarian broken, and the Kid sobbing at Mezk's feet, then he'd free the Dragon's Dagger and give him the Kid forever.

Once he shattered that blood bond, he'd break the last defense of the ivory blade, and the Demon Seed could devour it. That would break all ties between Mezk and his pact. He'll have fulfilled his part of the deal, freeing the incubating soul trapped within the dagger, and it could go its way to exact revenge on the ones who did this to it.

Mezk wasn't sure where he'd go next. Durgan's Keep sounded good, but he knew that cesspool too well, and wasn't sure if he wanted to bother taking it for his own.

Maybe he'd get a ship and take to the seas. They were dangerous, much more now than they were before the Downfall, but at least he'd be free.

The ends of the world were his only restrictions. He could go to Seawall City or cross the continent and see what lay there.

But another thought niggled at him. Mezk knew he'd be in the center of a huge power play. One well-placed knife, and his biggest rival would be gone. If he killed Klendrisia, everyone else would be a new player in the game. He'd be able to make alliances, form new connections, and perhaps even have them bow to him for a change.

Demons were tricky things, but they weren't infallible. They were so used to having the upper hand over humans, they never considered that the tables could be turned.

If Mezk could kill Klendrisia, he could control the portal annex. He would be the one making the deals and collecting the debts from the demons for a change. They would come to him, ask him for favors and passage.

And with his connections in Red Wind, Durgan's Keep, and the other communities, he could rule this entire part of the continent if he could control the portals to other realms and worlds.

This was food for thought, and the Demon Seed encouraged it. The dagger thought it was a good idea, and that the two of them could work together and bring great things to this world, one deal at a time.

Chapter 21

The city of Red Wind lay in smoking ruins. The demons had put most of the buildings to the torch, burning out anyone hiding within. When someone came out of a building, they were set upon by hordes of jedth or a crigth and torn apart.

The sooty clouds overhead moved with a mind of their own, dark tendrils reaching down to touch the ground and then pull back into the mass above. Ash fell across the city like a dirty flurry.

The splinter factions of the city had no chance; even if they'd been able to come together, it might not have helped.

Nathan wandered through the streets, helping anyone he could. Parents searching for children—or children searching for parents—were everywhere. The community came together now, but too late.

"The us and them mentally," the Kid said, and Nathan turned to regard him, "they were against each other, and it screwed them when someone else showed up. Now, they draw together, because there's a different *them* to battle their collective *us*."

"Well," Torrents looked over a smoldering pile of wet bodies, trying to puzzle what piece belonged to which corpse, "a little too little, a little too late, they just had their us'es handed to them."

"That's insensitive," Nathan said. "You shouldn't make fun of people who just faced this much death."

"They shouldn't have been pemties," Torrents shrugged, "if they'd been working together instead of trying to beat out the other guy, then more of them might've survived."

"You don't know that!" Nathan spun to face Torrents, jabbing the large man in the belly with a thick finger. "You don't have the right to say things like that. These were human beings, and they murdered them in the street for no reason. You have no right to come in here and insult their memory."

"Hey," the Kid put one hand on Nathan's shoulder, and pulled the poking finger from Torrents's stomach as the big man glared down at the rokairn, "hey, hey. I get what you're saying, but some of us deal with things in different ways, and that's okay, too. We can't expect everyone to be calm and not angry after living through something like this, can we?"

Fred moved between the Kid and the rokairn, lightly clicking his claws.

Nathan sighed, looked down, and shook his head.

"If I hadn't run," Nathan muttered.

"What?" The Kid turned Nathan to face him. "What are you talking about? You fought. You helped protect the church full of people, then you went out into the streets and hunted down dozens of demons, maybe hundreds. What do you mean, 'if you hadn't run'?"

"Not today," Nathan's voice tightened, "not now. When I first got here. I knew what I had to do. I knew I needed to go south. Find Klendrisia, kill her, and stop the demons from coming north. But I ran. I abandoned my responsibility, and because of that…all these people are dead. They're all dead, because of me."

"That's a load of bullbidj," Torrents spat, "you aren't responsible for the whole world. You're one man, or rokairn, and you can't think that you could've stopped a whole army of demons. That's ridiculous."

The Kid held a hand towards Torrents, gesturing for him to stop talking.

"You've done good here, Nathan," the Kid patted the rokairn's shoulder, "you've helped more people in one afternoon than most people help in their whole lives."

"You guys are right," Nathan said.

"I know we are," Torrents shot back.

"Hush," the Kid hissed at the barbarian, then turned back to Nathan, "what do you mean?"

"If I'd stopped her in the very beginning, it would've been different," Nathan looked the Kid in the eye, "even if I'd died fighting demons all alone, it would've been different. Klendrisia would've never come through here the first time, killing good people. She would've never taken your dagger, so that's my fault, too. She would've never gone to the Towers. She wouldn't have opened new portals. All that happened because I was a coward, and because I was a coward, people have died."

"No," the Kid said gently, "they died, because bad people do bad things…"

"I'm not done," Nathan interrupted, "and don't placate me with trite platitudes. They died because I didn't do something. It's that simple. But what I meant when I said you two are right, is that violence is the only way. Talking doesn't help. These people talked to each other, but it didn't help them, it tore them apart. Talking to Klendrisia won't help. The only thing this damned, pemtie world understands is blade and blood."

"Whoa," the Kid leaned away from Nathan, "such strong language. Did you just say the word 'damn'? Shouldn't you have said darn, or shucks, or golly gee whiz? Such a potty mouth, and from you Nathan. I expected better."

Nathan didn't laugh.

"Look," the Kid leaned back towards him, "we can't change the past, right? We can only do something different the next time. And what can we do right now?"

"We can go kill the demon bitch who caused all this," Nathan said through gritted teeth.

"You ain't gonna go alone," a deep, slow voice said from behind Nathan.

Nathan turned to look who it was, and behind him was a big man with a dull look on his face, a conical helmet on his head, and a shirt of chain mail.

"Nob?" Nathan breathed. "You're alive?"

"Yah," Nob nodded, "thanks to you. So, stop talking dumb. You can only help when you do things. Not after it happens. Okay?"

"Yah," Torrents's tone mimicked, "what he said, dork."

All three of the others looked at Torrents.

"Him," Torrents pointed at Nathan, "he's the dork, not you, Nob. You seem cool. He's a pemtie though."

"Yah," Nob nodded again, "but don't pick on him. It ain't easy being like that. I feel bad for him."

The Kid snickered and held his hand out to Nob.

"I'm the Kid," the Kid said, "and the other dummy behind me is Torrents."

Nob shook the Kid's hand.

"Whose kid are you?" Nob asked. "You don't look rokairn, or whatever Torrents is."

"No," the Kid laughed, "that's what they call me. I'm the Kid, no other name."

"Yah," Nob nodded at the Kid, and turned to the rokairn, "poor people can't afford fancy names like Nathan. Oh, and the priests at the temple want to see you, Nathan."

The Kid called Fred back to his side—the rock lobster had been diligently snapping the throats of any demons they came across, the acid blood not affecting his stony hide—and the group moved through the streets, taking time to help people they passed. It took almost an hour to travel the six blocks, and when they arrived, they had a group of twenty people with them.

The priests met them on the steps, taking the townsfolk into their care.

A thin, grey-haired man with a neatly trimmed beard stepped up to the group.

"This is Pelese," Nathan said to his friends. "He's the high priest here."

Each gave their greeting, introducing themselves.

"You folk," the priest's voice was full and rich, "have done a lot to help Red Wind, and I wanted to thank each of you."

Pelese held up his hand to forego any interruptions.

"I understand you've decided to go further into the storm," Pelese continued, "seeking the heart of this attack?"

"Yeah," the Kid's forehead wrinkled in confusion, "but we just decided that. How'd you hear about it already?"

"My son," the priest smiled, "Jonath protects, and he whispers to others to help when we can. And that's what I want to do."

"What does that mean?" Torrents asked.

"It means he wants to help," Nob grunted.

"It means," Pelese cut them off, "that I want to tend your wounds, give you supplies, offer the blessings of Jonath, and send as many able-bodied people with you as will volunteer to go."

"Like me," Nob smiled and nodded.

Torrents, Nathan, and the Kid exchanged looks.

"No," Nathan said, "no one needs to go with us. They've suffered enough, and too many have died."

"Hey," the Kid rested a hand on Nathan's arm, "this is their town, their world, and they're allowed to help defend it if they want."

"The child speaks wisely," Pelese said, earning him a sharp glare from the Kid, "and though you may seek the heart to destroy it, others can handle the arms of a many limbed foe."

"Ugh," Torrents muttered, "all the fancy talk. Is he reading poetry or something?"

"All things in life are poetry," Pelese smiled, "if you take the time to listen. Some are dark, some are hopeful, and all should be shared. Allow these people to share this burden, and the glory of the sagas that will be written and sung to recount the brave deeds, the lives lost, and the future that will come from it."

"How can we say no to that?" the Kid raised an eyebrow.

"No," Nathan said.

"That's how," Torrents muttered.

"This is my responsibility," Nathan ignored the barbarian's comment. "I can't ask anyone else to go with me!"

"My son," Pelese said, interrupting the Kid, who had opened his mouth to say something, "you aren't asking. They are going with you, or without you, to protect their homes and families. The ones who would not go are either unable to rise and hold sword and spear or have fled in hopes of not falling to the inevitable. Would you brand every man and woman a coward, and deny them the right to defend their loved ones?"

Nathan sighed and looked away.

"Then it is done," the priest smiled, "come inside so our chirurgeons may tend to your injuries. A hot meal and a warm bed also await."

The sun rose, breaking through the thick clouds in single rays, on two score of armed townsfolk. Others lined the streets. Any not gathered could not get out of bed or were tending to the injured.

It was a motley army, some barely old enough to fight, others much too old to wear a sword anymore, but they were prepared to face something that couldn't be beaten.

The crowd cheered, a ragged sound, grim along with hopeful, as the columns of people on horseback and a few supply wagons moved away and down the broken street.

Nathan rode a pony at the head of the procession, bracketed by Torrents and the Kid. The barbarian rode on a roan mare who pranced excitedly, and the Kid had a dapple who kept nuzzling him for treats. Fred scampered along on one side, making horses whiney and shy away. Nob rode behind Nathan, spear in a stirrup and sword on his side.

The temple gave each of them what healing they could spare and patched or replaced their equipment.

They'd travel east, across the Red Plains and the western portion of the Crescent Desert. When they hit the crag wasteland in the center of the desert, they'd veer southeast towards the Pyridom. The trip would take three weeks with the wagons and extra people.

It was on the tenth day of the journey, and the third day into the heat-blown sands, when the deserters left in the middle of the night, taking most of the supplies with them.

Chapter 22

"They took all the water," Nob's voice cut through the chill, desert, night air, "and the horses!"

"Stop yelling," Torrents hissed. "You'll bring them all down on us."

Nob quieted, looking around. Seeing Torrents crouched beside the wagon a few meters away, the burly man moved over to the barbarian and crouched as well.

"What're we gonna do?" Nob whispered, much too loud.

"The Kid is checking it out," Torrents reassured him. "We don't know what happened yet."

"Yes, we do," Nathan's bitter voice came from on top of the wagon. "They stole all the supplies and left us to die in the middle of the desert."

"Let's just wait until the Kid gets back," Torrents directed his voice to Nob to reassure him, "before we jump to conclusions, okay?"

Nob nodded.

"The only conclusion is," Nathan growled, "people are bidj."

The Kid hunched, moving along, keeping low so he wouldn't be seen over a dune from a distance. He wasn't sure if it was necessary. He wasn't worried about the deserters seeing him—they'd already be long gone since they were on horseback and had adequate light—but there were other things that hunted at night.

Fred was three paces behind him, shuffling along with natural ease in the desert. The Kid had thought that odd, considering lobsters were not especially graceful on land. Then again, he didn't know a lot about this magical construct he'd created by accident. The rock lobster seemed to be in his element in the sands. Literally.

It was a waning moon, almost down to a quarter, just ten days until the new moon. Not that the moonlight mattered, the green glow of the demon-lights—which is what they'd begun calling the atmospheric effect in this area that resembled the northern lights, except in color—lit the night sky, making the moon a blurred smear, sickly yellow beyond the dancing swirls of demonic energy.

The Kid still didn't understand how the deserters snuck out of camp without waking anyone. Leading that many horses away without making noise was an impossible task. And how did they pack everything with no one noticing?

Could they have used magic to silence themselves, or to keep everyone asleep?

The Kid didn't think magical skills were so common that anyone among the townsfolk would have the ability. There were the priests, but they had left the three of them behind with the camp. They also worshiped the god of protection, and that meant guard-duty was in their repertoire. Jonath often gifted his priests with extra abilities, including heightened awareness and perception. No one should have been able to sneak past them, let alone a bunch of people with fully loaded horses.

Besides the priests, the only people left behind had been the older men and women. That meant the deserters consisted of the young. Did that mean anything? Perhaps they were prone to rebellion, or easier to sway? And why would they leave now, anyway?

There was no way these people slipped away in a well-lit night, on a flat desert landscape, without help.

Or something taking them. But how did you snatch up two dozen people and forty horses without raising an alarm?

And Fred didn't sleep, and he knew to wake the Kid if something was happening. But Fred hadn't noticed anything, either.

When the Kid was woken—by Nob—the street thief had begun a search. The Kid had checked around the camp, easily finding the tracks of the horses leading into the night. But they'd ended less than twenty paces away.

The sands had been blowing, partially covering the tracks, but it hadn't blown enough to conceal them completely.

It made no sense.

Without the food, water, and supplies that were taken, people were going to die. Too many had died already, and now the people who'd come with them would likely be next. The old didn't travel well on foot through a desert with no water.

The Kid was sick and tired of losing people. Not in the way he lost the deserters when he was tracking them, but losing them to death. Death was the natural conclusion to life. Everyone had to take that irrevocable step sometime. But to see so many killed before their time was taking its toll on him.

Hope's Hollow, Durgan's Keep, Red Wind, and now they were taking a journey down the River Styx and into the belly of the beast. No one making this trip was likely to survive it, and there was a good chance the rest of the world wouldn't survive it, either.

It was exhausting, always having to deal with death.

Something caressed the Kid's mind, breaking him away from his thoughts, and he froze like a mouse hearing the cry of a hawk.

Fred, feeling something wrong with his creator, scurried over to the Kid and clacked his claws in a display meant to frighten a foe.

"You can still feel my mind," the Kid patted Fred, "can't you, boy? I wish I still had my other abilities, too, but at least we're still connected."

The Kid's lost his mind mage abilities when Mezk stabbed him with the cursed dagger. If something had touched his mind, and even Fred sensed it, that meant it could connect with any mind: mind mage, normal, or magical. What sort of thing could do that?

Something tickled at the back of the Kid's thoughts, like when doing a crossword, and couldn't remember the clue needed to fill in seven-down, thirteen letters. A being that could do those things, it could hunt anyone, and wouldn't leave a trace or raise an alarm.

"I'm a fool's pemtie," the Kid muttered, shaking his head as he rose.

He ran as fast as he could back towards the camp.

Time flew faster than the Kid's feet and he was within the circle of the encampment's abandoned wagons before he knew it. Fred, still beside him, reached up with a claw and pinched the Kid's inner thigh.

"Ow!" The Kid slapped at his thigh, glaring down at the construct. "What the hell was that for? And where is everyone? You see anyone, Fred?"

Fred danced left and right and turned in a circle.

"Yeah," the Kid looked around as he spoke, craning his neck to check the top of wagons, "I don't see anyone either."

He moved to where he'd left Torrents and Nathan, inspecting the sands beside the wagon. It showed an imprint where the barbarian had been kneeling, a thin line of his blade beside it.

Climbing atop the wagon, sand scattered across the canvas covered crates, showing where Nathan stood when the Kid saw him.

He turned, preparing to jump off the side to the sands below, and tripped over Fred. The thief stumbled, wind milling his arms as he swayed at the edge of the wagon. He regained his balance and dropped back on his heels.

"Fred!" the Kid growled, looking at the rock lobster. "What's gotten into you? And how'd you even get up here? Been practicing your jumps, or did you learn to levitate?"

The Kid turned back to the edge, preparing again to jump down, and stopped when he noticed the swirling patterns in the sand below.

"I swear I heard him," Torrents said, trailing a dagger in a spiral pattern in front of him, "like he was shouting at that damn crab. It didn't sound like it was far away, but it was faint."

"That makes no sense," Nathan said, still scanning the horizon, "but there's something else here, even if it's not the Kid."

"Perhaps," Nob said, "the two of you should go out into the night and find your friend. I can wait here; in case he returns."

"You might be right," Torrents stood, shoved his dagger back into its sheath, and brought his ebon blade up, resting the flat on his shoulder, "he's been gone too long."

"How long has he been gone?" Nathan was studying the clouds moving overhead, his voice serious and focused. "I mean, really Torrents, how much time has passed since we've been waiting?"

"I don't know," Torrents wrinkled his brow, "I really…don't know. That's odd."

"What's odd?" Nathan's voice was expectant, like he was looking for a specific answer. "What exactly are you finding odd at this moment?"

"It doesn't matter," Nob said, "you should find your friend. Perhaps one of you could go one direction, and the other can go the opposite direction. It would be quicker if you separated."

"I'm not sure." Each word was a separate sentence as Torrents spoke to them. "I can't put my finger on it exactly, but it's like…like this is just a single moment. I know the Kid's been gone for a while, but it feels like he just left."

"Go on," Nathan prodded, nodding, but still watching the sky, "how could that be, Torrents?"

"We've had an entire conversation, right?" The barbarian looked up at him and went on when he saw

Nathan nod. "Maybe more than one, but it's like no time passed. And, the wind is blowing, but the sand isn't moving. That's not really normal, is it?"

"You should go," Nob's voice was a command, "find your friend, leave here and go seek him."

"Not really," Nathan said, "and the wind isn't blowing up here, a meter off the ground, but the clouds are moving. And when did Nob start speaking in complete sentences?"

Torrents turned to look at the burly mercenary, but only glimpsed the deep green shadow surging towards him before screaming.

The shadow launched itself at the barbarian, enveloping him as he tumbled backwards onto the sands, bringing his sword to bear.

The weapon was no longer in his hands.

Torrents screamed.

Fred pinched the Kid again, harder this time, causing him to squeal.

"Fred!" the Kid sputtered through clenched teeth. "What's gotten into you?"

The lobster ran to the Kid. He didn't grab the man's clothes and pull himself up. He just ran up him, settled onto his chest, and seized the Kid's ears in his massive claws.

"Ow!" the Kid jerked away, but found his back flat against the ground, his elbow digging into the sand for a moment before he reached to grab Fred's pincers, "Wait, what just...how am I laying down, Fred?"

The canopy of the canvas tent above the Kid flapped in the wind.

Holding Fred's claws in place, the Kid sat up and looked around without turning his head, thus avoiding having the rock lobster tear his ears off.

"I'm…" the Kid enunciated slowly, "I'm in my bedroll, in my tent? How'd that happen? Where'd the cart go?"

Fred released the Kid's ears, scrambled backwards down his chest and sideways onto the sand beside him.

The Kid put both hands under him, pushed up, and stood, ducking in the enclosed space. He walked, while bent, to the door flap, and pushed out into the night air.

The dark, oily cloud he'd seen over Red Wind hung low in the sky above the camp, dirty tendrils quivering as they touched tents and guards on duty.

Each person the Kid could see stared straight ahead, their bodies relaxed, even if standing.

"Night hunters, Fred," the Kid said to the rock lobster who'd moved forward and pressed against his ankle, "dream hunters. Invisible, ethereal demons who devour hope and fear. That's what's here, but you can't see them when awake. They're like the…psychic assassins for the really, dark, slimy folks. And I'm pretty sure we have an infestation."

Fred clacked what the Kid assumed was an agreement.

"I think…" the Kid moved forward, one step at a time, "your bond with me, and maybe because you were touching me, allowed you to interact with me when I was, wherever I was. It could be because of my mind-mage abilities, but they don't seem to be around anymore."

The two moved through the camp, looking into tents where the cloud tentacles reached down and touched people, and at the comatose guards still standing and staring into the distance, taking stock of the situation.

The Kid saw the horses, in a tight group, about twenty meters away from the camp on a dune. The animals were whinnying and stamping nervously, shaking their heads and rolling their eyes.

Passing a wagon, the Kid spotted Nob standing on the other side, a tendril from above obscuring his head.

Moving closer, the rogue heard noises from underneath. Drawing two daggers, he bent to look beneath the buckboard.

Torrents and Nathan lay underneath, back to back, curled in their bedrolls, both twitching in their sleep.

The barbarian's ebon blade lay an arm's length from the man, and the rokairn clutched his axe, but his magical amulet was half buried in the sand at his feet.

The Kid stooped under the wagon, duck-walking forward. He slid the blade to Torrents's hand with his foot, while reaching out to retrieve the amulet and set it on Nathan's bare chest.

Chapter 23

Torrents fell backwards, screaming in surprise. It turned into a cry of rage, as he somersaulted heels over head and came up on his feet.

The shadow spirit was on him, a mouthful of black mist teeth stretching the creature's features until nothing more than a maw trying to devour Torrents's face was where its head had been.

The barbarian shoved both fists forward, attempting to hold the thing away from him, but his hands slipped into the mist, going numb and falling to his sides.

Then Nathan was there, swinging his axe at the ephemeral body of the spirit. The blade passed through harmlessly, but when the shaft touched the being's form, it shot a spray of green flashes resembling fireworks.

The creature spun towards the rokairn, a hiss that sounded like a distant teakettle issuing from above it. A wispy image of a tendril flashed into existence, extending from the sky.

Nathan flipped his axe and stabbed the vine wrapped handle at the thing as it pulsed towards him. The spirit flowed to the left, moving around the shaft. The rokairn swept the weapon's handle sideways, cutting through the ethereal demon.

Green fireworks burst around the creature and the hissing noise filled the air, the tentacle of smoke appearing above it again.

Torrents stepped backwards, looking around for something to use as a weapon, when he noticed his sword was now in his grip and his hands were no longer numb. He raised the blade, staring at it in surprise.

With a shrug, the barbarian brought the sword to bear in a double handed hold, angling it diagonally across his chest in a full body defensive posture.

The thing surged towards Nathan again and crashed against an invisible bubble surrounding him.

Looking down in surprise, Nathan saw his black shield amulet resting against his breastbone.

An ebon blade slashed across the specter, and the thing melted into tattered wisps of smoke with a sigh.

The Kid was crouched beside Torrents when the barbarian's eyes fluttered open. Beside him, Nathan moaned and sat up from his bedroll.

Fred danced back and forth anxiously.

"Good morning, sleepyheads," the Kid smiled, "when you clear the cobwebs from your head, I need some help to wake the others."

"What was that?" Nathan twisted to look over his shoulder at the other two, blinking in the chilly night. "Were we dreaming?"

"Sorta," the Kid duck-walked backwards to get out from under the wagon, Fred scurrying to one side, "I think you were facing a Night Hunter, it's a demon spirit, and probably working with the folks we're going after."

"How many are there?" Torrents asked, crawling out from under the shelter.

"Not sure," the Kid held out one hand to help the big man to his feet, pointing towards the sky with his other hand, "but I think that ominous cloud is a nest of them. Some sort of hive mind, or something where they all gather. See the tendrils, like what we saw back in Red Wind?"

Nathan emerged from the other side of the wagon, looking up, and holding his chain mail shirt in one hand, his axe in the other. The black amulet still clung to his hairy chest.

"Do you know how to stop it?" Nathan asked, pulling his pack to him and strapping on various pieces of his armor.

"I think you guys can do that," the Kid pointed at Nob, who was standing a meter from Nathan, an even-more blank look than usual on his face. "I think your trinket blocks them, and Torrents bigger, blacker…sword can send them back to where they come from."

"Then let's do this." Torrents raised his blade.

"You want pants first?" the Kid laughed, pointing at the barbarian's minimal night clothes.

"Nope," Torrents said over his shoulder and strode around the wagon.

By the time the barbarian got around the wagon, Nathan had removed his amulet, slid his gambeson over his head, followed by his chain mail shirt, and pressed the magical shield to the center of his chest.

Torrents looked Nob up and down, the burly man staring slack-jawed into the distance, a streamer of oily smoke wrapped around his head.

The barbarian raised his sword and swung it with one hand through the tendril, splitting it. The tentacle jerked upward and away like a living thing, retreating into the swirling mass above.

Nob gasped and fell to his hands and knees, the big man's conical helm tumbling from his head to the sand. The guard vomited between his splayed hands.

Nathan put a hand on Nob's shoulder, steadying him.

"You go," Nathan looked up at Torrents's worried face, and the Kid behind him. "I'll stay with him for a moment. Everyone may react differently, so we'll need to get the ones who aren't too bad to stay with the ones who are."

Torrents nodded and turned away, striding towards the closest grey tentacle.

"You sure?" the Kid asked. "Are you okay?"

"Yeah," Nathan grunted, rubbing Nob's shoulder, "go on, I'm fine, and I'll make sure that Nob's doing okay, then I'll be right there to help."

The Kid took a step backwards, then turned and jogged after Torrents who was already severing the next tendril.

He caught up in time to check on the young guardsman who'd just been freed from the demon's grasp.

Torrents had already moved on to the next person.

They continued this pattern, Nathan, Nob, and others joining as they freed more people.

When they had a dozen people released, the Kid and a handful of others went to retrieve the horses and bring them back to the camp.

Within fifteen minutes, every person who could be woken and freed from the grip of the spirit cloud had been. The camp was a flurry of activity as friends checked on one another.

"Fourteen dead," Nathan reported, his arms held behind his back as he stared at his feet, "and seven others who probably won't ever be right again. They're sick, confused, and dazed. Like that thing took part of them. No one wants to go back to sleep, they're afraid."

"That's what it fed on," the Kid was leaning against a wagon wheel, Fred running in circles around his feet, pausing every few seconds to look for danger, "that and hope. It seems like people who were touching others were less…damaged. But this thing is attracted to strong emotion, and the people who were the most positive or negative were the ones to get the worst of it. It focused on the young more than the old, too; I guess because young people have more intense emotional reactions."

"How do you know so much about these things?" Torrents asked from where he squatted in front of a fire, poking at the burning dung with his dagger.

"It's part of being a mind-mage," the Kid shrugged. "These things hunt active minds, and abilities like that can draw them to you. I suspect if I hadn't lost my powers, I would've been quite a treat for them."

"I hated them," Nathan interrupted.

"What?" Torrents looked up from the fire.

"These people," Nathan waved an arm towards the people huddled in small groups, and the pile of canvas wrapped corpses at the edge of the encampment, "in that…dream, or whatever it was, I thought that a bunch of them had taken the horses and water, and just abandoned the rest of us."

"Yeah," the Kid nodded, "I did too. So? That's what the things were feeding us to create fear."

"But…I hated these people," Nathan said again. "I didn't care if they lived or died. That's not true. I wanted them to die, and even suffer for what they'd done."

"Okay," Torrents said, "I was right there with you, in the dream, and in that sort of mindset, too. It was just part of what was going on. It's no big deal."

"It is a big deal," Nathan hissed. "I don't hate anyone. I don't want to see people hurt. But everything you guys had said, you know, about violence being the answer, I really felt that way about these people. And now, half of them are dead or…broken."

"You didn't do that to them, though," the Kid said.

"Doesn't matter." Nathan shook his head.

"Get over it," Torrents stared straight at the rokairn, and everyone turned to look at the barbarian, "this isn't all about you. Look, I know you're Mister Sensitive and all that, and you're all about being nice, and that's fine. But this isn't all about you. You're whining and crying about pemtie bidj that doesn't matter. You didn't do this, and you're allowed to feel angry once in a while. Suck it up, we have a job to do. And we can't do it if you're all emo and bidj. You'll become the burden, the one who's abandoning us, even though you're right beside us."

Nathan stared at Torrents with slitted eyes, chewing on his lip, and fingering the haft of his axe.

Torrents stared back, his face tight.

"Wow," the Kid said, "there's some thick tension right now. How about we all just hug it out and be friends again?"

Nathan turned on heel and walked away.

The Kid moved to follow.

"Let him go," Torrents said, his tone short, "this is something he has to work out. Words aren't gonna fix this one. You should know that. We've all gone through some bidj, but in the end we all had to figure it out for ourselves."

The Kid watched Nathan walk away, Nob trailing after him.

"You know," the Kid muttered, "you're a real asshole, and I want to say you're wrong. But I can't find a good way to prove that right now. But I don't have to hang around you either way. I think I'll go find someone that I can help. Have a good night, Torrents the barbarian."

The Kid turned and walked towards the opposite side of camp from where Nathan went.

No one slept again that night, and they were on the move an hour before daylight, leaving behind a pyre of sixteen bodies. Though only fourteen died in the attack, two more had taken their life before the night was done.

Three others escorted the seven people who couldn't function anymore back west, including a priest of Jonath to provide extra protection, heading to Red Wind. They took the wagons, which meant they needed fewer horses to carry the same amount of people. They distributed the remaining supplies between the horses going the other direction.

The Kid, Torrents, Nathan, Nob, and the ten people from Red Wind that could still ride and fight, turned their horses and wagons to the east, heading for the rocky crags that dominated the center of the Crescent Desert.

The people of Red Wind spoke of the monsters of the crags, horrible creatures that hunted any who entered the rocky area.

The townsfolk had gained a new respect for the three men who had been nothing more than strangers to them when this all started.

Ichaelson—the higher ranked of the two remaining clerics of Jonath—took the lead, guiding the meandering line of horses across the dunes. The older man with the gap in his teeth knew the sands and called upon the guidance of his patron deity, who ruled over the element of earth, to help him find a true path.

The second, Vindalai, was a solid woman who always carried her signature weapon, a meter-long shafted handle with a steel head shaped like a brick—halfway between a maul and war hammer—with the symbol of Jonath stamped on the side. She took up the rear, always on the watch for signs of anything approaching.

The two clerics gravitated to Nathan, and one or the other would call to the rokairn, waving him over whenever they saw him looking in their direction. When he went over, the priests would instruct him about the ways of their god, telling him tales or lessons from their religion. But they also sought to learn from him, asking him questions of faith and encouraging stories of willpower and determination. The rokairn brushed them both off, remaining surly and withdrawn.

Three of the younger men—Dodd, Shad, and Tradler—imitated Torrents, shedding armor in favor of less cumbersome furs.

"What the hell are you wearing?" Torrents sneered, scrunching his face up as they rode up beside him. "You're gonna get yourselves killed, dressed like that. If the heat of the desert doesn't get you, then the first demon you come across will cut you open in a split second. You're all pemties."

"But," Tradler's eyes were wide with a panicked look, "you never need armor."

"And I get really cool scars because I don't wear any, pemtie," Torrents sighed. "You trained using armor. I didn't. I was raised using agility and getting the hell out of the way."

"We could learn to do that," Shad chimed in, "you can teach us."

"Really?" Torrents leaned back, wiping a hand across his brow. "Whew! I was worried that we could face a horde of demons any time now! I didn't realize we had years, or at least months, to teach you three a whole new fighting style!

"Look, geniuses," Torrents slowed his horse and turned in the saddle to look at the three, "you don't change your strategy in the fourth quarter unless you have to, okay?"

"Uh, I don't know what that means," Dodd sounded whiney every time he spoke, but Torrents thought he sounded spoiled and entitled, "but I find it easier without the armor."

"It means," Torrents stared down the greasy-haired teen, "get your damned armor and put it on. Did you ever stop to think why I use this gigantic sword? It keeps things further away from me. You boys are using short blades. Anything attacking you will be right up on you if you want a chance to hit it. By not wearing your armor, especially with that type of weapon, you're inviting something in close enough to do more damage than you could handle. Is that clear enough? Get your chuzzing armor back on, you pemtie bidjs."

The Kid kept the remaining half entertained with wild stories—some from this world, others from TV sitcoms—and the antics of Fred.

The rock lobster would act out any story the Kid told, though its limited actions often made no sense in relation to the tale. Varina and Dinwiddie—a couple who'd lost their three children in the battle at Red Wind—always clapped and talked about how their kids would have loved the performance.

Mecklen was sour about the little stories and shows, complaining that they should be 'saving their spit' to help survive the desert heat. He was an older man, a veteran of the Demon Front who constantly grumped about things, his words drawled as he chewed on the thick pinch of tobacco in his right cheek.

The last two didn't speak much. The young woman, Ablemarle, was polite and to the point. But the slim man traveling with her never spoke, and the Kid didn't think anyone even knew his name.

By the afternoon of the second day after leaving the nightmare camp, as they came to call it—the younger men had dubbed it 'the Battle of the Nightmare Camp'—the crags were visible as small, jutting shapes in the distance.

Everyone took to riding with the hoods of their cloaks up to protect them from the brutal sun, and anyone without a cloak fashioned some sort of head covering from whatever cloth they could find.

They traveled from sunrise to about noon, then set up shade tarps to shelter from the most intense part of the day. Ichaelson, who had some elementalist gifts in addition to the holy magics of Jonath, combined the two things to help find water whenever he could. A few hours before sunset, they'd mount up and move again, until they set camp for the night a few hours after the sunset.

It tinted the sands green from the energies blanketing the land to the south. The light of the Demon Front had been intensifying as they drew nearer to it, and closer to the new moon.

Vindalai, a veteran of many years and battles on the Demon Front, told the others that she'd never seen it like this. The desert was barren most times, but now there was no sign of life creeping across it or flying above it. Even the cacti had withered and drying to husks.

The sun was most of the way across the sky, with just a couple hours of daylight remaining, the sands transitioning to rock under the hooves of their mounts.

More than one of them sighed audibly, relieved to have something besides the hot shifting sands under their horse's hooves.

They rode in silence, each wrapped in their own thoughts, approaching the elevated crags in the center of the desert. Their shadows grew long in front of them as the sun moved further west behind them.

Sand erupted in plumes and sprayed around the riders. Figures burst from the gullies along the side of the road, throwing off canvas cloaks that blended with the sands and raising crossbows at the group. Other forms dropped dun-colored tarps and moved from recesses in the surrounding rocks.

A score of stout men and women surrounded the haggard group. Spears, javelins, crossbows, and bows pointed at the group.

The riders bunched together, their horses bumping against one another, making the animals whicker and shy away from the edges, pushing to the center.

Ichaelson's head snapped to the side, a stone ricocheting off his head. The priest slid backwards in his saddle and then toppled to the ground.

Vindalai slid from her roan mare to land near her fellow priest, pushing horses' rumps and bridles, trying to stop her friend from being trampled.

Shad's horse reared, as he jerked hard on his reins, and fell to the ground in reward for his efforts.

Dodd was spinning in circles, struggling to pull his sword from its sheath, his horse jerking its head back and forth, trying to free itself from the control of its rider.

"Kreelon ghrust!" Nathan commanded in a strange language with his rumbling baritone, then repeated, "Stay still!"

"Troj?" A gruff figure pushed forward from the crags, pointing at Nathan over his crossbow, "Trojet Bellstamp? Is that you? We thought you were dead!"

Chapter 24

"Gretna," the short, stout man shouted, "watch the hills! Dandron and Galax, you two take the sands, one to north, one to south, eyes on the sky and your feet. Let's not have a repeat of last month when we lost track of this dimwit. Troj, where the hell have you been?"

The rokairn that surrounded them broke into organized groups. The three the leader tasked moved to lookout positions, the other sixteen set up a perimeter around the horses.

"It's me, Grundy," the rokairn who had spoken moved towards Nathan, his head tilted. "Grundy Stonegap, your squad commander and friend of fifty years. Maybe you recall some of that?"

Nathan looked between the Kid, Torrents, and Nob, shrugging, then slid out of the saddle and dropped to the ground. The wind whistled through the rocks surrounding them and a small dust devil danced across the trail ahead.

"Sorry, Grundy Stonegap? Trojet Bellstamp, that's me?" Nathan asked, shaking his head.

Something chewed at his mind, a familiar ring to the names he repeated. They were right, they fit. Memories swelled, and Nathan stumbled as the weight of it came over him.

This man, this rokairn, walking towards him, was someone he had known. He'd known him for most of the life that belonged to his rokairn body. Recollections of Grundy gaining a squad leader position ten years before Nathan—or Trojet—was allowed to go on patrol rose in his mind. His past from this world filled his mind, washing over him and overwhelming him.

Nathan knew he'd accepted his first position assigned by the Crescent Crag Clan under this man, and images of the rokairn warrens under the desert flooded back to him. His people lived here, hidden from the heat and dangers under the sands.

He'd saved Grundy's hide, and some of the others, many times, and they'd done the same for him, usually when fighting demons or undead from the south.

A hand on his shoulder brought him back to the present.

"You alright, khaudarn?" Grundy steadied Nathan. "You don't look too good. You're pale. Did you see a ghost?"

"Sorry, it's complicated," Nathan mumbled. "I've gone through a lot since we last patrolled together. I'm not the same rokairn you knew."

"Really?" Grundy laughed. "How is that? Did these pemtie humans do something to you? Last I knew, you went off on some crazy quest to Seawall City, thinking you could take on the whole Demon Front by yourself."

Grundy put his hands on Nathan's shoulders and turned him to face him. Growing serious, he searched Nathan's face.

"It's alright," the patrol leader shook Nathan, "the council will overlook it, maybe give you a mild reprimand, but they'll let you come back."

"No," Nathan's voice firmed, "I can't go back. Not now, maybe not at all."

"What?" Grundy smiled. "Of course you can. It'll be alright. You're an excellent warrior, you're just going through something."

The Kid traded looks with Torrents.

The barbarian shrugged, and moved his horse closer to Dodd, grabbing the bridle of the man's mount to calm it. Shad and Tradler moved to each side of their friend.

"Control your horses," Torrents called out. "Nathan'll work this out, then we can be on our way."

Vindalai helped Ichaelson to his feet, as the older priest rubbed his head.

The Kid moved closer to Varina and Dinwiddie, who were helping Ablemarle and her friend calm their mounts.

The Kid threw a glance at Nathan, understanding what he was going through. The Kid had gone through a similar thing when he'd met people who knew him before…before he'd been in this body. It was easier for the Kid, though, because the Kid had eagerly thrown himself into this world and embraced the change, going with it.

Nathan struggled, confused by the duality of his mind and his body, and the memories he could access when needed, but usually suppressed.

"Nathan?" Grundy watched Torrents, then looked back to the other rokairn in front of him. "Is that some sort of human name they gave you?"

"It's hard to explain." Nathan squared his shoulders, visibly calming, as he focused on the patrol leader. "I think I've had a calling from Jonath. The god. The one of protection."

"Yes, Troj," Grundy smiled, speaking like he was addressing a child, "I know who Jonath is. What is this calling, though?"

"I've had…" Nathan hesitated, "a vision, and given knowledge from beyond. There is another spirit within me. I did die, but this other soul saved me, and now we're bonded. Sorry, I know that doesn't make much sense.

"Before you say anything," Nathan continued, moving Grundy's hands from his shoulders, "you need to understand that I'm going south to the Demon Front. You've seen the lights, and probably noticed that there are more demons than ever before. Things are coming to a head, and I need to go do whatever I can to stop what's causing this. I have to do this."

Grundy took a step back, looking Nathan up and down, squinting, his face moving from concerned to determined.

"Yes," Grundy nodded, "I see that you've changed, but I don't like the idea of you running into the mouth of hell with a bunch of grassland humans. They'll run; you know. These people aren't known for their dedication. They're short-lived, and don't understand our ways, and how we focus and achieve what others cannot."

"The demons attacked Red Wind," Nathan gestured at the people behind him, "and these people came with me from there to fight, in any way we can. Our people, the Crescent Clan, will be next. We will not remain untouched; the demons will come."

"They can't reach us," Grundy scoffed. "We can collapse the tunnels and stay underground for a century without blinking. Their problems are not ours."

"Yes," Nathan nodded slowly, "but in a century, when we reemerge, the enemy will still be here. It won't be our world anymore. It's time to fight, to defend our world. And I'm going to do that, with humans, rokairn, and anyone else who will stand with me. I'd rather die than let my world be taken by these creatures who want nothing but destruction. We rokairn are built to create and protect, not hide and let others destroy. If we hide now, we won't have the chance to recover."

"Are you trying to convince me?" Grundy turned away, crossed his arms, and look to the green glow in the southern sky. "I hear you, brother. But I don't know that the council would agree. They think to choose this fight would be akin to choosing to die. I feel your words though, and they…have passion, but I'm not sure of the wisdom of them."

"Will you stop us?" Nathan asked, and Grundy turned his gaze back. "I know we cannot fight you and the demons. I would ask that you allow us to pass in peace if you will not join us. But I plead for you to call the clan and march with us."

"No," Grundy said flatly. "I will not stop you, but I will not dedicate the clan to your cause. It is not my place to do so."

The wind rose, and sand scattered across the group. A hawk called in the distance, its hunting cry echoing off the rocks.

Grundy seemed to consider something, looking towards the sound.

"A sign, the call to hunt. We will give you what we can," the patrol leader gestured to the rokairn who'd created the perimeter, "water, food, and some weapons if you need them. Then I must return to the tunnels and let the council know what we've found."

"I understand," Nathan sighed, "and thank you for the safe passage."

Grundy recalled his lookouts while the humans mounted their horses. The two groups exchanged introductions and goods, and within an hour moved deeper into the Crescent Crags and parted ways.

The humans and Nathan set camp, as the other rokairn disappeared into the broken landscape.

After two days, they reached the southern edge of the crags, another two days brought them to the northern edge of Tull's Swamp.

They moved along the western edge of the swamp, curving to the southeast. The Pyridom once stood in the center of the swamp, but the magics and demon incursion caused the wetlands to wither and recede, creating an alcove of desert in the center of what once was home to thriving life.

The northern arm of the swamp turned fetid, reeking of stagnant pools and dead or dying life.

In the distance, the sky changed from green to an emerald canopy overhead, reaching from horizon to horizon.

Packs of jedth roamed the desert to the south, and the group veered into the marsh to avoid them. They saw crigth also, usually solitary, but now appearing in threes, hunting for sport.

The group from Red Wind grew more nervous. Even Shad, Tradler, and Dodd lost their bravado, growing quiet as they came closer to their final destination.

The priests, Ichaelson and Vindalai, called upon the blessing of Jonath frequently to help the group pass unnoticed.

Mecklen sharpened his sword as they rode, rarely putting it away, and the others took no comfort in the war-grizzled veteran's actions.

"What's the plan?" The Kid asked once they could see the Pyridom in the distance, indicating they were less than a day from their destination, "Do we even have one? Or are we just charging in and hoping to find a huge power outlet that we can pull the plug from?"

The Pyridom was an inverted cone in the distance, standing alone on the plain of sand. Lightning lanced down, curling around the tall spire. The once reddish stone had a sickly, glazed look and had taken on an orange tint, contrasting with the green clouds around it.

"We go in," Torrents's tone was grim, "find the leaders, and cut off the head of the snake. Maybe if we do that, the rest will fall into chaos, and we'll have a chance of surviving."

"Surviving?" The Kid scoffed. "I was hoping we'd win, not just survive."

Torrents didn't answer, not looking over. He stared ahead, studying their destination.

"We'll camp," Nathan brought his horse up beside the other two, Nob trailing behind him, "at least for this evening. I don't want to go in and have night follow us. I think a morning attack will be best."

"Attack?" It was Torrents's turn to scoff, though his was harsher than the Kid's. "We're lucky we got this far without running into some of these things. It's almost like they were avoiding us. We can hope to make a surgical strike and do some good, but I wouldn't think of it as an attack. The Kid doesn't have his powers. We lost half our force to the nightmare demons. The rokairn turned their backs on the whole situation. We don't have the numbers to do anything but charge in and pray we find the one person, or creature, we need to find to stop this mess. If we make it to the Pyridom without getting killed first, and if we find that person, and if we can kill them before they kill us, then maybe we can stop this. But I think it'll be like kicking a hornet's nest from the inside, and making it back out will be…"

The barbarian trailed off.

"We can do this," Nathan's voice was quiet, but firm, "we were brought here for a reason, and it wasn't to fail. And we were all dying when we came here, so maybe we can do one last bit of good before that time comes. I won't give up, not now, and not even with my last breath."

"Give up?" Torrents turned in the saddle to look at the rokairn, a grim smile on his face. "I didn't say bidj about giving up. I'm gonna go in and give 'em hell, shove their own hell right back down their damned throats. I'm never giving up again."

"That's my boy," the Kid murmured. "We got this, even if it gets us before we're done."

Chapter 25

The sun rose on thirteen humans and one rokairn riding across the sands from the edge of Tull's Swamp towards the Pyridom of Power.

Dark green clouds roiled, purple lightning arcing through them, the smell of ozone and decay hanging in a warm humid miasma below them.

The sands at the base of the Pyridom mimicked the movement of the clouds above, alive with thousands of jedth and hundreds of gnohls and crigth. Winged creatures circled the pinnacle of the structure, their screeches rolling across the sands, making the horses dance and nicker.

Bright blue orbs dotted the bottom of the ancient structure, showing the seeds to the portals that would open. One sphere, ten times larger than the others, acted as a beacon at the top of a flight of stairs for the group to follow.

Torrents led the group, his sword that severed demon ties to this plane in his hand.

Nathan rode beside him, his amulet glistening and sparking as they drew closer, repelling the demonic energies in the air. The rokairn held Marcid in his hands, the vine-wrapped handle glowing a vibrant shade of green.

The Kid dropped from his horse, handing his reins to Varina. He took his place beside the others, twin daggers in his hands. Fred scurried along beside him.

The townsfolk clumped together in two groups, except Mecklen, who rode a short distance apart, to have room to swing his sword.

Shad, Dodd, and Tradler rode in a wedge of their own, as the remaining four followed closely behind the priests.

The gnohl and demon horde parted as the group approached, clearing a path to the bottom of the Pyridom, and the steps and raised platform on which it stood.

The structure was old, constructed before modern people inhabited the land. Built by ancient peoples for long forgotten purposes, by the time modern civilization arrived, time and weather scoured the runes and hieroglyphs from the structure.

"That's odd…" the Kid watched the mass of demons extended along each side of them, "they're just letting us through."

"Do you think it's the magical things we got from the Tower of Onyx?" Nathan asked, turning in his saddle to crane his neck and see the wall of creatures close behind them.

"I have a bad feeling about this," Torrents said, his voice barely audible over the chattering and screeches of the mob surrounding them.

"Really? You're pulling that line out now?" The Kid said without humor. "Just don't shout 'It's a trap!' and order all fighters to protect the cruisers."

"Lando said that last part," Nathan murmured without enthusiasm.

The enemy ranks parted, and the group could see the base of the Pyridom, a single figure silhouetted in front of the large portal seed.

Klendrisia stood waiting, the smile on her face turning to a frown.

The group—except for the Kid, who was already on foot—slid from their saddles, readying weapons.

"Is this all you brought?" the demoness demanded as the group drew closer. "Where's the armies?"

"At least we have our target," the Kid mumbled, then raised his voice to address the cambion. "We're all you get, unless you'd like to go home and come back in a couple years so we can raise an army for you."

The woman sneered.

"Why?" Nathan called to her. "Why did you want us to bring armies? Why did you let us get this close?"

"Because," Klendrisia answered conversationally, her voice carrying across the distance, "I needed a sacrifice to open the gates. I guess your pitiful group will have to do. It won't let as many pass through, but it'll be a start."

"It's a trap," Nob nodded.

"It always is," the Kid sighed, "isn't it?"

"At least," Nathan hefted his axe, "she won't get everything she wanted."

Torrents nodded along with Nob, raising his double-handed sword.

"Get her..." Torrents's shout cut off.

Horns wailed from the west, and all heads turned in that direction. A cloud of dust rose in the distance, raised by men on horseback charging towards the demonic horde.

The sickly rays of sun that cut through the clouds glinted off steel weapons held high.

"There's got to be a couple hundred riders," Torrents gasped. "Where did they all come from?"

"I sent for them," Klendrisia's voice was smug, "weeks ago, I sent messengers to Durgan's Keep, and beyond, even to Diaz City and Runsk. Made sure they knew they had to be here for the battle on the new moon."

The ground rumbled, and Nathan pointed to the north.

"There's more," the rokairn sounded grim, "the Crescent Clan is coming, too."

"Are they riding…" the Kid squinted, his voice filling with wonder, "waves of sand?"

"They brought their priests of Jonath." Ichaelson's tone was awestruck. "Our human priests haven't been able to do that for generations!"

They watched the humans reach the edge of the otherworldly force to the west, and the rokairn crashed into the wall of creatures behind the group.

"Now," Klendrisia smirked, "this is a party. Thank you for convincing the rokairn to attend. It'll make the perfect invitation to all my people. They won't miss this for the world. Which, by the way, will be mine when this is over."

"Kaleb triot, den'al venitier!" Nathan roared, raised his axe, and rushed Klendrisia.

Nob followed his friend.

Torrents followed suit, gripping his blade in two hands.

The Kid ushered the small group past him as he guarded their backs.

The demons and gnohls between the group and their mistress pressed backwards, scattering.

Nathan took the steps two at a time.

"Now my pets," the demoness purred, "kill them all, but leave these three for Mezk!"

She swirled her fingers at Torrents, the Kid, and Nathan.

"Oh, Mezk, my sweet, you're on," Klendrisia trilled, turning and disappearing into a fold in the air.

The tall, thin dark-clad form with carrot-orange hair burst from the space Klendrisia had been a moment before.

As Nathan reached the top step, Mezk thrust Demon Seed into the warrior-priest's chest.

The rokairn's momentum carried him forward, and Mezk sidestepped, thrusting a foot across Nathan's path.

The warrior-priest went down, face-first, onto the stone platform.

"Your blood shall wash these steps," Mezk growled, grinning as the demonic dagger pulsed black with red veins in his right hand, the velvet-wrapped blade of the Dragon's Dagger gripped in his left, "you damn dirty dwarf!"

The assassin dropped into a crouch and spun to face the oncoming rush of the barbarian.

Torrents slowed to a stop before reaching the top step, Nob beside him.

"Too afraid to face your own death after watching your friend die?" Mezk sneered.

"Nuh uh," Nob shook his head.

"You missed something." Torrents pointed behind the thief with his blade. "It might be important."

Mezk opened his mouth to say something, stopping as he heard a metallic rustle of chain mail behind him.

He shot a look over his shoulder.

Nathan stood behind him, feet shoulder-width apart, Marcid held in both hands across his body. The magical amulet on his chest shone black, a scratch marring its surface.

"Guess your dagger counts as a demon," Nathan shrugged, and raised his axe. "My turn."

The rokairn took two quick steps forward, lifting his axe overhead and chopping downward.

Torrents took two steps forward, thrusting with his sword at the same time.

The two weapons tore into Mezk's black form and clashed into one another, the assassin melting into the shadows to slide away.

Mezk rose from a pool of shade behind Nob—still coming up the steps—the assassin's black blade swiping across the man's lower back.

Nob screamed and tumbled forward, smoke rising from the bone-deep gash.

Demon Seed pulsed as it fed, Mezk breathing in deeply through his nose, as if experiencing the rush of feeding on a soul.

The mass of monsters at the foot of the steps swept over the people of Red Wind and Fred, who disappeared amongst the feet of the gnohls and demons, his claws clacking.

Gnohls, hyenas, and demons frenzied and attacked, horses torn apart as they backed away, screaming.

Varina shrieked, claws and teeth tearing into her. Dinwiddie leapt from his horse towards her. The man never reached his lover, wife, and partner, as one of the flying creatures snatched him. Dragged upward, high into the air, three of the creatures pulled on his body, tearing limbs loose, blood raining down on the mob of demons below, feeding its frenzy.

The abominations had the look of sleek hunting cats crossbred with vipers. They were the size of racing hounds, slim and muscled with leathery wings covered in a fine down of fur. The colors of that fur spread across the spectrum, giving them a beauty that belayed their deadliness.

Vindalai, the priestess, stood back-to-back with Mecklen, Ablemarle and her companion doing the same a few steps from them. The four fought valiantly. Mecklen used decades of combat experience to place precise blows, taking down the small jedth with ease.

The priestess screamed war cries between blows; her face red, her breath coming in forced puffs. Her massive maul crushed the cat-snake beasts diving from above, knocking them into the swirling mass of demons trying to claw their way to the group.

Ablemarle and her partner moved like oil over a hot skillet, sliding from one place to another, separating, then coming back together. They never left each other's sight but moved to strike, then to cross with the other.

Ichaelson prayed, loudly chanting words lost in the battle's tumult. He called to Jonath, beseeching the god's protection for his companions. Dodd, Shad, and Tradler stood in a loose triangle formation around the older man, shielding him as he prayed for their safety.

Shad shouted in surprise, his feet going out from under him. Dodd turned to look, moving towards his friend, only to see him dragged into the breaking tide of monsters that surrounded them.

Shad's shout stretched into a scream, as Dodd saw his friend's arm stop moving. The rest of the body disappeared, but that one arm lay where it had fallen, severed, spurting blood onto the sand-coated steps of the Pyridom.

Voices wafted past the young man, like scents of dinner burning on the wind, a memory from his childhood, each moving past him, barely noticed. Tradler yelled a warning. Dodd never saw the segmented claws of the crigth reaching over the others and enclosing his head in a scaly hand, twisting. Flesh and sinew creaked and tore. Dodd's body fell under a wave of smaller jedth, the larger demon popping the man's head into its maw like some sort of macabre candy. The creature made slurping noises, followed by a throaty 'yummy' sound.

The remaining friend, Tradler, felt his mind stretch, the world around him distorting, and then snap back into place. Almost audible to the young man, he physically felt it in the back of his skull. His eyes blurred, and he screamed as he raised his sword and plunged into the surrounding mob.

It crushed him to the ground and held him down.

"…won't do any good," a familiar voice was shouting at him, "damn it, Tradler, stop fighting me. You can't save them now!"

Ichaelson had one foot on Tradler's back, standing over the young man, fighting the demons with two tonfa—short staves, each the length of his forearms with a handle jutting perpendicular to the shaft—knocking the monsters away in rapid strikes.

Mezk raised the dagger and stabbed it down into Nob again, draining him of any remnants of the energies that made him who he was.

A sharp scream came from below the assassin, and a form shot up the steps.

The Kid leapt at his nemesis, a dagger held in each hand, blades pointed down.

Torrents moved towards Mezk, thrusting forward with his enormous blade.

Nathan ran to Nob's side, fell to his knees, and checked on his friend. He turned the body over, and Nob's eyes rolled in his head, sightless and lifeless.

Mezk moved, side-stepping the attacks, shifting in the sight of the others. The Demon Seed sparked, blocking the demon-slaying sword of the barbarian, and the assassin's left hand flashed with an ivory blade toward the Kid.

Mezk ran his shorter blade down Torrents's longer weapon, catching the sword's cross guard, then twisted his wrist to deflect the barbarian's great sword, causing it to miss and strike the ground a hair's breadth to his right. The assassin continued the movement, running the demon blade along the back of Torrents's hand.

The barbarian screamed and jerked backwards. His arm went numb to the shoulder as he felt the pull of the Demon Seed and the buffering protection of his weapon.

The Kid looked down, following the path of the assassin's second attack aimed at him. Mezk buried the white blade of Edsumar to its hilt in the Kid's chest.

Chapter 26

Falling to his knees, the Kid saw it all.

To his right, on the steps, Nathan knelt over Nob, tears blinding the rokairn, his axe abandoned beside him. Torrents clutched his arm, the gash along his hand and forearm red with blood and demonic energy. The mass of demons at the bottom of the stairs swarmed over the small group of people who'd come from Red Wind. Fred had disappeared into the mass shortly after the fray began and hadn't been seen since.

The armies clashing with the demons and gnohls in the distance were lost in flashing lightning, green roiling mists, and dust clouds of sand.

The blue, glowing portal seeds pulsed and expanded, Klendrisia's sacrifices feeding them.

Mezk pulled Edsumar from the wound in the Kid's chest and lifted the blade to plunge it in again.

The Kid's head pounded, white light expanding to cover his vision.

There you are, a voice said in the Kid's head. *Ah, this feels so much better. You been doing okay?*

The Kid blinked, but internally. He was inside his head, the outside world receding.

"Edsumar?" The Kid laughed. "Yeah, I guess I'm alright, though I'm in a bit of a tough spot right now. Maybe things just look worse than they are. What about you?"

Been stuck in the dark with no one to talk to. It was boring, and I hate to say, a little lonely. You think I'd be used to it, after spending all those years in the temple until you showed up. I've gotten used to chatting with you.

"Yeah," the Kid smiled, "you're just an old softy. So, what's the plan?"

No plan. Mezk still has control over me, so I get to just hang out and see what happens.

"If only I had my powers," the Kid sighed, "this would turn out totally different."

You do have them. Edsumar's voice sounded amused to the Kid. *You never lost them. You just…invested them.*

"What's that mean? Invested them? Is there a brain trust somewhere I wasn't aware of?"

Oh, you got jokes now! Edsumar teased. *No, you did that thing, made Fred, and most of your abilities are tied up in him. When the Demon Seed pricked you back at PepperGarten's, your remaining abilities went dormant as it blocked the dagger from pulling your soul from you.*

"Fred?" the Kid asked. "Fred has my abilities?"

The Kid was on his knees, the real world coming back into focus with a jolt that pulled him back to the here and now. The stone edge of the steps bit into his shins, and a hot breeze swirled around him.

Mezk stood above him, a maniacal grin on his face as he brought Edsumar down for the killing stroke.

A grey streak, accompanied by a clattering stone on stone sound, rushed towards the Kid from the side of the stairs. Something hit him like a boulder, and the Kid fell as the ivory dagger came down.

Fred, now standing on the prone form of his master, clacked his claws at the oncoming weapon.

"Cla-clack, clack," came the familiar tattoo of sound.

The blade bit into the stone-hide of the construct, sinking between the plates.

Mezk hissed and pulled on the weapon, trying to free it to strike again. It didn't budge.

The dagger sunk further into the massive rock lobster, and Fred scrambled away from Mezk. The little protector scampered off the steps, into the flowing mass of demons, and disappeared, the dagger embedded in his carapace.

The Kid had felt Fred. He felt the rock lobster coming when he'd thought of him while talking to Edsumar. He felt the little protector knock him over and Edsumar bite into the stony creature, the connection with Edsumar's mind interrupted when it happened, and so had the link to Fred.

As those were severed, the Kid's mind flooded with awareness. It was like waking up to realize you'd been sleeping on your arm, and it was numb. When you move, it tingled, then became pins and needles as feeling returned to it.

The mind-mage abilities, once closeted away, rushed back into the Kid's mental grasp. His brain made connections it hadn't before, knowledge of how to use his gifts in ways he hadn't used before.

Was this from the time that the magics held Fred together? Or from the brush with demonic powers? It reminded him of when he'd first come to this world and done things with his powers that the original soul who inhabited the body never thought to do.

His mind probed his body, knitting muscle and tying nerve endings back together. He did it in a blink of an eye, a single moment where tissue and organs sealed, pushing blood and bone back into their accustomed places, and it was excruciating!

The Kid screamed, clutching his chest, awareness of his surroundings rushing back to him.

Mezk stood over him, staring toward where Fred disappeared into the crowd. The scream brought the assassin's attention back to him.

Demon Seed flashed, the ebony blade slashed towards the Kid…and reflected off an invisible barrier.

The Kid thrust his hand forward, and Mezk flew backwards. The mind mage picked up his daggers, which he had dropped on the steps, and rose to his feet. He threw them underhand, one at a time, taking control of their flight with his mind.

The blades flew in wide curving arcs, weaving around Mezk, cutting the assassin again and again.

Clenching his fists, the Kid raised them, and the daggers mimicked his actions, rising above the black-clad enemy. The mind mage brought his hands down, then crossed them in front of himself.

The twin blades plummeted, embedding into the flesh between Mezk's collarbone and neck, cutting across the man's throat.

Mezk's mouth moved, trying to cry out. Blood poured from his severed neck instead, and red bubbles of the viscous liquid frothed on his lips.

The demon dagger in the assassin's hand pulsed with red veins, siphoning off his life essence.

The Kid's daggers flew around his nemesis, slicing into his forearms—leaving deep cuts from wrist to elbow, severing tendons—and causing the demon blade to clatter to the stone parapet as Mezk's hands lost the ability to grip.

The weapons spun in the air and darted behind the assassin, sliding across his calves, opening the meaty muscle and cutting the Achille's tendon.

Mezk fell forward on top of the Demon Seed. Convulsing, his body withered and shriveled as the dagger fed on the man who'd been its master.

The Kid looked around—his daggers spinning in the air and blood flying from the blades, leaving them clean before returning to his hands—and took stock of his surroundings.

Nathan knelt beside Nob, cradling the dead man's head. Torrents was on his knees—his sword on the ground next to him—clutching his injured hand, the muscles in his neck standing out. Fred was nowhere to be seen.

"Nathan!" the Kid barked, "Torrents needs you; can you do something about that soul sucking thing?"

The rokairn looked up at the Kid, his eyes lost in grief, then looked at Torrents. He looked at the Kid again, nodded, and eased Nob's head to the stone floor before standing.

Nathan moved to Torrents, touching the barbarian's injured arm, his lips moving in prayer. A mist of red rose from the limb, and the Kid thought it was blood before realizing it wasn't liquid. The pulsing energy darted in one direction, then another, then flew at Mezk and slammed into the body, causing it to jerk.

The Kid looked down the steps.

Tradler lay on the stair, Ichaelson standing over him, with Vindalai standing next to the senior priest. Mecklen, Ablemarle, and her silent companion held off the horde on the other side.

Injured, they all looked close to falling under the onslaught of demons around them.

The rokairn and human armies had fought their way closer, and though diminished, it looked like they were beating the demon army.

The portal seeds had stopped pulsing and were blossoming in spasms of sparks and color.

"You've done well," Klendrisia's voice came from above, "you've made the ultimate sacrifice. One of a dark soul, tainted with desperation, their blood shed by someone of purity."

The demoness, floating in the air above the battlefield, gestured to the portals.

"My gateways open," Klendrisia's throaty voice was ecstatic as she threw her arms wide, "and all who come through shall be under my contract!"

The portals opened, forms coming out in a trickle at first, then a stream, then a flood. Like a dam bursting, the blue portals became cracks in reality, then spread to become fissures before finally tearing a rift between worlds. Creatures of all sizes and shapes poured from the extra-dimensional doors.

The large glowing gateway at the top of the steps pulsed, a final doorway waiting to open. Then it winked out of existence.

Mezk's body jerked, his flesh rippling and expanding. His leather armor tore, splitting at the seams. Leathery wings erupted from his back, and an extra set of arms burst from his ribcage. The body pushed up from the ground from where it had lain and rose to one knee.

It stood, metamorphosing.

"I have a host," a deep voice intoned from Mezk's husk as skin sloughed from the bone carapace growing from his body, "I am free of the dagger that was my prison. I am Zklypyllik and I shall take my vengeance on the…"

A two-handed blade sliding through their abdomen interrupted the newly formed demon.

Torrents stood behind them, holding the pommel of the weapon.

"Vengeance this, bitch," the barbarian growled.

A throaty chuckle came from the form as they continued to grow, now the height of two men. The demon reached behind them and pulled the sword from their back, dropping the weapon onto the stone platform.

"That petty toy will not banish me in this form," the figure boomed. "I cultivated the seed in the dagger on this plane. I am native to this world, and you cannot send me away. You shall all become my first feast as I conquer this realm."

"Within the constraints of our contract," Klendrisia said, "you are bound by our agreement. I didn't think I'd need to remind you of that, Inciter Demon."

The rokairn and human armies reached the Pyridom as the portals opened, and the flood of demons swarmed across them, attacking and feeding.

The priests of Jonath called upon the gifts of the element of earth to defend the land, causing rock and sand to burst upward. Spears of stone launched into the air, piercing demons, and dust devils swirled across the landscape, enveloping the invaders.

"Chuz this," Torrents shouted, snatching up his sword and swinging at the gigantic demon in front of him. "Maybe I can't banish you, but I can kill you."

Nathan planted his feet at shoulder width, gripped his double-headed battle axe in both hands, hoisted the weapon, and took a step forward to attack.

The Kid watched the small group at the bottom of the stairs retreat upward, fighting their way up the steps and closer to the still-growing demon.

The overwhelmed armies were being torn apart by the hordes of thousands of demons swarming across the desert. Klendrisia hovered over the scene, a victorious smile on her face.

The Kid sighed.

He had his powers back but didn't have Edsumar or Fred. A demon, which appeared to have finally stopped growing, that couldn't be banished, was towering above him. Oh, and they were conjuring a flaming sword into existence, how Voltron of them. Huge, curled horns spiraled from their head, and their face contorted, so a bear-like snout—complete with a triple set of fangs—jutted out.

The demon grasped the fiery weapon with all four hands, and when they pulled them apart again, the being held four blades of fire. Flames erupted along their bone carapace, and something resembling lava dripped from the red veins pulsing on their surface.

Nathan hacked at the giant demon, his axe cutting deep into the being's calf, green sprouts appearing in the wound.

A flaming sword bashed the rokairn, but did nothing more than knock him sprawling, the amulet on his chest absorbing the demonic energy of the weapon.

The rokairn heard Klendrisia laugh and clap from above. The cambion alternately shouted orders to the chaotic battlefield—her magic projecting her voice across the massacre from her vantage point—and spoke in a foreign language, seemingly to herself. Each time she did the latter, another demon group came through one of the portals lining the base of the Pyridom.

"Kid!" Nathan shouted, standing up and stepping in front of the street thief, "you got your hole?"

"What?" the Kid's attention snapped back to his surroundings. "Not since I got this body!"

"What?" Nathan said, then shook his head. "No, your magic hole. Do you have it?"

"Like I said," the Kid's eyes widened, "oh, yeah, yeah. Why?"

"Give it to me," Nathan shouted over the sounds of battle. "I have an idea!"

"Don't use it," the Kid fumbled the magical artifact from a pouch, and handed it over, "remember, it can have weird results."

"I'm counting on it." The rokairn pointed at the Demon Seed laying on the ground between the giant demon's feet. "Can you get that dagger for me?"

Before the Kid could answer, Nathan turned to Torrents. The street thief grabbed at the blade with his mind—the tainted magics of the weapon making him queasy—and pulled it to his hand.

"Torrents!" the warrior-priest shouted, and the barbarian gave him a quick glance as he parried flaming swords from the demon. "Trade me!"

The rokairn threw his axe to the barbarian, and the barbarian tossed his sword to the warrior-priest without hesitation or question, his face tight with the pressure of combat. Torrents knew his ebony blade wasn't doing much good, even with its enchantments. Maybe the priest's nature-blessed blade would be more effective. Both caught the other's weapon at the same time.

"Now," Nathan turned back to the Kid, reaching for the dagger the thief held, "hand me that."

Chapter 27

Nathan took the Demon Seed dagger from the Kid. Made of some dense, unknown metal, it felt heavy and cold in his hand.

The rokairn pulled the amulet from his chest and attached it to Torrents's sword and lifted the magical black material of the hole with his other hand.

"Klendrisia," Nathan shouted up at the demoness, "you control all the portals, right? They do as you will, is that right?"

The half-demon looked down at him, her face scrunching up in confusion.

"I do control them," she sneered, "and the beings who use them. I shall control this entire world!"

"Remember when you said you tasted hope because of me," Nathan fumbled with the hole in one hand, the demon dagger in the same hand, and the two-handed blade in the other, "and it was bitter?"

"What are you babbling about, dwarf?" Klendrisia snapped.

"Well, sorry about this," Nathan dropped the magical hole on the ground at his feet, "but I hope you're getting used to that bitter taste."

A dark round circle opened behind the hovering woman, who turned to look behind her at the rift in the air.

Nathan took the sword in both hands, still fumbling to keep the ebony dagger in his grip at the same time and stabbed it downward into the hole.

The blade disappeared into the blue-black darkness, reappearing out of the hole in the sky. Piercing the levitating demoness's breastbone, Nathan jerked the sword back. Klendrisia's body folded almost in half as she was pulled into the magical rift.

The top part of her body emerged from the hole at the Nathan's feet, and he jammed the cold, dark dagger into Klendrisia's eye socket. The woman screamed, and her legs—still dangling in the air—kicked.

Nathan watched as many things happened at once. The banishing magic of the two-handed sword pulled at Klendrisia's essence; the shield-amulet blocked her control and commands of the portals and demon army; the empty prison known as the Demon Seed activated, seeking to fill the void inside it with Klendrisia's soul; and the magical hole on the ground wavered.

Nathan shoved the sword forward again, back into the hole.

Klendrisia scrambled at the edge of the aperture, clawing at the sand covered platform, nails digging gouges into the stone, causing both to crack and split. With nothing to grip, she slipped further into the midnight orifice. Above, her legs were drawn into the hole.

Her scream cut off as she disappeared into the dark. The hole folded behind her, drawing closed as if something in another world pulled at the center of the cloth and drew it through a knothole in time and space.

It disappeared without a sound.

The ground shook, sand dancing along the stone walkway as the earth rumbled. A glossy sheen crept up the Pyridom, coating the sloped walls of the structure. The stone's sickly orange color deepened, becoming black and smooth in blotchy patches—like some sort of time lapse fungus—claiming the shady side of the structure until the whole magical landmark was a midnight hue.

The portals lining the base of the Pyridom flared and blossomed outward, disintegrating the closest demons.

The massive demon in front of Torrents hesitated, his forked tongue tasting the air.

The barbarian, the warrior-priest, and the street thief looked out across the land.

On the battlefield, screeching fiends and demons scrambled away from the Pyridom. Lifted by an invisible force—a mystical wind catching them in its power—they flew towards the blue gateways. Without Klendrisia to control the magic, Nathan watched the creatures sucked into the portals.

Overhead, the flying cat-snake demons crumpled into balls under the crushing force and plummeted at downward angles into the closest.

In less than ninety seconds, only a few gnohls and proto-hyenas remained of the enemy forces.

The green clouds broke apart, the purple lightning fading, and sunbeams shone through like spotlights.

Less than a hundred humans and a few dozen rokairn, scattered across a mostly empty battlefield, looked around. With a shout, they raised their weapons and attacked the remaining enemies.

"The contract," the demon boomed, and the Kid, Torrents, and Nathan looked up at him, surprised that he was still here, "has been broken. I am free of it, and the bonds that the demon bitch used to restrain me!"

"Aw, damn it," the Kid muttered, "they left the worst one behind."

"It's all good," Torrents smiled and pointed with Nathan's axe. "He's lost his hellfire stuff. I don't think he's got it all going on anymore. I'll take care of this. But, just in case, feel free to help out."

The massive demon swung two swords at the barbarian. The blades no longer guttered flame, instead resembling cooling volcanic rock.

Torrents stepped back and swept the battle axe sideways, catching both swords in the weapon's arc and guiding them to where he'd stood a moment before.

Vibrant green light sparked where the weapons touched. Vines erupted from the demon's swords, flowers bursting into full bloom. The blades crumpled to the ground with a noise like wet snow falling from an eave. Where they landed, a dark, rich soil was all that remained.

The demon screamed, slashing with their remaining two weapons. Torrents rolled under the swords and between the giant's legs, slashing, severing a leg at the knee.

Nathan drew hand axes from his belt and charged forward.

The Kid telekinetically lifted his blades, bee-lining them to the demon's head.

The three danced the tango of combat with the giant foe. Marcid's magic claimed the demon's last two blades. The demon went on the defensive from a kneeling position due to the missing half of one of their legs.

Vindalai and Ichaelson joined the group, followed by Ablemarle. Mecklen trailed behind with Ablemarle's silent friend, both injured and leaning on one another for support.

The rest of the rokairn army joined the fray. From the sands at the feet of the Pyridom, stone spears flew over the heads of the group and pierced the monster's chest. A giant hand of sand, almost as large as the enemy, rose from the desert and grabbed the invader and dragged them down the steps, weaving between the combatants still attacking the massive invader, and onto the desert floor.

Nathan, Torrents, and the Kid lost sight of the demon as humans and rokairn from both armies swarmed the monster.

Looking across the desolate landscape, the Kid saw outriders chasing down the stragglers of the enemy army, and others checking the dead and making sure they wouldn't get back up again.

The Kid put a hand up to shade his eyes, searching the sands for Fred.

"That's a good sign," Nathan said, pointing at the Kid. When the Kid looked confused, the rokairn explained, "You, shading your eyes. That means the sun is out. Been a while since we've seen that."

Ichaelson looked up from where he was binding Mecklen's knee. The limb looked shattered, bending backwards at an unnatural angle, and the grizzled warrior grimaced as the priest set it.

"Nathan," Ichaelson's voice was somber, "would you like me to say the parting prayer over your friend Nob, or would you like to do it?"

Nathan looked over at Nob's body. The demon had stepped on him, crushing him during the fight. Most of the guard's body was a broken and twisted heap, withered and drained.

"No," Nathan said slowly, not moving, "I'll take care of him. I'll return him to the earth, as is Jonath's way. From ash and dirt, we grow, and so we shall return, renewing the land."

Ichaelson nodded, then called to Ablemarle, asking how Tradler was doing. The younger man was in a state of shock, and though his body would heal, his mind might never recover.

Vindalai stood next to the silent man who'd never spoken a word, and both—already bandaged—watched over the battlefield for any threats.

"Do you think we should go look for Varina, Dinwiddie, Dodd, and Shad?" Vindalai asked the man next to her. "Try to recover their bodies, or whatever we can find of them?"

The slim man shook his head, pointing at small groups that had broken from the armies of both races.

Parties of a half dozen soldiers roamed the battlefield, already stacking bodies to be burned, before they could scatter the ashes. They took the boots, weapons, and any useful items from the dead, piling them separately. In a land where the dead walked, only a body burned to ashes couldn't rise again.

"You seen Fred?" the Kid looked at Torrents.

"Nuh uh," the barbarian grunted, "can't you just call him, or think to him, or something?"

"Not anymore," the Kid shook his head, "that stopped working when he was stabbed with Edsumar."

"Edsumar?" Torrents's face brightened. "You got him back?"

"Nope," the Kid sighed. "He was embedded in Fred when Fred ran off."

"Need help finding them?" Torrents offered.

"Naw," the Kid hooked his thumbs—hands resting on the dagger hilts—through his belt, "I think the walk alone will do me good. Thanks though."

"Yeah," Torrents watched the Kid, shoulders slumped, turn away and move down the stairs.

"Hey Kid," Torrents said.

The Kid stopped and turned to look at him, squinting in the sun.

"You okay?" Torrents asked.

"Just exhausted," the Kid said, and Torrents nodded, "not just my body, but everything. So much death. I'm just so tired of it, you know? Just so tired of it all."

The Kid turned away and moved down the steps to the desert floor. He moved in a zig-zag pattern, widening each pass as he went further from the Pyridom, which was now a sleek, black pillar on a smooth black base. It looked cleaner, but more ominous at the same time. A looming mystery for some other time.

The Kid meandered back and forth, turning the idea of life and death over and over in his mind, searching for Fred or Edsumar.

Something moved. The Kid turned towards it, shading his eyes.

A large, flat, grey stone—about a pace wide, by two paces long—shifted in the sand. It rose at an angle, silt sliding down its uneven surface to collect on the ground. The stone shifted again, a crack forming down the middle as the single rock face became two, then spread apart.

A rocky, reptilian neck and head extended from the top edge, and a long tail emerged from the sands, twitching.

"What the hell?" the Kid murmured, drawing his blades and crouching, ready to attack.

The draconic head swiveled towards him, grey, sandy eyelids blinking over faceted stone eyes.

"Kid?" The voice sounded like chalk screeching on a slate chalkboard. "Is that you?"

"You know me?" The Kid asked, still ready to defend himself. "Do I know you?"

"Yes," the screeching changed, shifting to the sound of a rock scratching a sidewalk to make a hopscotch board on a hot summer day, "we know you. We've been with you a short while, though maybe long in your terms. It's very confusing for us right now, and we can't be sure."

"We? Us?" The Kid stood up, cocking his head, the wheels in his mind turning.

The rock monster stood, sand sliding from its body, which was about the size of a horse, if horses had wings. Which they might here. The Kid wasn't sure. But this was a dragon, a small stone dragon.

Yes. We, us. We know you, a familiar voice said in his head, though it had an odd echo, like someone added reverb to it before broadcasting it into the Kid's brain.

Chapter 28

Red Wind was bustling in ways it hadn't in decades. It was a building boom; the city was experiencing growth in more than one way.

Most of the buildings were damaged, and more than half destroyed. The city was rebuilding but doing it a little better since the Church of Jonath had a controlling factor.

Before the invasion, crime syndicates controlled the community. Since the invasion, those same groups fled before the final battle, were killed, or were too scattered to wrest control from the priests.

The people loved the church and the priests, because they were the ones helping rebuild everyone's homes and businesses. They brought in food, supplies, and protected the people while the city had no walls or militia.

It had some sort of law, though. After the Battle of the Pyridom, they awarded Mecklen the office of Reeve. He immediately complained about it, and then deputized Ablemarle and her silent partner, who the Kid had nicknamed Teller.

Ichaelson and Vindalai were local heroes, and their presence brought more people—especially the younger folk—to church services than anything else.

Tradler was a lost soul, though. The young man wandered the streets in the dawn and dusk hours, shuffling through the dusty lanes, like he was haunting the town. During the day, he would sit in whatever tavern, pub, or drinking hole he could find, pickling himself with a mug or glass of anything he could wrap a shaking hand around. Anything to not remember, not think, not care. At night, he slept wherever he fell, sometimes at a bar, other times on the side of the street.

Logs were being brought down the Lasso River, cut into planks at the sawmill on the banks, and hauled across the plains and fields to the city.

The rokairn opened trade talks with Red Wind, and in a show of good faith sent priests of Jonath to the city to teach the human priests how to work stone in ways only one with the blessing of Jonath could.

With these resources, they rebuilt the outer wall of the city, parts of it raised from the stones of the ground itself.

"It's only a matter of time," Nathan said, "like you guys told me, people are poo."

"I don't think we said it quite like that, though," Torrents laughed, "but we get the idea."

"You're telling us," the Kid leaned on double-width planks set on two barrels to create a makeshift table, "that they offered you the jeweler's shop, and the old owner is dead, and you could just have it?"

"Yes," Nathan nodded, "they consider it fair payment for what I did for Red Wind."

"And you said no," the Kid continued, flapping his hand at Nathan, "because you think that one day, crime will return here and ruin it all."

"Something like that," Nathan nodded again, "it always does. Might not be now, or even soon, but it'll come."

"But…" the Kid started again, and Torrents elbowed him.

"Maybe, Kid," the barbarian leaned down, his breath reeking of ale, and looked at the Kid pointedly, "maybe Nathan doesn't want the jewelry store because he'd have to run it alone."

"He could hire people to help him," the Kid's voice went shrill as he continued to wave his hands, "I mean, gee-willikers! It can't be that hard!"

"Maybe," a voice that sounded like gravel falling downhill said, "he misses his friend Nob, and doesn't want to be reminded of him every day in the shop where they met."

The three looked at the stone-hide dragon who lay curled on the ground at the foot of the table, head raised to look over the edge of the planks.

"Fredsumar," the Kid wobbled, turning to look at his friend, "egg-cellent point!"

"Fredsumar?" the dragon rumbled. "When did we get that name?"

"It fits," the Kid picked up a chunk of cheese and popped it in his mouth, talking between chewing, "You were Edsumar, then Fred absorbed you, my psychic magics bonding the two of you, and so Fred and Edsumar, becomes; Fredsumar!"

"Hmmm," the dragon lowered his head again to his fore-claws, "we'll talk about later, when you're a bit more sober."

The dragon had grown since the last new moon, when they'd left the Pyridom of Power, its sleek, black structure looking suspiciously like a Tower of Onyx.

When the Kid first found him, Fredsumar had been the size of a horse. In the past four weeks, he grew to the size of an ox, or maybe a buffalo. He was now twice as wide as a horse, his body one and half times as long, and that much again in length with his neck and tail. His wingspan was the most impressive part though: snout to tail Fredsumar was about the length of two pickup trucks, but his wings from tip to tip wider than eight pickup trucks end to end when he spread them to full length.

"So, Nathan," Torrents broke the uncomfortable silence, "if you aren't setting up shop here, what will you do?"

Nathan considered, chewing on a strip of jerky.

"I think I'll go east," the rokairn nodded, "I have previous memories of the Seawall City, and it sounds like something straight out of a fairy tale. It has mages, priests, wizards, sorcerers, and a fine-tuned, organized military. I think I'd like to see this firsthand again."

"Can we go?" The Kid leaned over the table, his chin in his palm, elbow resting on the stained planks, squinting and smiling. "Or is this a private thing where we're not allowed to join you, even though it's not like it's your city and you have any authority to stop us? Why would you want to, anyway? That's just being silly, Nathan. You aren't the boss of me…"

"Yes," Nathan interrupted.

The Kid tried to focus on the rokairn, blinking and swaying.

"Yes?" The Kid asked. "Yes, what?"

"Of course you can come." Nathan took a long pull from his ale, wrinkling his nose at the bitter taste. "I can't believe rokairn are legendary for loving this stuff, it's horrible. It's so bitter. It's like liquid Torrents."

"What did you just say?" The barbarian cocked his head downward towards Nathan. "Did you just say what I think you said? Did you just say…a joke? And without apologizing before it? And after it?"

The three laughed together, Fredsumar snorting a small dust cloud on their feet.

"And during it," the Kid added, "and ten minutes after it."

"Yeah," Torrents dropped a hand onto the Kid's shoulder, "we get it, Kid. Drop it, you've gone too far with it now. It's no longer funny."

"But," the rogue tried to move the hand from his shoulder, but missed the barbarian's arm, "why was it funny when you said it then?"

"Because," Torrents moved his hand, and the Kid almost fell over without its support, "I said it. You know, Kid, you really lose all sense of comedic timing when you drink. I mean, you're like anti-funny."

Nathan and Torrents laughed again.

"Your face is anti-funny," the Kid said, then burst into exaggerated laughter.

"So, let me get this straight," Torrents said slowly, "if my face is anti-funny, then it's not funny looking at all? Maybe even handsome? Is that right?"

"I didn't say all that," the Kid cocked his head and furrowed his brow, "did I? I just meant, your face isn't a laughing thing, it's not funny. That means your mouth, too. Like all the things that come of it, isn't funny. Your words are anti-funny. And yes, maybe you're a little handsome. But you're not funny looking. Maybe a little funny looking, in a handsome way."

"Okay, Kid," Torrents sighed, "stop now, you did it again. You over explained and took the joke too far. Just stop…talking."

"Oops," the Kid hiccupped, "I did it again."

Torrents facepalmed with one hand, and gently shoved the Kid with the other. The thief slid sideways and fell to the floor.

Laughter bubbled up from under the table.

"I've fallen," the Kid's giggling voice said, "and I can't get up."

Epilogue

The canvas walls of the pavilion flapped and popped in the wind. The sun in the west cast long shadows across the oasis, the lines of palms duplicated along the sands, stretching for the east like they were searching for the sunrise.

The cloth building had three poles, the center one slightly higher than the other two. It was oval, nestled in the sparse grass and the tall, slim trees of the watering hole.

The smell of roasting mutton came and went with the wind, the greasy smudge of smoke ripped away from the vent hole as soon as it drifted out.

"That's odd," Torrents said, "I don't recall there being sanctuary at this oasis."

"What do we know?" The Kid shrugged. "Things change so quickly in the desert. And it's a tent. How hard could it be to set it up and take it down? It could be anywhere tomorrow."

"But we just left the rokairn lands in the crags." Torrents shifted the weight of the new sword on his back. "And we're on the border of the Seawall City territory. And there's no pack animals or wagons to transport it. Plus, the grass is still fresh around it, not worn, so it hasn't been here long. Don't you think anyone setting up here is just asking for trouble?"

"I know that smell," Fredsumar rumbled as he trundled along behind the trio.

"Lamb?" Nathan asked, looking over his shoulder. "I do too. My grannie used to make it. Super simple and basic, but it was wonderful. Always reminds me of Chanukah, and the sounds of family bickering and judging you."

"Ah," the Kid sighed, "the good old days. Shall we go in?"

The two humans and the rokairn moved to enter, reaching for the tied flap of a door.

"What about us?" Fredsumar tilted his head to look at the tent as it swayed in the wind.

The others turned back to look at the stone dragon.

"It won't be a problem," a new voice said, making all three jump, and Nathan to let out a loud squeak, "I'll roll up the side for you, old friend."

A man stood in the doorway, holding the flap open and to one side. He was human, between thirty and fifty years old, of medium height, and wore a turban-style head wrap over his pale face.

"Torrents, Kid," the man nodded at them, "it's good to see you again."

"Jack?" The Kid's voice rose with surprise. "Jack Tucker?"

"What the hell are you doing here?" Torrents laughed and clapped the shorter man on the shoulder.

"Welcome to the Traveller's Inn. Come inside," Jack stepped out of their way, and gestured to the interior with a wave of his hand, "and we'll talk once you each have eaten have a plate of mutton, hot potatoes, and some green vegetable thing I picked up. They're like Brussels sprouts, but the size of a racquetball."

The three filed in, their eyes adjusting to the dim light. Behind them, the wall was lit with the setting sun, and the wall across from them was the mellow blue of shadow.

The tent was spacious for a tent. The ground, covered with overlapping rugs, had six rough wooden plank tables scattered around, with no obvious organization.

A third of the interior space—from the pole to the right, to the far wall—created a separate room with a curtain. Tapestries and banners hung from the ropes along the top of the cloth walls.

A table—littered with pitchers, bottles, carafes, glasses, mugs, cups, and a small keg—in front of the opening to the private room created a makeshift bar.

On the left, between the center pole and the support pole, stood a spit—two metal 'y-shaped' poles standing on each side, with a cross-pole supported between them—over an oval rock-framed firepit.

A thin old man stared at the three and slowly turned the handle, roasting a goat over the fire.

"You?" The Kid froze, staring at the man, eyes wide.

"Oh, damn!" Torrents stumbled, catching himself on a table before he fell. "Really? You're here? I'm gonna need a drink."

Nathan pushed past the other two, trying to see who they were talking to and about.

"Yeah," a voice cackled, "PepperGarten is here. Did you expect somebody else? Mother Teresa, maybe? The Pope? Gandhi? Gloria Steinem?"

"You didn't die," Nathan whispered, "but I buried you. And built a cairn. A big one. With lots of rocks.

They were heavy, too. My back hurt for three days after that. How are you here?"

"PepperGarten got better!" The old man giggled. "It's hard to keep a good man down, and it's good to keep a hard man down. Or is it down to hard a good man? Well, whatever, something like that."

"Gentleman, and Kid," Jack said from across the tent, "I have a table here for you. Why don't you get some food, and then we'll talk."

Jack stood at a table beside a rolled up and tied panel of the tent to the far left. Fredsumar sat on his haunches outside, his head on the edge of the table closest to the wall.

"Fredsumar," Jack addressed the dragon, "I have an extra goat or two if you're hungry."

Their host scrunched up his face and tilted his head, eying the dragon.

"Do you eat?" the innkeeper asked.

"You bet he does," Torrents interrupted, moving to the table, but making a wide berth of PepperGarten. "He's grown a bunch since he…"

The barbarian trailed off.

"What do we call it?" Torrents asked. "Since you were born? Metamorphosed? Well, since he got this way, instead of being a knife and silly rock crab."

"Fred was a rock lobster," the Kid moved past the old man, but watched him the whole time, "and now that we're talking about it, I haven't seen Fredsumar eat at all. Do you eat?"

"We were a dagger, thank you very much," Fredsumar grumbled, "and we take sustenance, but not like others. Not like we did when we were an actual dragon."

Nathan walked to PepperGarten and looked him in the eye. The withered old man wasn't much taller than the rokairn, but Nathan still had to look up.

The rokairn thrust out his hand, and PepperGarten looked down at it, a grin splitting his face.

"Welcome back, PepperGarten," Nathan said. "I'm pleased to see you have returned from…wherever you were."

PepperGarten grabbed the rokairn's meaty hand in both of his and pumped it up and down.

"PepperGarten is pleased, too!" The old man's voice was shrill and excited. "Oh, the things PepperGarten has seen and done since coming here. PepperGarten remembers when Jack first brought PepperGarten here…"

"Wait," the Kid cut the man off, stopping halfway to a seated position, "Jack brought you here also?"

"He was the first one," Jack's voice was wistful and warm, like he was remembering something fondly, "and he's proven his worth many times over."

"Was he always this weird?" Torrents asked, sitting on the bench seat furthest from the old man and keeping a wary eye on him.

"Oh, yes," Jack laughed, "always. PepperGarten lived for years on the streets of New York City before coming here. But man, he took to the nature magics with a passion!"

The Kid dropped onto the bench across from Torrents, sitting as close to Fredsumar as possible.

PepperGarten was still pumping Nathan's hand, and the rokairn gripped the man's wrist with his other hand and tugged his trapped hand free.

The four new arrivals settled around the table, as Jack served them plates piled with food, and mugs full of mead, wine, beer, or spirits; each as they requested.

The evening passed into night, and the group told of the events since they'd last seen Jack. They also filled Nathan in on who Jack was, and how the man could bring people from their world to this one.

When the meal was done, the six settled around a table beside the firepit with mugs of hot tea, or small glasses of digestifs. The conversation lulled into comfortable silence.

"Okay," Jack said, slapping his thighs and standing up, "I guess it's time to get to it."

"Get to what?" Nathan asked, smiling.

"Oh," the Kid said quietly, looking down, "you're going to ask, aren't you?"

"Yes," Jack nodded, "I am. But it's still your choice, as always."

"Ask what?" Nathan urged.

"Do any of you want to go home?" Jack looked at each of the three in turn, pausing to gauge their reactions.

"Nope," Torrents said, leaning back on the bench, belching, and rubbing his stomach. "I'm good. I think I'll stick around. Thanks for asking, though!"

"PepperGarten wants to stay!" the old man said, his voice solemn and serious for once. "PepperGarten likes it here, better than New York. This is home now, and PepperGarten never wants to go back to that other place. And PepperGarten would appreciate it if you quit asking."

"Nathan?" Jack looked at the rokairn. "What about you?"

"We have a choice?" Nathan asked. "I mean, is it like Wizard of Oz where we click our heels together and say, 'There's no place like home,' and we shoot back to where we were before?"

"Not quite," Jack laughed, "but something like that."

"Well," Nathan took a deep breath, and let it out slowly, "I think I'd like to stay, for a while at least. I need to find out what happened to me in Seawall City before I came here. Well, what happened to Trojet Bellstamp before I took over his body."

Jack nodded, then turned to look at the Kid, who was still staring down, wringing his hands in his lap.

"Kid?" Jack spoke softly. "Do you want to go, or would you like to stay?"

"I don't want to go," the Kid spoke slowly, "but I don't want to keep doing this. This stuff, these things, we've been doing. There's been so much death, and I don't think I want to handle it anymore. I just want to live and enjoy life. Is that an option? I don't want to go back, because I'm dying there. Esperanza had a chance of living when she went back. Torrence or Nathan could survive what happened to them. Me? I'm a dead person if I return to that other world. Can I stay, but not have to do…all these things anymore?"

"Yeah," Jack nodded, "any of you can walk away anytime. I mean, you're drawn to each other because of the connection of your home…reality. But, yeah, you can go anywhere you choose to go. You don't have to stay."

"Really?" the Kid's voice flooded with relief. "It's okay to just…leave?"

"Yeah," Jack smiled and nodded, "I'll even pack you a bagged lunch of leftovers to take with you."

"We'll go with you," the gravel-rumble of Fredsumar filled the room. "We should be able to fly soon, and we can take you anywhere we choose to go."

"It's settled then," PepperGarten cackled and clapped his hands, "PepperGarten agrees to join the two of you, and help you on your journey to somewhere that isn't here!"

Fredsumar and the Kid exchanged looks, then the Kid shrugged, and the dragon nodded once.

"Okay," the Kid smiled, "you can go with us, PepperGarten."

"PepperGarten knows PepperGarten can go," the old man huffed. "That's why PepperGarten said that PepperGarten would go with you. You're welcome."

The group settled around the table with their drinks and conversation and talked late into the night. They discussed their world and the things they missed, which mostly were certain foods; the differences in this world, and the beauty of both worlds; the fact that they had magic items and lost them; and the night ended with talk of how to save this world and make it…less apocalyptic.

They bedded down on the carpets, moving the tables to cloth walls, and fell asleep to the crickets and night birds of the oasis.

In the morning, Nathan and Torrents woke to find that the Kid, PepperGarten, and Fredsumar were gone.

Jack sat in the only chair in the tent, leaning back on two legs. The man puffed on a pipe—a huge wooden pipe, deep brown in color, with swirls of grain along the bowl, and long bent stem—and blew smoke rings, sorta. The rings wobbled and broke apart with the slightest breeze.

"They're gone," Torrents said, stating a fact, not asking a question, as he stood and stretched.

"Uh huh," Jack grunted, pulling on his pipe again.

"Where'd they go?" Nathan asked, sitting up.

"Dunno," Jack mumbled around the stem of his pipe.

"Will we see them again?" Nathan rubbed at his neck.

"Maybe," Jack shrugged, "if you need to, or they need to see you. Never know with these things."

"What do we do now?" Nathan asked.

"Same thing we do every day, Natie," Torrents said in a snide, stiff accent. "Try and save the world."

281

End of Portals, Book 2

Sneak Peek of Portals, Book 3: Mystics &

Monoliths

Chapter 1

Torrents the barbarian threw his arms around the stone pillar, hauling himself up the corner of a building on the northern side of the city square. He wanted a better view of the hanging that was about to take place.

He swung his muscled leg over the wide railing and pulled himself over and onto the stone balcony. The crowd backed up a step. The newcomer shouldered his way through the throng of figures, most of them politicians and robed councilors, and claimed a space at the opposite edge of the railing overlooking the common area below.

People moved aside for the broad-shouldered figure with two swords on his back. The weapons had replaced his usual double-handed sword that was lost a few months ago at the Demon Front, battling otherworldly invaders. A long dirk was inside of each of the large man's knee-high boots, and a cudgel swung from his wide leather belt.

The man blew a strand of his black hair from his eyes, and it fell back across his face. He reached up and pulled his shoulder length hair into a ponytail and tied it back with a leather cord.

"Torrents the Barbarian," someone behind him uttered his name in quiet awe. The young councilman leaned over to a woman, explaining who the warrior was in a conspiratorial whisper, "Hero of Durgan's Keep when it was invaded by a necromancer and her undead army. Defender of portals at Land's End when the demonic horde burst through it and into this world."

The barbarian ignored them and raised his hands to smooth the furs that he traditionally wore. His hands dropped awkwardly as he realized they weren't there.

Torrents had traded his usual grey furs for pale leathers. The outfit was still warm to wear but was better protection. It was worth sweating a little to avoid getting a blade in the gut.

Autumn was setting in but wasn't like back home on Earth. It was muggier, and the humidity lent itself to sweating profusely, short tempers, and fighting. He could spot at least three different squabbles below him. His hand dropped to the cudgel on his belt without him thinking about it.

He scanned the crowd for his partner, Nathan, the rokairn priest. Torrents couldn't help to think 'dwarf' in place of the word rokairn, because that's what his friend's people looked like to him. The term dwarf was hurtful in this world, just as was calling an aeifain or a dasism an elf was rude. It was an ethnic slur and using the term could cause trouble.

Torrents spotted Nathan pushing his way through the mob of people. Almost everyone was a head-and-shoulders taller than the rokairn, and the priest squeezed past clumps and groups of humans who didn't bother to acknowledge the polite apologies of the smaller man.

Torrents could see the head of the double-bladed axe on the rokairn's back, its wooden handle wrapped with living vines and leaves. Nathan stood out for more reasons than his height, his thick, braided beard, and the massive weapon. The priest had taken to adapting Earth fashions to this world.

The rokairn wore a doublet with lapels, in a checked pattern in brown shades, and loose pants that matched in color, but was the style worn by sailors. All of Nathan's accessories—from his belt and leather wrist cuffs to his hat and boots—were black, though he had a bright green feather that bobbed on the wide-brimmed hat that made Torrents think of pirate movies.

The rokairn, who was a jeweler back home on Earth, had a variety of rings, necklaces, bracelets, and earrings on him. All were excellent quality, though few were flashy, and most were just simple works of art.

Nathan had a bead on their target, tracking the new person down like a fat kid who smelled popcorn, using the abilities given upon him by his god.

There were gods in this world, real ones that did things. As in, deities who interacted with and affected their faithful. Torrents was still wrapping his head around that, even though he'd hung around with a priest or priestess since he'd arrived in this reality. People could pray to the gods, and they answered, giving help, causing miracles, and answering requests of their followers and worshipers. It was a weird concept after seeing so many evangelists, social media posts, and politicians talking about praying to help others and getting no measurable results.

But Nathan got results from his god, Jonath. Jonath was a god of many talents, or as Nathan said, areas of influence. It meant magical realms, skill sets, and a few other things. Jonath was the master of the element of earth, agriculture, protection, guards, and of all things…perception. Torrents didn't know how it all related but thought of it in the same way that big business diversified. Sometimes, you got ahold of something by association rather than intent.

The crowd was cheering and jeering, excited about the impending hanging. They jostled for a better view of the wooden platform and noose, as street vendors wove their way through the throng, shouting out their wares and prices that couldn't be beaten.

People were people, and this—in Torrents's mind—was no different from a sporting event back home. They came to see a spectacle, and there was a chance they'd go overboard and even riot. It didn't matter if their team won or lost, emotions ran high, and people rode that wave. Families came—children held in the protective circle of adults—and they shouted and booed along with drunken louts, city officials, and famous or infamous figures in the crowd.

Those individuals would each give commentary in their own specific arena after the event. Some in the city square with the body swinging lifelessly behind them, some in bars and taverns with the drunks singing lively behind them, and others in shadowed rooms, whispers slithering around them.

Gambling was common and scattered throughout the crowd—usually near the food and souvenir vendors—were people collecting bets. Taking down names, gathering money, and scribbling on a chalkboard or a wax tablet, these people fed off the crowd the same way a remora would feed off a shark— or a drug dealer off people looking for an escape.

Bottom feeders, welcomed by the population, who had the delusion of pulling one over on the inevitable odds. It happened occasionally, but more often they paid the price in gold or flesh.

Seawall City was different from any other city that Torrents had seen since he'd come to this world. It was built almost exclusively with stone, and most of the roofs made of baked ceramic tiles that reminded him of the Spanish roofs of the southwest United States.

The city lorded over an angry sea to its east. Stone docks jutting out into the ocean, incessant waves breaking against the pylons. They'd constructed higher docks since the Downfall, when everything in the world had changed as the comet that orbited the planet altered all the rules of magic and might. Now, the waters raged like a living beast, trying to tear down the stone that mere humans had constructed.

There were three tiers of docks used. They used the lowest in the winter; they were the thickest, and the most reinforced, to avoid being destroyed by violently tossed ice floes. The middle ones were for the spring and autumn, though it was the seasons of storms. The highest was for the summer, when ice melted, and the seas rose to the halfway mark on the hundred-meter-tall walls that the city perched atop.

They'd built the metropolis with the combined force of magic, and the blood and sweat of men. They'd laid it according to a grand plan; the streets in orderly grids and spokes that resembled a wagon wheel, the farmlands outside the walls and sheltered with rock formations grown from the bones of the land.

The outer wall of the city was a wonder. It was thick enough that two wagons could pass one another when on top, and most entrances that led into the building-thick wall were wide to allow a single wagon entry. The wall was a castle unto itself, built to shelter most of the city's populace if needed.

Seawall City had its own currency, a rare thing in an age struggling to survive in a time after this world's apocalypse. They traded in gold, silver, copper, and brass, whereas the other cities that Torrents had visited mostly bartered and traded in goods and services. Commerce was returning, but it wasn't where it had been before society collapsed.

The barbarian scanned the crowd again, spotting Nathan, who was nervously fiddling with his beard with one hand and clutching the symbol of his god with the other. The rokairn's mouth moved, and Torrents could almost hear his companion apologizing to each person he brushed against as he passed.

The priest followed his holy symbol the way a woodsman would follow a compass, glancing down at it, looking around, then turning and moving in a new direction.

Shouts from the crowd erupted.

A group of eight men-at-arms surrounding a figure appeared in the portcullised entrance from the thick stone outer wall of the city. A wizard—or a mage, sorcerer, or something, Torrents never knew which was which, or which witch was which—led the procession.

In the center of the group was a pale, thin woman. At least, Torrents thought it was a woman; it could have been a lithe and delicate man. But any way you looked at them, this person was beaten and broken under the lash, and possibly other tortures. It could have even been magic; after all, magic-using elitists—

spellslingers to uneducated masses like the barbarian—controlled the city.

With an intake of breath, Torrents realized that the person about to be hung was an elf. *Aeifain*, the word echoed through his mind. They were their own species, though thought to be related to the Dasism, who roamed the wild, open spaces of the world.

Out of curiosity, Torrents focused on the figure—knowing it couldn't be the one they'd come here to find—his sharp eyes picking out details. Looking closely, he could see the aeifain was female. She held her head high and haughty, ignoring most of the crowd, and looking down on the few she did glance at, though she was a half head shorter than most of the adults.

He'd never met an aeifain but heard they were an arrogant bunch who treated everyone else like they were ghetto-trash. Torrents dealt with that sort of attitude often enough before he'd come to this world. As a black high-school student and athlete, he'd seen how people would look down on others.

Torrents shrugged off thoughts about the woman who was about to be hung and scanned the crowd for Nathan again.

He saw the rokairn moving through the mass of people, a valley in the waves of humanity, the crests rolling in to fill the space he'd occupied only a moment before.

Nathan stopped, looking from his holy symbol to the gibbet, where the aeifain was being led to the noose.

Torrents scanned the guards, then looked closely at the mage (or wizard, or whatever) who led the procession, wondering he'd be the one they'd need to contact and bring into their little group.

Looking back at Nathan, the rokairn was gesticulating wildly, pointing towards the raised platform.

The barbarian looked at the group surrounding the prisoner again. When he and Nathan came into this world from their own, they'd inhabited a body that had just died. The energy transfer of their souls had healed the physical wounds of the body they'd taken over and allowed them to have a second chance at life.

Torrents studied the group. It'd be nice to have another sword-swinging warrior beside him, muscle to back him up. Nathan kinda filled that role, but was much too meek to offer any real intimidation factor. He did okay when it came down to brass tacks, but not so much when he was trying to not get into a fight. The best way to do that was by flexing before your enemy got enough balls to draw and throw down; Nathan did it wrong and came off as a wimp for it.

Then again, maybe it'd be the spellslinger. Torrents had hung out with priests, and the Kid (who had travelled north and west a few months ago), and they all had some magical abilities, but each was prone to rely on a weapon rather than magic. Someone who could just whip out a fireball to clear the way through the fodder before Torrents got there to take out the mastermind with his sword might be a nice change of pace.

Torrents had been all-state football and basketball—and had even run some track and field—before his car accident severed his spinal column, paralyzed him from the waist down, and confined him to a wheelchair. He knew that sort of thinking wasn't

PC, and people told him he shouldn't think of himself as restricted and limited. They didn't know what it was like, but he did, and he'd look at it however he felt like looking at it. Screw those hopeful wusses that preached that the world was all chuzzing puppies and rainbows.

He just wanted his life to mean something. It wasn't in his nature to be selfish and self-centered. He'd learned that the hard way. But life had to mean something, and that meant doing big things that others considered worthwhile, right? Or did it? Could he live his life for himself, doing what he wanted while helping others? His thoughts wandered to the Kid, and what he was doing right now.

The Kid had been his opposite but had also become his best friend. He'd never told him, because that wasn't manly, and would be ridiculed. Wouldn't it?

The barbarian pulled his mind from the bitter tar pit of his thoughts, focusing on his original idea, building their team. He liked teams. And it was always three of them brought together to face some problem, or army, or world-threatening event for some reason.

He'd faced an undead horde and things that put zombies and vampires to shame. He'd fought back an invading force of demons from another dimension, all to save a world he'd never asked to be a part of. But here he was, facing things down and being a hero, when in the real world, he rode the aluminum rails of a chair.

But he'd liked Esperanza, the priestess of Latress, (who apparently was a goddess married to Jonath) before she'd returned to their world where she'd just attempted suicide. He missed the Kid, though he'd never say it out loud. The Kid had been a cancer-riddled old lady in the body of a street-thief boy who had magical powers that let him make illusions and jump around like he had trampolines on his feet.

Now it was just him and Nathan. He liked the guy, but in the real-world Nathan owned a jewelry shop, and been—to put it bluntly—a wimp. The man had no spine, no guts, and no backbone. He'd apologize for breathing. Not that he didn't have some skills, but he'd never admit to them.

That annoyed Torrents.

The lead guard assisted the aeifain in stepping up on a bench so he could drape the noose around her neck. The man tightened the rope so it was snug around the woman's throat.

The barbarian looked back to the rokairn, trying to decipher which person was destined to join them. He knew it wasn't the prisoner, but couldn't figure out which of the seven other people the priest meant.

He also wondered how that person would die. Would the crowd riot? Would the aeifain lash out, knocking one of them to the ground?

The spellslinger in charge of the death-squad rested his hand on the lever that opened the trapdoor under the prisoner. He shouted something to the crowd, lost in the excited shouts and screams of the bloodthirsty mob, then pulled the control.

The floor dropped away, and the body fell, jerking. The crowd went quiet with a gasp, and the crack of the bones and sinew in the aeifain's neck was heard in that moment of silence.

Then the crowd cheered, drowning out all other noises.

Torrents looked back at Nathan, raising his hands in confusion, indicating he didn't know which one was their new companion.

The rokairn pointed at the spasming body hanging under the wooden platform as her death throes waned and she stilled.

Torrents looked at the prisoner in confusion and saw her eyes open and focus on the crowd.

Then terror crossed her face, and she let out a strangled scream.

Calendar

The basic calendar is a lunar calendar. There are thirteen months in each year. There are twenty-eight days in each month. There is a new moon on the first day of every month. The first day of spring is on the Equinox.

Seasons	**Months**	**Days**	
Spring	Loen	1.	Ginof
	Hapok	2.	Bestuf
	Axara	3.	Midā
		4.	Therin
Summer	Surem	5.	Uthr
	Santara	6.	Dunwith
	Xaco	7.	Lasin
Autumn	Harton		
	Thon		
	Ault		
Winter	Witen		
	Maleo		
	Frear		
Thaw	Milwen		

Glossary

Aborgas: Small hamlet near Red City.

Aeifain: Willowy race of beings with almond eyes, pale skin, and slightly pointed ears. Often more advanced in arts, culture, and magic than the lesser races.

Akar Lake: Body of water near Ruger Whitley Estates.

Ault: Ninth month of the year, and the third month of the autumn season.

Axara: Third month of the year, and the spring season.

Bestuf: Second day of the week.

Bidj: A swear word mean waste or offal.

Chuz: A harsh swear word.

Dangrazio: Subterranean metropolis and trading post.

Dasism: A race who follow the path of elements and nature. Physically, they are slighter than humans, with olive skin, pointed ears, and almond eyes.

Dioneze City: A broken city on the eastern part of the continent run by slavers. Known for its gladiatorial ring.

Dragon Estates: An ancient castle rumored to have a dragon residing in the caverns below it.

Dargaon's Hole: Ancestral home of dragons in the Wandering Hills.

Dunwith: Sixth day of the week.

Durgan's Keep: A city-state in the far east that was founded by a rokairn and his adventuring companions.

Edgewater: Medium port town on the coast of the Sea of Seron.

Everyway: Largest city on the continent of Teurone.

Ez'rainia-fromton: City of the dead located in the Great Desert. Was the city in which Verl'zen-luk had been imprisoned before his rise to godhood.

Fate's Run: Dockside gambling hall in Tarnish. Run by a woman named Fate.

Frear: Twelfth month of the year, and the third month of the winter season.

Ginof: First day of the week.

Glass Valley: A valley made of glass in the slim desert that was formed when a stone dragon fell from the heavens.

Gray Lands: Home of the Aeifain.

Great Desert: A large desert east of the southern Rolling Mountains, which is home to Rogen the Plague and the Great Desert Empire.

Great Desert Empire: A civilization built by Rogen the Plague and his nation slaves, located in the Great Desert.

Hapok: Second month of the year, and of the spring season.

Harton: Seventh month of the year, and the first month of the autumn season.

Highest Spire: A structure that is fifty kilometers at the base and spirals upward. Doors that lead to other places in time and space are spaced every six meters. The height of this tower in unmeasured.

Hope's Hollow: A small village on the on the borders of the Black Wood and the Wandering Hills.

Humbrey: A Kingdom of thirteen houses that embodies nobility and honor.

Icon Hall: Aeifain home on the eastern portion of Teurone.

Jonath: God of justice, protection, strength, and earth. His symbol is a trident and balanced scales.

Kez'et-dual: A demon enslaved by the Trööds.

Khelikian: God of Insects.

Kord: A twisted gold wire that is the standard currency.

Land's End: A demon-ridden peninsula on the south-eastern most portion of the continent.

Lasin: Seventh day of the week.

Ley-lines: Elemental energy currents, invisible to the naked eye, from which wizards can draw energy.

Loen: First month of the year, and of the spring season. It begins on the spring equinox.

Mage, Mind: Practitioner of the art of psychic magics such as body alteration, telekinesis, telepathy, etc.

Maleo: Eleventh month of the year, and the second month of the winter season.

Malvor: Duchy in the Kingdom of Trysteria, south of the Kingdom of Humbrey. Run by Duke Malvornick.

Mida: Third day of the week.

Milwen: The thirteenth month of the year, and the transition month between winter and spring.

Nine Towers of Magic: Abandoned during the Wizard Wars, this secluded and elite university was dedicated to teaching magic. Located east of the Black Wood.

Nomed: A demon-human-aeifain hybrid.

Northwood Community: The largest city in Northwood, founded by humans, dasism, and other races.

Obsidian/Onyx: God of Magic who came to power when the Talisman appeared in the sky.

Obsidian/Onyx Towers: Black towers raised by the God of Magic to distribute magical tools, goods, and weapons.

Ocean Wood: Lands reclaimed by the Dasism from humans under Kala the Black.

Olde Kingdom: A fallen Kingdom in the southern portion of the Everyway Plains.

Oracle Plain: Grasslands north of the Common Wood, east of the Slim Desert, and west of the Rolling Mountains. Home of the mystical order of the Oracle.

Pantageas: City run by mages and wizards in the northern Everyway Plains, just south of the Kingdom of Humbrey.

Paradise Island: An island created by a dead volcano. Now a refuge for pirates and seagoing folk. Run by small governments and individuals, known for its waterfalls.

Parsay Gevies: God of Luck, Chance, and Dreams. Referred to as Parsay by adults, who pray to him for luck, and as Mister Gevies by children, who pray to him for dreams to come true.

Pek: A silver coin, worth one-tenth of a gold kord.

Pemtie: A moron, ignorant, or stupid person, idea, or event.

Phaz, Day of: A day that happens once every four years. Shrouded with myth and superstition.

Promethene: Goddess of Song and Light. Her clergy is almost always women.

Pyridom of Power: A landmark on the east coast of the continent that focuses magical energies.

Red City: Run down city once plagued by lycanthropes and undead. Located on the coast of the

Red Wind: Located in the Red Plains, this city is known for its crime lords and drug trade.

Rock Crag Wastes: a rocky area geographically located west of the Great Desert and east of the southern Rolling Mountains.

Rogen the Plague: Rokairn slave master and lord of The Great Desert Empire.

Rokairn: The Stone Folk. A short, stout race known for their attention to detail, organization, and dedication to fine craftsmanship. Both sexes are known to have beards.

Rolling Mountains: An immense mountain range east of the Oracle Plain, and west of the Northwood.

Rondarius the Foul: Insane Necromancer

Royale Bay: A bay north of the Sea of Seron and east of the Everyway Plains.

Rugber Whitley Estates: A small community known for the mind mages born there.

Rumay Bay: A shanty town on the shores of the Broken Sea that was once a hub of trade before The Downfall.

Runsk: A warlord-controlled city nestled between the Grey Forest and Diaz Wood.

Santara: Fifth month of the year, and the second month of the summer season.

Sea of the Great Plague: A body of water south of the Great Desert.

Sea of Seron: A body of water south of the Everyway Plains.

Seawall City: A fortified city run by spellslingers in a military fashion, located on the east coast of Teurone on the Eastern Ocean.

Sharp: A brass coin, with one one-hundredth of a gold kord.

Shuglak (shug-lak): Horse-sized herd creature with large round ears, a single nose horn on a flat hog-like snout, and two tusks jutting from the bottom jaw of males.

Shulyar City: Dasism name for Silver City.

Silver Castle: One-time home of the god, Jonath, who built it.

Silver City: Also known as Shulyar City, a city built by the god Jonath.

Sinking Swamp: A swamp that hides the Library of time, west of Trysteria and north of the Everyway Plains.

Slim Desert: A thin desert between Everyway Plains and Oracle Plain.

Spellslinger: A generalized term for a wielder of one of the five types of magic; alchemy, mind magic, holy, conjuring, and elemental.

Stadia Isle: A pirate island in the Sea of Seron.

Surem: Fourth month of the year, and the first month of the summer season.

Talisman: A comet that returns on a regular basis, but now is in orbit around the planet.

Tarnish: Run-down desert city on the coast of the Sea of the Great Plague.

Tarra: Goddess of water and healing. Twin of Torr.

Teurone: Continent detailed in this book.

Therin: Fourth day of the week.

Thon: Eighth month of the year, and the second month of the autumn season.

Torgoth: God of Trade and Commerce.

Torr: God of fire and combat. Twin of Tarra.

Transvartius: A wise and benevolent man sometimes known as the Traveller, the Hidden Diplomat, and disciple of the Walking God.

Traveling God, The: God of innate magic, such as mind mages and wizards. Also known as the Walking God.

Troöd: A race from another dimension, that are reptilian in features. They have two distinct species, greys and greens. The former deal in summoning magics, and the latter are chameleon like soldiers.

Trysteria: Kingdom in the northern portion of the Everyway Plains.

Uthr: Fifth day of the week.

Velentian Brandy: A strong alcohol drink.

Verl'zen-luk: God of ritual Magic.

Witen: Tenth month of the year, and the first month of the winter season.

Wizard: Practitioner of elemental magics which tap into the energy of ley-lines.

Xaco: Sixth month of the year, and the third month of the summer season.

About the Author

Travis I. Sivart writes Fantasy, Science Fiction (including Steampunk, Cyberpunk, Dystopian, & Post-Apocalyptic), Speculative Fiction, Social DIY, and more. You can sometimes find him live-streaming the writing and editing of his latest project from his home in Central Virginia, surrounded by too many cats.

You can find Travis on Amazon, Barnes and Noble, Books-A-Million, and other literary retailers.

9 781954 214217